MALCOLM CAHPRA

AND THE

RISE OF THE FORSAKEN

BY

C. Iannuzzi

DEDICATION

To my mother for your unending support. You believed in me even when I didn't believe in myself. You stuck by me through all my endeavors and without you, I would be nothing. I'm blessed to have such a wonderful person in my life.
To my best friend in the world, Mya. You were beside me the whole time and I cannot put into words just what you mean to me. I truly don't believe that I'm deserving of such an amazing companion.
I will love you for eternity.

TABLE OF CONTENTS

PROLOGUE

Strange occurrences have become more common here on Cahpra Isle. The island is one of four continents that make up the magical world of ShadowCrest. Its lands are hidden by a veil of storms that keep the outside world from ever finding them. It's known to the inhabitants as the Four Shadows. Many races of beings live here, some with powers that rival the gods.

Years ago, the people of Cahpra isle were forced to fight for their lives against a massive rebel army from the neighboring land of Halicon. The now banished king of the isle viciously cursed their entire army to live in misery and torment. He thought that they would never reach the isle, but they landed on its shores and the curse they bore only made them a more ruthless enemy.

The Battle for Cahpra isle was brutal, but the people of the isle were victorious. Their kingdom in the north was ruined and it held many painful memories so the newly appointed king, William Cahpra, chose to move the people south and rebuild.

His only son Malcolm went off to fight the remaining enemy abroad as the leader of a group of fighters that came to be known as the Brave Hundred. Tales of their crusades spanned the world. They spoke of fearsome battles of magic and steel. Beings with the ability to control the elements and others who could heal the mortally wounded.

It's been ten years since he's been away fighting and the lingering curse that was meant for the rebel army's demise has now brought them back. A prophecy told by clerics mentioned that the son of a king would return at a time when he was needed to lead his people against a risen army of the dead. The prophecy has begun to unfold and the signs across the Isle are clear. Evil is upon them, and this is where the journey begins.

CORAL
ISLAND

PIRATES
COVE

HEREX'S
COTTAGE

ANGEL LAKE

STARLITE
VALLEY

DYRE
MOUNTAINS

THE RUINED CASTLE

TWILIGHT FOREST

ANCIENT PLAINS

REBECCA'S
HOUSE

TWILIGHT
PLATEAU

MERCHANT LAKE

WATERTOWN

WATERTOWN
CORRIDOR

VOODOO'S
HUT

TEARDROP
FOREST

BRIGHTWATER
CAVERN

TEARDROP
LAKE

TWILIGHT
PENINSULA

WHISPERING PLAINS

SORROW
LAKE

THE NEW KINGDOM

EVERDARK
DEPTHS

BECK'S
HOUSE

STORM RIDGE
MOUNTAINS

KINGS
PORT

BARRIER
ISLAND

N
W   E
S

Cahpra Isle

CHAPTER 1
AN UNEXPECTED ABDUCTION

Hidden in the vibrant foliage of a secluded valley sat a small log cabin with a puff of smoke rising from its chimney. Sleeping peacefully inside was a burly man by the name of Arthur Beckman, better known to his friends as Beck. He awoke in a fluster and quickly sat up in bed.

"Whoosa-da-whatsa," he muttered incoherently.

He wore brown overalls with a red T-shirt and his thick ginger hair and beard were a mess as he looked around the room curiously, but then he realized where he was.

"Ahh. Home sweet home," he said contently.

Beck was a humble, backwoods kind of fellow. He wasn't one for the crowded life that came with living inside the kingdom. He enjoyed nature and cooking and preferred to keep a little distance from the rest of the world.

He cleared his throat in a large hack and hung his legs off the side of the bed. His feet dangled over the floor even though he was a taller dwarf at about five feet. He stretched his arms over his head and let out a wailing yawn that spooked his dog who was sleeping on the floor.

"Good morning, Mya," he said as he stepped into his boots, then he straightened his hair and walked out into a sitting room where others were still fast asleep.

A woman named Helaina slept on a plush sofa by the fire. She was known to all as the fairest and most powerful sorceress in the lands. She wore a long white gown with a floral pattern that was stitched in gold. Raven color hair covered most of her face and a wand was tucked safely in her belt. On the floor, not far away was a man named Archer with short brown hair and a neatly trimmed beard. He was dressed in black leather armor and snored peacefully while clinching an old wooden bow in his hand.

Beck went over to Helaina and pulled her blanket up to tuck her in and she snuggled deeper into the couch. When he turned to walk away, he noticed that Archer's blanket had also fallen off him. He thought of pulling it up, but then he stopped and gestured that he was fine as he giggled and walked away. Mya followed behind him as she wagged her tail happily.

Inside the kitchen there was a warlock by the name of Herex who kept an endless watch out the back door. He wore a black robe with a fiery pattern at the base and a belt that was lined with rubies and emeralds. His mace leaned against the wall beside him. It looked much like a steel mallet with large rubies imbedded around the top.

Herex was a man cursed a few years ago by a potion that separated his spirit from his body. His spirit was the only part of him present now which made him unable to speak and eat or even feel, but he is conscious, and he is powerful. These are Malcolm Cahpra's most loyal companions and together they form the mightiest battle group in all the lands.

When he got to the door, Herex was standing there motionless. He waved his hand in front of him to see if he would answer and suddenly Herex lunged forward.

"Ahh!" shrieked Beck. "Just makin sure you're still with us, buddy. I'm headin out to get some breakfast. Haven't been back to stock the place in some time, so I need to go out and get it. Not that it matters to you, but I promise when ya get your body back, I'll cook ya a feast!"

Herex shook his head to acknowledge him as Beck put on his coat. He threw an old backpack over his shoulder then he grabbed his rifle and headed out the door.

He exited the valley into a dark part of the forest. The sun dimly lit the sky but not a ray of light made it through the thick canopy of the trees as he strolled down the trail with his rifle over his shoulder.

Birds were perched in the trees and a family of monkeys sat together in another. A swarm of tiny dragons swooped in and started to attack him, but they were so small he barely paid them any mind as he shooed them away. He went along on his way and started to sing a song.

"Gonna shoot me - some breakfast - out here in these woods. Gonna take it home - and cook it up -

and eat it with ma friends."

He whistled the melody as he made his way deeper into the forest. Soon after, he reached a large clearing not far from Sorrow Lake and scanned the area for movement. He found a spot to sit in some thick brush and waited for a boar to cross his path.

After a little while he became drowsy, and his head sank as he began to doze off. He heard the sound of footsteps, and he immediately took aim with his rifle. He looked intently through the scope but saw nothing, so he slowly settled back in and not long after, he started to doze off again.

Suddenly the sound of cracking branches awoke him, and he was tackled from behind by a gang of skeletal beings with glowing red eyes. They were dressed in the ragged remains of the clothing and armor they had died in. They held him down and bound his hands and feet, then they ripped him from the brush and dragged him toward the lake. He kicked and squirmed to try to get away but there were too many of them. They pulled him into the shallows and Beck struggled to keep his head above the water. A whirlpool in the center led into an old cave system known as the Everdark depths and they pulled him down inside, down into the depths.

A short while later the sun rose over the valley and the others started to wake up. Helaina was nestled into the couch, comfortably wrapped in her blanket. Archer awoke with a chill, and he quickly ripped his

4

blanket back up to his neck. A sigh of relief came over his face from the warmth then he shook off a chill. They got up and slowly made their way out to the porch. To their disappointment, Beck wasn't outside cooking breakfast like usual. They began to search the cabin inside and out, but they didn't find him anywhere.

"That's not like him to be gone for so long," said Helaina with concern as she looked out at the valley.

Helaina was the unspoken mother of the group. She cared deeply for each of them, and also kept them in line, so what she said went. They'd become a family over the years and now a part of it was missing. Herex went to the railing of the porch and pointed to the trail he had left on.

Immediately they all made their way down the stairs and went off to find him. They questioned everyone they came across for miles and before they knew it, they had spent the whole day searching for him. The daylight had come and gone, and they were no closer to finding him. They found themselves at the shore of Sorrow Lake and deeply worried for Beck.

"I wish Malcolm were here. He would know what to do," said Helaina.

"He'll be arriving at the new kingdom soon. We will regroup with him in the morning. Beck can hold his own, for a little while," replied Archer.

They all reluctantly agreed and were about to head

back when Herex noticed a group of trolls on the far side of the lake, and he pointed to them.

"Good eye, Herex. Let's go see if they saw anything," said Helaina with the slightest look of hope that she could muster.

They headed over and as they arrived, the trolls bowed to them with respect.

"Lady Helaina. I know why you're here and I regret to be the one to tell you, but your friend was pulled into Sorrow Lake by the undead."

Helaina turned back to Archer and Herex with a dismal look on her face as the worst possible scenario had begun to unfold.

"Thank you," she replied as she quickly turned away.

Herex threw his arms into the air and his portal rose up from the ground. It resembled a tall black mirror with an intricate frame. A swirling blue cloud formed inside as a smoky aura began to linger off the top of it. Without hesitation Helaina walked inside and Archer and Herex followed. In a flash, they disappeared, and the portal sank back into the grass. Veins of energy coursed through the ground from where it stood. They exited the portal back at Beck's house and started to prepare for what would surely be a long and restless night.

Not far to the east, Malcolm Cahpra traveled down a dark and windy trail high up in the Storm Ridge Mountains. A blue aura lingered in the air from his thick plate armor. On his back were two large battle axes that kept the same tone. Bullhorns protruded from the sides of his helmet and his cloak drifted in the wind behind him.

As he trudged on down the trail, he heard a rustle in the brush nearby. The thick trees shut out the moonlight as the sounds grew closer and closer. He gazed to the side where the noise had been coming from and then he turned to face his predator. A pack of wolves only a few feet away were crouched and ready to attack.

The aura from his armor became a blazing red as if it were on fire and it lit up the trail. He let out a vicious growl that echoed through the mountain and the wolves quickly backed off trembling. He watched as they stumbled over each other and disappeared into the darkness. He could have ended the wolves, but after all the fierce battles he's fought, they were no threat to him. His armor faded back to the blue aura, and he continued down the trail.

Soon after, he reached a cliff that looked out over a massive valley. In the center was a grand white stone castle with towers that reached high over the surrounding hills. Small orbs of light floated around it and lit the castle walls brightly. It shined onto a lake below and the ripples of water reflected into the hills, illuminating the crystalline leaves on the trees. A gentle breeze caused the valley to glisten. Malcolm had never seen the new kingdom with his own eyes.

He stood at the edge of the cliff and took in the amazing sight for a while before he turned away and went on down the mountain.

Inside the castle there was a gathering in the great hall that marked the night of the kingdom's most anticipated prophecy. The room was lined with white stone columns and statues of elder fighters were placed in between. Paintings of famous warriors and wizards hung over the mantles of a dozen large fireplaces that burned around the outer walls. On the far side of the hall was a stage with an old hand carved wood podium. The men and women of the king's army filled long tables as the glowing aura from their weapons and armor gleamed throughout the hall.

The huge doors slowly opened behind the stage. Everyone stood and turned to face king William Cahpra as he walked through to the podium. They all clinched a fist to their chests and dropped to a knee to show their respect for him. They bowed their heads and awaited his words as he looked out over the crowd.

The king was an older man with thick gray hair under his crown. He wore a long red robe with a golden sash around his neck that reached down to the floor. He carried an old wooden staff that had been used in battle many times before and although still powerful, it was now mostly used for a walking stick. He stared fondly around the room at all the men and women.

"Welcome brave fighters, good friends! You have all proven your courage and loyalty to this kingdom many times, and I am honored to have been your king these many years. As you all know, the return of my son is nearby. There have been sightings of the undead in the north, and more recently, here in the south. Attack is now eminent. The prophecies spoke of a risen army of the dead, and this kingdom will not be safe until this foe is defeated once and for all. Another battlefield awaits, but we will overcome this enemy. When my son returns, he will lead us to victory!"

Everyone cheered and held their weapons into the air as they began to glow brightly. The king lifted his staff over his head, and everyone quieted down.

"For now, feast my friends. My son is almost here."

Everyone saluted him once more, then he walked back out as the doors slowly closed behind him.

Now at the base of the mountain, Malcolm continued down a path lit by small globes that would take him right to the main gate of the town surrounding the castle. A group of people celebrated just outside the entrance. Some enjoyed a laugh by a bonfire as a few others sang and danced. Carriages were parked along the path and tents were scattered around the grass.

A group of children played in the forest nearby.

They formed colored orbs of energy in their hands and fired them back and forth at each other. Upon impact, the orbs would only burst and fizzle away. The orbs they were able to conjure at a young age were harmless, but when their powers matured, they became lethal and were only used for their protection or in battle if they chose that route. Many of the beings on the Isle had use of these powers.

The color of the orb identified if the magic was summoned from the light or from the darkness. Spells from the light would glow green or blue or yellow and the auras from dark magic were red and purple or black. Only a small few had the ability to use both.

Others excelled in different areas such as healing or potion making. Some wielded powerful weapons like swords and axes or maces and staffs. A few were brilliant inventors and many were just humble carpenters, but they all lived together peacefully.

As he walked through the white stone entrance and onto the cobblestone road, he observed all the neatly kept shops and the colorful manicured gardens. Potted trees and plants were meticulously pruned and placed in every corner throughout the town. The groundskeepers even left the perfect amount of ivy to climb the walls on a few of the shops along the road.

Elaborate architecture and masonry graced each structure throughout the town. Every single stone seemed to be nurtured into its final immaculate position. From the tall white columns and the grand archways to the opulent crown moldings and stained-glass windows, not a single detail was overlooked inside this beautiful town.

Every road he passed off the main strip seemed to have its own little nook. Whether it was an eatery or a fountain or a small park, each had its own treasure. He walked beside a large park that was separated from the road by a stone wall. He looked through the iron railings and delighted at the sight of the green and blue and purple leaves of the trees. Some were even bio-luminescent, which created a peaceful ambient lighting in the darker corners of the park. He only needed to look up to see the tall white towers of the castle above the trees.

As he made his way further down the road, he saw a large crowd of people and decided to take a detour through the park. He went through an opening in the wall and traveled down a footpath with the luminous green leaves of weeping trees hanging overhead. The gentle green light that emanated from the ends of the leaves lit the path for him. A few benches sat below the trees and looked out onto a small pond that was illuminated by white water lilies that floated on the surface. He contemplated staying for a while to take in the view, but his pending family reunion was the main thing on his mind.

After a few minutes in the park, he reached the other side and exited onto another road. Purple banners with the Cahpra family crest hung from the many lamp posts along the road. In the light of the lamps were vendors with wooden stands full of books and a line of wooden carriages. Some had candy and chocolates and others had potions that bubbled into the air. Finally getting to see the new kingdom and how the people were able to live in peace was instant gratification that his journey was never in vain.

As he went further down the road, he arrived at a stable where large birds were perched all over a tall tree that stood high above the town. A man working there called out to him.

"Hello, sir! Can I interest you in a new mode of transportation? We have some of the most beautiful Gryphons you'll ever see in these parts!"

A dozen birds stared down at him from the tree. They resemble an eagle but stand six to ten feet tall with wing spans of around twenty feet. Gryphons were bred in black and white, and yellow and brown. There were gray ones with white bellies and rarely seen was the golden gryphon that only a few people had ever been able to tame.

The people in the kingdom adapted to this way of transportation some time ago. Just a whistle and they could fly off anywhere they desired. At a young age, the children were paired with a bird that they would grow up with. At first the birds would fly them to their lessons and around with friends, but as they grew, the birds became loyal companions. For some they would be a source of transportation and for others, a trusted friend they could take into battle.

He looked up at all the birds then back at the man.

"No, but thank you, friend. I'm rather attached to the one I have," said Malcolm kindly, then he turned away and continued down the road.

When he reached the center of the town there was a festival inside the square. A man in a black and white stripe suit walked around on stilts that made him twenty feet tall and an old woman scared some children with a ghost story as they were gathered by a campfire. Another man waved his wand at his pet squirrel, and it transformed into a drooling beast that seemed just as friendly as the squirrel. It became unstable and its eyes began to cross. Another wave of the wand and he changed him back, then it quickly scurried away down an alleyway between the shops.

The townspeople stopped to watch him as he walked past, and they pondered to each other about who he was. A mother pulled her son away when he tried to approach him out of curiosity, but Malcolm kept on walking, the blue aura still radiating from his armor.

He looked around at all the people who were now staring at him, then he placed his fingers to his mouth and whistled out loud. From what seemed to come out of thin air, a golden gryphon in heavy plate armor landed beside him and bowed its head to Malcolm with respect.

"Sorry, Star. I just felt like walking tonight, but I

saw you behind me the whole time," he said.

He gently pets his beak, then he climbed on and gazed up at the castle. The people stared at the bird's shiny golden armor and a large star sapphire gem that gleamed brightly on its chest. Slowly they began to recognize that it was the same bird from the tales of the brave hundred and the man before them was Malcolm Cahpra, leader of the group who has kept their kingdom safe for the last ten years.

They began to cheer and praise him as many took a knee to show their respect. Malcolm bowed his head back to them, then he gently tugged on the reins. Star leapt straight up into the air and with a swipe of his powerful wings, they flew off toward the castle.

CHAPTER 2
THE RETURN OF MALCOLM CAHPRA

King William looked out into the sky from a balcony high up in the castle, eagerly awaiting the arrival of his son. As he stared out into the darkness, he noticed the large golden bird come into sight. He saw the blue aura from Malcolm's armor, and he yelled down to the guards.

"Open the gates!"

The men swung them wide open, and Malcolm flew through and landed on the steps of the castle. He dismounted the bird and fed him some fresh bread from his satchel. Star graciously took it in his mouth and bowed to Malcolm, then he flew off into the hillside.

King William quickly made his way down through the castle. When he reached the great hall, he shoved open the doors and went right to the podium, never once taking his eyes off the outer door. As it slowly opened, there stood his son, for the first time in years.

"He has arrived," said the king.

Malcolm slowly walked past the fighters in the hall. As he reached the stage he knelt to the king and took off his helmet. He was strong and handsome with golden blond hair that fell over his face as he bowed to the king.

"Welcome home, son."

A smile came across Malcolm's face as he looked

up at the king.

"Hello, father," he replied with content.

He stood and walked up the steps to him. They grabbed each other's forearms firmly and gazed at each other happily before sharing a warm embrace for the first time in ten years. After a few moments, they both turned toward the fighters.

"Ladies and gentlemen, my son, Malcolm Cahpra," said the king proudly.

They all dropped to a knee in loyalty of the man who would now lead them against the forsaken army.

"Thank you. Please, enjoy your feast. We have a long journey ahead of us, but we will bring peace back to this great kingdom," said Malcolm confidently.

Everybody applauded him and sat back down to eat.

"It's good to have you home, son. I've been looking forward to this and your mother cannot wait to see you. When you left, you were teenagers. Now you return a man who I'm so proud to call my son."

"Thank you, father. It is good to be home. I would really like to take off this armor. It's been a long trip."

"Of course," replied the king.

He looked over at one of the butlers.

"Will you call on the blacksmith, Monroe?"

"That won't be necessary, father," Malcolm interrupted. "I trust only one man with my armor.

16

Some friends will be arriving early in the morning," he added.

"I will have preparations made for them," replied the king as they walked back through the doors and up a grand staircase.

"Your quarters are at the end of the corridor. I'm sure that you'll be comfortable. I'll leave you to get settled. Your mother and I will be in the dining room off the bottom of the stairway when you're ready."

"Thank you, father. Then I will see you shortly."

The king smiled at him as he walked away then he went off in the other direction. As Malcolm reached the middle of the corridor, he noticed a thick steel door that had the engraving of a crystal ball with an eye inside it.

He went over curiously and opened it up to peek inside. When he did, the wood in the fireplace ignited and lit up the room. There were dark wooden shelves that covered every wall and held numerous glowing crystal balls.

One of them floated over a pillar in the center of the room. A circular glass ceiling above it lets the eye of the ball see all the things that happened on the isle. In the corner of the room was a large table with a slot for them to be placed inside. Each of them would tell the story of a certain time or event and the table reenacted it in perfect detail.

He walked closer to observe it when the door suddenly opened, and the king walked inside.

"I'm sorry! I didn't realize you were in here," he said with surprise. "I find myself in this room often. There's so much history in here."

"Father, I know what lies ahead. How many fighters do we have?"

After a brief pause, the king replied.

"We have just over twenty thousand loyal, well-trained men and women. They will make you proud, son. Please, go and get settled. Your mother is extremely anxious to see you."

As they exited the room, Monroe was standing outside.

"Monroe will show you to your room," said the king.

They both went their separate ways and Malcolm followed him down the long corridor. There were large white columns along the walls. Portraits of his relatives hung between them along with beautiful tapestries and porcelain vases. They arrived at two large doors and Monroe opened them into the room.

"These are your quarters, my lord."

Malcolm entered the room and saw the plush bed and a warm fireplace. He hadn't seen such luxury in a long time. He was used to sleeping out in the forest and moving camps often.

"Thank you, Monroe," he said graciously.

"You're welcome. I bid you a good night, sir," he replied as he pulled the doors closed.

Draped over a shiny wooden table in the center of the room was a red robe with the golden emblem of his family crest embroidered on the chest. He picked it up and looked closely at the symbol, then he put it back down and began taking off his armor. As he removed each piece the blue aura faded away and he placed it all on a rack by the fire.

He put on the robe and went to the window to look out at the town. He watched the smoke leaving the chimneys of the people's homes throughout the town. It humbled him to see them living safe and happily in the kingdom that was built in his absence. He glanced up at the moon and took a deep breath, then he left the room and went back down the corridor.

Inside the dining hall the king and queen had just arrived. Queen Talia wore a bright yellow gown with a diamond tiara in her fiery red hair. They went to the table and Monroe pulled out her chair. She sat down and the king sat after her.

"Where is he, William?" asked the queen impatiently.

"He will be here soon. He only arrived a few minutes ago," he replied.

The door suddenly opened across the room and a smile of joy spread across the queen's face as Malcolm walked inside. She got up and ran over to him.

"My son! My son! You're home!" she chanted, with excitement.

19

She gave him a hug and stood back in front of him. She gently touched his face, noticing it was now years older than the last time she saw it.

"Hello, mother," said Malcolm as he smiled back.

A sigh of relief came across her face, and she hugged him tightly again.

"It's so good to have you home. I've missed you so much," she said as she grabbed his arm and pulled him over to the table. "Please, sit. We have so much to talk about."

Malcolm smiled at her and looked over at his father.

"All in good time, mother. Besides, the last ten years don't make for a good dinner conversation, but what I will tell you is that I have truly been blessed with the greatest friends who stood by my side all these years. You will surely love them as I do."

"Is there a maiden who has caught my son's eye?" she asked, seeming very interested in his response.

"Darling! He'll tell us about that when he's ready," said the king.

The queen turned to him with a smirk and the king acknowledged it submissively as he looked back at Malcolm.

"Malcolm, the arrangements are made for your friends. They will be given a feast and a comfortable place to rest when they arrive. They will be right at home here."

Malcolm laughed as he thought of the conditions that they were used to.

"In order for them to feel at home, they would need a dark forest and a pile of hay below a tree," he replied. "It's been a long time since we've had accommodations like this. This will be a welcomed change."

While he spoke, a bottle of wine floated across the table and poured itself into one of the glasses. Malcolm was caught by surprise as he found the use of magic entertaining since the only magic he was used to was in battle and not for the simple pleasantries like that. Monroe came back into the room followed by others with large platters of food. Malcolm stared at the feast as his mouth started to water and the king saw it.

"I'm sure you're hungry, Malcolm. Please, dig in!"

He took a piece of steak and began to eat it with his hands. He took a gulp of wine to wash it down and he went right back to the steak. The king and queen turned to each other and smiled. Both were just happy to see their son sitting down having a meal with them, even if it wasn't with the fork and knife that sat beside his plate. They started eating too and glancing over at him from time to time. He ate as if he hadn't eaten in days and soon after, a stack of bones filled his plate.

"That was quite delicious! Thank you, Monroe,"

Malcolm said.

"You're welcome, my lord."

He turned to his mother and father as he wiped his mouth with his sleeve.

"May I be excused?" he asked.

"Of course," said the king.

He drank the last gulp of wine and stood up.

"I'll tell you all about my travels soon, mother. I'd really like to rest now. It was nice to eat together again, and I'll see you both in the morning."

He went to his mother and kissed her on the cheek, then he gave his father's shoulder a gentle squeeze and left the room.

When he got back to his quarters he went right to the window and looked out at the kingdom once more. After a few moments, he went to bed and stretched out on top of the covers. He capped a candle on the nightstand and quickly fell asleep.

In the morning, the sun rose up over the hills and shined onto the castle. Inside the room, the light reached Malcolm's face. He sat up and looked around, unfamiliar with his surroundings, but then he remembered where he was, and he promptly climbed out of the bed.

He rushed out of the room toward a large double door at the end of the hall. His father heard the racket and he turned to the queen.

"I'll be right back," he said as he grabbed his staff

from next to the door and started down the corridor behind him.

Malcolm reached the outer doors, and he swung them open. The light was so bright it seemed to the king as if he had disappeared. Then he walked out behind him and as his eyes adjusted, he saw Malcolm by the railing, looking out into the distance.

"What's the matter?" asked the king.

Malcolm pointed into the sky.

"They're here."

They both stood beside each other and looked toward the sunrise as three gryphons flew into sight. As they got closer, Malcolm saw each of his friends on their backs.

Archer soared in on a gray bird and beside him was Helaina on a beautiful bird that was as white as snow. On the other side of her was Herex, and his bird was as dark as night. As they reached the balcony, the birds perched themselves on top of the railing. They took a step down to the floor and crouched for everyone to dismount. They stepped down and immediately they put their fists to their chests and dropped to a knee to show their respect to Malcolm and the king.

Two of the birds flew off into the sunrise and Herex's bird transformed into a floating black orb that he took and placed into his satchel.

"You don't have to bow here my friends," said Malcolm. "If it weren't for each of you, I would not be here today. Father, this is Helaina. She's the one who's kept us all alive these many years. She's the most powerful sorceress in the lands with powers to heal, along with the ability to manipulate nature, and who knows what else?" he said as he looked over at her.

She smirked back at him as the king reached out and took her hand.

"Thank you for all that you have done, Helaina. It's an honor to meet you."

"It's an honor to meet you, my lord," she replied as she bowed her head graciously and smiled back.

"This is Archer," said Malcolm. "You will never find a better bowman. He never misses his target!"

"Archer, it is nice to meet you," said the king as he shook his hand. "I have some experience with a bow myself. Maybe we can shoot together sometime," he asked.

"I will look forward to it! It would be an honor," Archer replied kindly.

"And this is Herex," Malcolm said. "He cannot speak in his present state. Years ago, he was crossed by king Westmore's son, Morgan and his soul was separated from his body. It's now being preserved in a safe place till the day we can find the potion that will let him return to it. His powers were of the light, but since this has happened, he can summon from the dark as well. He is truly a fierce fighter and a great friend."

"Herex, I'm sorry to hear of this. I hope that one day this can be remedied. It is truly an honor to meet you," said the king as he shook his hand and tried to see into his hood.

"There is one more person, but he's often a bit tardy. Where is Beck?" asked Malcolm.

They all dropped their heads at the same time.

"We fear that the undead have taken him. He went out to get breakfast, like usual and when we awoke, he was gone," said Helaina.

"We looked all over the forest for him," said Archer. "We came across some trolls while searching the Whispering plains, and they told us that the undead pulled him down into Sorrow Lake. You know what that means."

"The Everdark Depths," replied Malcolm in a solemn tone.

"But that stronghold was taken out years ago!"

"I'm afraid, it still remains," Archer replied.

Malcolm grinned in anger and darted back into the castle.

"If you would all accompany me to the dining hall. I've had the chefs prepare a meal for all of you," said the king as he went back through the doors.

They followed him down a corridor to a set of doors that opened into the dining hall. Inside was a feast that was fit for a king.

"Please, make yourselves at home and eat till your content," said the king.

The three of them thanked him and bowed in appreciation, then Archer and Helaina began to pick. Herex sat down with them even though he didn't eat. Another bottle lifted off the table and took them all by surprise as it poured itself into their glasses. The king smiled at their reactions.

"If you would excuse me? I need to speak to my son," he said.

"It was nice to meet you all."

The three of them stood up as the king left the room, then they sat back down and continued to eat. The king went straight to Malcolm's quarters and knocked on the door.

"Come in," said Malcolm from inside.

He opened the door to see Malcolm writing on a scroll.

"Son, I am sorry for your loss," said the king.

"Beck is not lost, father, but we do need to act soon," he replied.

The king went closer to the table and saw an intricate set of plans he was drawing to infiltrate the Everdark Depths.

"We will cut down every undead fighter inside this stronghold. We will retrieve our man and leave nothing behind," Malcolm said without even lifting his eyes from the plan.

"Very well. I will have our fighters prepare for battle."

"No father. Let them rest. The four of us will take the Depths alone."

The king looked at him in amazement at his bravery and confidence. He placed his hand on Malcolm's shoulder.

"Well then, I will let you prepare."

He walked over to the door and looked back at him.

"Your friends are in the dining hall when you're finished. If I can help in any way, please don't hesitate to ask," said the king.

Malcolm looked up for a moment.

"Thank you, father," he replied then he continued with the plan.

The king left the room and went back to his quarters.

Inside the dining hall, everyone was finished eating and they eagerly waited to see the plan that Malcolm devised to save Beck.

A short time after, the door swung open, and he walked inside. Everyone stood up to greet him.

"By sunrise tomorrow, the Everdark Depths will no longer exist. We will tear down the walls and destroy anything that gets in our way. We will get Beck out of their grasp. We leave tonight."

He threw the scroll onto the table, and everyone

leaned in to see his plan.

"Herex, I'll need you to summon our friend, Gamon," said Malcolm.

Herex quickly stood up, seeming excited. He lifted his arms into the air and his portal rose up from the floor. A moment later a man could be heard screaming in the distance. Slowly it got louder and louder then suddenly a gnome no more than two feet tall came flying through the portal and landed on his backside. He slid along the floor and came to a stop with his legs in the air. He sat up as a cloud of dust billowed around him and he coughed and waved his hands to clear the air, then he looked up and saw Herex.

"Herex! You could've at least given me a little warning before you suck me through one of your bloody portals!" he hollered.

Gamon was a brilliant inventor and perhaps the most versatile person in the group. He wore a pair of green overalls with a white t-shirt and a pair of goggles around his head of thick white hair.

Everyone began to laugh. Herex giggled as he lifted his arms up again. Suddenly, a noise was heard of something grinding across the floor. It started to get louder and louder. The portal lit up again and a large old wooden trunk came sliding out at Gamon. He rolled out of the way just as the trunk stopped where he was sitting. He struggled to his feet and walked back out from around the trunk, yelling at

Herex.

"You know you're reckless sometimes!"

He kicked the side of the trunk and it opened to reveal his entire workstation. All his tools hung on the walls and an anvil sat beside a little work bench.

"My anvil too! Was that really necessary, Herex?"

"He's trying to make you feel at home," said Malcolm.

"Well, I do now!" replied Gamon. "My entire shop is here except for the building!"

Herex lifted his arms up into the air again.

"No! Don't do it!" yelled Gamon as he ran away from the portal.

"We have a shop here that you can use," said Malcolm.

Herex put his arms down and giggled under his hood as everyone else started to laugh at them again. Gamon stood with his arms crossed, tapping his foot on the ground as he stared at Herex.

"I'm glad you're all enjoying this," he said.

"Okay everyone. Gamon has a lot of work to do," said Malcolm. "It's good to see you friend. Help yourself to some breakfast. Afterward I will need you to gather up the armor and weapons to be repaired. It needs to be ready for tonight."

Gamon went to the table and climbed up to the top of a chair. He took a piece of bread and looked over at Malcolm.

"Consider it done!" he said as he took a bite.

"Thank you," Malcolm replied.

Everyone sat back down at the table with him. He stared out of the corner of his eye and saw Herex looking at him.

"Stop looking at me like that or I'll melt your mace into putty! And get rid of that portal! It's freaking me out! I feel like something else is gonna come flying out at me!"

Herex giggled and swiped his arm over Gamon's head. Gamon tucked into a ball in case he was playing another trick, but the portal sank back into the ground and disappeared in a flash of light. Gamon looked back over and was relieved to see that it was gone as he continued eating.

"Herex, would you leave him alone," said Helaina as she held back her laugh.

Gamon tore a piece of bread in his mouth and glared at Herex.

"He only does it because he likes you," said Archer.

"Well, that's a heck of a way to show somebody you like them," Gamon replied.

Herex patted him on the back and startled him again. Everyone started to laugh, except for Gamon.

"By the way. Where is Beck?" he asked.

Everyone looked around at each other, unsure of what to say.

"Beck will be here tomorrow," replied Malcolm. "He got caught up. But he'll be back tomorrow."

"Oh, good! I have something for him that I think he's gonna love. I've been working on it for weeks," he said with excitement.

"I'm sure he will be very happy with it," added Helaina.

As soon as they all finished eating, Monroe came back into the room.

"If you would all accompany me to the great room, please?"

They followed him into the room, and they all sat down in front of a tall stone fireplace. The entire kingdom could be seen through the massive windows. They all looked out at the town as the people went on with their daily routines.

"Please call on me if there's anything you require," said Monroe as he walked back out of the room.

Malcolm stood in front of the fireplace and looked up at a picture of his relatives that hung above.

"Once again, I must ask you to put yourselves in harm's way," he said. "The outcome of our journey over the next few days will become the premise of the future of this isle. Tonight, we will travel to the Everdark Depths and get Beck out of the undead's grasp."

"The undead took, Beck?" yelled Gamon. "Oh, I got a few things for them rotten corpses. How dare they!"

"Don't worry. We will get him back," said Malcolm. "What I need is for you to work your magic on the weapons and armor. We'll take care of the rest."

"Oh, I'll get right to it," replied Gamon.

"I'm sure you can find your way to the shop. Your tools are already there waiting."

"I'll find it!"

"Thank you, Gamon. You're the only person I trust with our precious metals," Malcolm replied.

"Thank you, I won't disappoint you."

"We leave at midnight," said Malcolm.

"The gear will be like new by the time you're ready," added Gamon.

"I have some things to do myself. I will see you all tonight," said Malcolm as he walked out of the room. Everyone else looked around at each other.

"Midnight it is," said Helaina. "Gamon, I know you're busy today and I wish you could join us, but is anyone up to seeing some sights?" she asked.

Gamon shook his head in agreement.

"That sounds like a good idea. I wouldn't mind exploring the new kingdom a bit," replied Archer.

They all headed back out to the balcony they arrived on, and they stared out at the new kingdom below.

CHAPTER 3
THE NEW KINGDOM

Helaina and Archer whistled for their birds and Herex released his orb out in front of himself. It floated into the air and in a flash, his black bird appeared.

They all got on and they leapt from the balcony and flew off toward the town. They glided over the rooftops and soared around the perimeter before landing in the center of the town square. They all got off their birds and looked around as people stared back at them curiously but continued what they were doing.

The road was lined with small shops and the carriages of traveling salespeople filled the square. As they walked down the road, two older men on a bench noticed who they were, and they began whispering to each other.

"Is that Lady Helaina, Herex, and Archer?" asked one of the men.

The other man looked up and put on a thick pair of spectacles.

"I think it is! Lord Cahpra's most loyal fighters!" replied the other man as they went past.

They came up to a small shop with a small wooden sign above the door that read, 'Marta's Antique Trinkets and Such.'

Helaina saw an old woman glaring at them from inside the window. She walked up and stared right back as Herex and Archer stood behind her, wondering who she was. The woman disappeared back into the shop and Helaina quickly walked in the door, but the old woman was nowhere to be found.

There were shelves full of antiques and portraits of famous wizards hanging on the walls. They noticed a large rectangular table that sat in a dark corner of the shop, so they went over to take a closer look. An engraving on a copper tag read, 'The battle for Cahpra Isle,' and they all looked around at each other with curiosity.

Archer found a small button on the side, and he pressed it. Suddenly the top of the table lit up and a holographic model of the north castle and the surrounding land appeared in amazing detail. Seconds later, a reenactment of the entire battle began to play out. Tiny people fought all over the land as orbs fired back and forth. Airships filled the air and fired on the castle as others fell from the sky.

A creek was heard in the floor, and they all turned to see the little old lady standing just behind them. She wore a long black dress with a cloak and a pointed black hat. A pair of old square frame glasses rested on the tip of her nose.

"Why did you have to push the button? Do you know how long that battle took?" She asked.

"Uhh. About four days?" replied Archer.

"That's right! Now it has to go through the whole battle and now I'm the one who gets to listen to it the entire time!"

"I'm sorry, but what is this?" asked Archer.

"It's a reenactment table. There's only three in existence. The king has one of them and the other is somewhere oversea. I'll sell you this one if you want?" She asked.

"No thanks. I don't have anywhere to put it," Archer replied.

"I'm Marta Pimroe, the owner of this establishment."

She began to stare at Herex, and she tried to see into his hood, then she realized what he was.

"Hmm. There's an interesting story to you isn't there, friend?"

Marta walked away through a red curtain in the back of the shop, and everyone followed her into a dimly lit room. Shelves covered the walls and were filled with trinkets and figurines. A glass case with small potion bottles sat in the center of a round table in the middle of the room.

"How long has he been like this?" she asked.

"Almost five years," Helaina replied. "Is there anything we can do?" she asked nervously.

"I'm afraid not, and that's the longest I've ever heard of anyone lasting outside their body," she said as she spun the glass case.

She looked through all the potions then she opened a door and took out a small white flask that was carved into a skull.

"This will buy you some time," Marta said. "When you begin to fade, take a swig of this potion each day or else you could disappear forever. It will never run out, so you won't need to refill it, but someday, it won't work anymore. Maybe a year or so, if you're lucky."

She handed Herex the bottle and he graciously took it and bowed his head to her.

"Thank you for your kindness," said Helaina.

"You're welcome. It's the least I can do for one of the brave hundred. Well, it's time for me to open the shop so if you would excuse me," said Marta as she walked off into another room.

Everyone went back through the front and out the door. Herex looked at the skull flask closer, then he placed it safely into his satchel and they went on down the road. There was a noticeably sad look on Helaina's face as she thought of the small amount of time that Herex had left.

They came up to an old traveling salesman whose carriage was a large glass tank on wheels. The wooden sides of the cart folded up into overhangs and hundreds of paper cranes flew in circles inside the tank. It was surrounded by shelves that were filled with origami flowers and trays of candy and many types of chocolates. The man noticed the sad expression on Helaina's face as she watched the cranes.

He took a flower from a vase and handed it to her. She looked up at him and smiled as she took it in her hand. The paper it was made from became a real flower as the petals turned pink and they started to glisten. Helaina thanked the man as she took a gentle sniff of its pleasant aroma, then she grabbed his arm and gave a gentle squeeze to show her appreciation for his kind gesture. He smiled back and she walked off a little happier with Archer and Herex.

Further down the road there was a little girl sitting on a bench outside of a shop. She seemed shy and nervous as she looked around at all the people in the town. Helaina went over and handed her the flower. The little girl's eyes widened, and she smiled brightly as she took the flower and smelled it. She looked up at Helaina and thanked her and giggled as the color of the petals changed to yellow.

Herex and Archer saw a weapon shop nearby and quickly went to the window to see inside. They both turned to each other for a moment and then went straight in the door. Helaina rolled her eyes and laughed as she followed them inside.

The walls were covered with swords, axes, staffs, maces, and every other kind of weapon. Magic wands filled a large glass case near the back of the shop. Some were made of wood and some from bone.

Others were forged from different metals and no doubt very powerful.

Archer and Herex stood in the center of the shop and looked up at a sword that was suspended in the air. It was a long and shiny, double blade sword. At the base of the blade was a glowing blue orb that floated between a serration of the blades. The handle was covered with a tan leather twine and its metal radiated a bright blue aura.

"Would ya look at that," said Archer.

The shop owner saw them admiring the sword and he went over to offer his help. He was an older man with a white beard, and he wore a long gray robe. He held a cane with a dragon carved into it. Its head was the handle, and its body and tail wrapped all the way around to the bottom.

"Looking for a change of pace?" asked the man as he noticed the empty quiver on Archer's back.

"You never know, but for now, I need to stick with what I know," he replied.

"A bow man, I see!"

"Yes! All my life!" replied Archer proudly.

"Nothing can hide from a well-placed arrow," said the man as he turned to his side, revealing a bow on his own back. It was made from cherry wood and quite worn from use.

"Ahh! A fellow bowman!" said Archer.

"It's my weapon of choice as well. If you are ever

in need of a new one, I have a lot to choose from," he said as he pointed to a wall full of them.

"If any of you need anything, anything at all, just give the bell a ring and I'll be right in the back."

"Thank you," Archer replied as he looked over at the bows.

Herex inspected the maces as Helaina browsed the wands inside the showcase. After a few minutes, she went over to Herex and Archer and whispered to them.

"You both realize that Gamon could build any of these weapons if we ask him, right?"

"Yea, you're right. But there's some nice stuff here!" said Archer as Herex shook his head in agreement.

"Maybe it's time to go," he added.

They all walked out in front of the shop and looked down the road at all the people in town.

"I'd like go to the south shore for a little while," said Helaina. "It's been so long since we've sat by the beach."

"That sounds nice! Might as well," replied Archer.

They both looked at Herex and again he shook his head in agreement. They called their birds and flew off over the rest of the town and the lake as they exited the lush green valley.

They soared over the hillside to a sprawling green plain and soon after, the ocean came into sight. The plain ended and they flew out over a white sand beach.

King's Port was seen in the distance. A dozen ships were docked and unloading their goods into a fleet of carriages. They descended and landed on the sand beside the surf. Not far from the beach was a large island filled with tall redwood trees.

"Do you remember the light festival they had on Barrier Island when we were young?" asked Helaina.

"I do!" replied Archer. "Every tree on the island was covered in lights. I remember wishing that *that* night would never end!"

"In a few days, we will be able to do all those things again. We'll bring peace back to the Isle and our kingdom will endure," replied Helaina.

They spent some time sitting on the beach and enjoying the beautiful afternoon. Herex watched the seagulls overhead. At times, they seemed as if they weren't even moving as they hovered in the wind. The beach wasn't as pleasing to Herex since he wasn't able to feel the breeze or even take in the scent of the ocean. Being there was only a reminder of his reality and the likely fact that he may not be around much longer.

One of the ships departed from the port and floated by them. The ship caught the wind in its sails, and it pushed them out past Barrier Island.

An airship rose up high into the sky over the port.

The crew on deck prepared the ship to make way as it turned and headed off into the clouds.

"Maybe we should get back to town now. We'll come back and spend the day when Beck is here and I could go for a cup of tea right about now," Helaina added.

"I think I'll join you. I'd have a brew, but I'll wait for Beck to do that," said Archer.

Herex shook his head in agreement, just happy to leave the beach. He let his orb out in front of him and in a flash his bird appeared, and he climbed on. Helaina and Archer both whistled to their birds, and they landed on the beach beside them. They climbed on and flew back over the plain. When they reached the town, they landed in a quiet corner with a small cafe. They sat at a table in front and watched as all the people made their way around the town.

"It would have been a better day if Beck were here. It's still nice to be back though," said Helaina as she sipped her cup of tea.

"Yes, it is. It's nice to be in friendly territory," Archer said.

"This is what we've been fighting for. Every single battle was worth it to protect this isle," said Helaina.

"I agree. It was all worth it," replied Archer.

"The sun is setting so we should get back to the castle. I'd imagine they'll be wondering where we are," said Helaina.

"I guess it is about that time," replied Archer.

They called their birds and climbed on. Suddenly all the people in the area gathered around them and started to clap and cheer to show their appreciation for the sacrifices they made for the kingdom. A woman from the group placed a wreath of flowers around the neck of Helaina's bird. Another woman tried to place one on Herex's bird, but he shook his hands to gesture that he didn't want it. The woman smiled kindly and turned to Archer. He felt obligated to accept it after Herex denied her and the woman placed the flowers around his bird's neck too, then they all backed up and waved goodbye to them.

All at once the birds hopped into the air and they flew off into the sky. Helaina stopped for a moment and hovered in place to look at the kingdom one last time before they went back to the castle. The others stopped beside her to see what she was doing.

"What is it, Helaina?" Archer asked.

"Would you look at that," she said.

They looked out at the valley as the trees and the plant-life started to glow when the sun fell behind the hill.

"It's so beautiful here. We can never let it fall to the undead," said Helaina.

"We will preserve the way of life here. Like we always have," replied Archer.

Herex again, nodded in agreement.

"Let's get back to the castle. We have a long night ahead of us. Beck is coming home," said Helaina cheerfully.

They turned away and flew back to the castle. They landed back on the balcony and Herex's bird disappeared into the black orb as the other birds flew off into the hillside. They stood there for a moment looking down at the colorful valley. Shades of blue, green and purple from the glowing foliage reflected onto the walls of the castle, forming a collage of color for the people in the kingdom to watch each night.

They took in the beautiful sight for a short time then they went inside. They joined everyone else for dinner and they talked together for a while. It wasn't an overly joyous meal with the journey that lay ahead, but they still enjoyed each other's company. It was getting late so the king and the queen gave everyone their blessing then they retired to their quarters for the night.

"I'd like to go look over the maps one last time then I'll meet you all here before midnight," said Malcolm.

"I have to make a few finishing touches on the gear, and I'll bring it up when I'm finished," said Gamon as he left the table.

They both walked out of the room and everyone else went and sat by the fire for a while. The time seemed to drag as they waited for midnight, but it slowly came closer and closer. The door suddenly opened and Gamon came marching into the room.

"Boy, do I have some treats for you guys!" he said.

Some of the men from the shop helped him carry in all the armor and weapons and they placed it on a table. They slowly walked away, and they took their time leaving to admire Helaina for a bit longer.

"Come and see what I have for all of you," he said.

Everyone got up and went over to see.

"Ladies first," said Gamon. "For you, Helaina. I have strengthened your wand to cast further and stronger than ever!"

As he placed it in her hand it sent a pulse of energy up her arm, then it faded away.

"What was that?" she asked.

"It mended itself to you and now only you can use its powers."

She looked it over and placed it safely in her belt.

"Thank you, Gamon, I have a feeling I'll get to test it out soon," she said.

"You're welcome! For you, Herex. I made your mace lighter and stronger. I also added a more powerful ruby and polished it up a bit and I restrung the handle too!"

Herex took the mace and held it up. The new ruby started to glow brightly, and he looked over at Gamon and nodded to show that he was thankful.

"Explosive tip spreading arrows for you, Archer.

These babies will take out anything within twenty feet of your main target."

"Really? I like that idea! Thank you, Gamon," he happily replied.

"Oh, and I put a new chord on it too! It'll shoot a little further now."

"You never cease to amaze me. I don't know what we'd do without you," said Archer.

"Well, you wouldn't have such good weapons and armor to start," replied Gamon.

They all began to laugh together.

Gamon looked over at Herex and saw that he wasn't laughing with them.

"What's the matter? No humor?"

Herex looked at him for a moment then patted him on his shoulder and startled him again. Herex then started to laugh to himself under his hood.

Just then the door opened, and Malcolm came inside.

"So, my friend. What surprises do you have for us this time?"

"Ahh, Malcolm! For you, that new sword you've been asking for. It's made of the strongest and lightest metal in existence. It is unbreakable! When you are ready to attack the blade will extend and make you able to reach more enemies with every swing."

Malcolm examined the sword from its handle all the way up to the tip of the blade.

"It's beautiful, Gamon. I've been wanting to put down those axes for a while now. Thank you."

"You're welcome," he replied.

Everyone put on their gear and a four-barrel rifle sat by itself on top of the table. Everyone noticed and it saddened them as they thought about Beck.

"I'm sure he will love it, Gamon," Malcolm said.

"I've been working on it for weeks. I can't wait to give it to him. You guys gotta get him back, you just gotta," he pleaded.

"Well with that said, let's go get Beck. Mount up!" said Malcolm.

They walked away and Gamon noticed that Malcolm had left his helmet.

"Aren't you forgetting something?" Gamon asked.

"No. I think I'll leave it here. Besides, it takes away from my peripheral vision," said Malcolm.

"Is that so? I'll have to fix that for ya!"

They went out to the balcony, and everyone called to their birds. All at once they descended in from the sky. Herex let his orb into the air and his bird appeared. They all climbed on and with a swipe of their wings, they all flew off, side by side, toward the moon. Gamon watched from the balcony until they were out of sight.

"Good luck, you guys. They're coming to get you, Beck. Don't worry. They're coming to get ya," Gamon whispered into the night.

46

He turned away and walked back into the castle as the doors slowly closed behind him.

CHAPTER 4
THE EVERDARK DEPTHS.

Glowing vegetation lit their way as they flew over the land. The rivers and lakes sparkled, and colorful plants and flowers outlined the trails through the forest below. In the distance, there was a part of land that dropped off from the bright forest. All that could be seen was darkness.

"We're almost there," said Malcolm. "Just a little further. I'm not sure of what to expect, so be ready for anything."

They all looked ahead into the darkness. As they flew into the Whispering plains, they immediately felt the beady eyes of creatures staring up at them from below. As they reached Sorrow Lake they flew out over the water and buzzed by a dwarf who was fishing in a canoe. The boat rocked so much that the man fell right in. When he came back up, he shook his fist and spat some water as they hastily disappeared into the distance.

"Alright everyone, stay close in the tunnel," said Malcolm. "Herex, I need you to lead the way. Be on guard, there will be undead here."

Herex moved to the front of the pack, and they all formed a line, one behind the other. As the entrance came up, they all crouched down and flew straight up over the opening to the depths. One by one they dropped inside a vortex of water in tight formation.

As soon as they reached the tunnel, the undead fighters covered the walls and stared back at them with their glowing red eyes. Herex pointed his mace ahead of them and he fired a slew of red orbs into the tunnel. After a bright flash, a flame spread across the walls and ignited the bones of the undead.

They flew swiftly through the rest of the tunnel and as they reached the end the birds spread their wings to slow themselves as they dropped inside a massive cave. They landed with so much force that the ground trembled and dust rose up all around them. Everyone dismounted the birds and stood inside a small circle of light that shined down from the tunnel.

Helaina formed a white orb in her hands and fired it into the air. It illuminated the entire cave and they saw hundreds of undead fighters crawling along the walls toward them. They began leaping from every direction. Helaina quickly waved her wand and a dome formed around them. The undead landed on top and hacked on it with their weapons, trying relentlessly to get at them.

"I'm going to explode the dome outward, and it should take down some of them," said Helaina.

"Everyone, prepare yourselves," said Malcolm. "Leave nothing behind. Let's get our man back."

Helaina took a deep breath and looked around to see that they were all ready. She threw her arms into the air and the dome exploded. The burst of energy

---

was so strong it ripped through the entire cave and wiped out every single fighter. They all looked around then back at Helaina, impressed with the outcome.

"Well, that worked! Great job!" said Archer.

They all looked around for where to go next.

"There's only one way out of this cave and it's on the north wall," said Malcolm.

They all turned to see the tunnel already filling with more undead fighters. Dozens emerged with their glowing red eyes and weapons drawn. They crawled and ran frantically into the cave as everyone prepared for their next attack. Archer took an arrow from his quiver and loaded it into his bow. The rubies on Herex's mace began to glow and his eyes turned red under his dark hood as he focused on the fighters that were closing in. Helaina turned toward the tunnel and formed a green orb in her hands.

"It's time," said Malcolm as he pulled out his sword.

The aura of his armor changed to fiery red. He held up his sword and the blade extended to double his reach. He gazed at it closely as the fiery aura slowly spread to the tip of the blade.

"Very nice, Gamon," he whispered to himself.

Everyone spread out as the undead got closer. The first group began to attack but they were quickly cut down by Malcolm's fiery blade. More undead fighters kept piling out of the tunnel. Helaina fired her orb at them, and it struck the ground at their feet. Green moss began to grow all around them as thick roots shot up and ripped them down to the ground. The vine encompassed them till they were completely overcome.

Malcolm walked to the entrance of the tunnel and slashed through all the fighters in reach of his blade. The flame enveloped their bones and their skeletal bodies crumbled.

Archer took aim at the fighters that were crawling along the ceiling. As he pulled back the arrow it began to glow. He saw it out of the corner of his eye then he released it at the fighters. It soared through the air and split into a dozen more arrows. They took down his target along with every fighter around it. He pulled out another arrow and looked at it closely as it let off a slight glisten.

"That Gamon did it again," he said as he loaded it into the bow and fired.

Herex held up his mace and fired a shiny red orb over the heads of the undead. When it exploded, a red dust rained over them and caused them to go mad. They began hacking away at each other with their weapons till only one of them remained, then he pointed his mace and finished off the last one with a single orb. The fighter burst into flames and its old torn robe dropped to the floor, clearing the cave of the undead fighters.

"That wasn't so bad," said Archer.

"No, it wasn't, but I don't think it will be that easy as we get further into the depths," Malcolm replied.

Helaina formed another white orb and fired it down the tunnel. They continued inside and found some stray fighters, but Herex took them out before they became any trouble.

The end of the tunnel opened into another large cave. Water poured from the ceiling and passed straight through a hole in the floor that led into another cave below.

A giant ogre slept in a chair on the far side of the cave and a large group of undead fighters blocked their way into the next tunnel.

"Archer, I need you to take out some of these fighters," said Malcolm.

"My pleasure," he replied as he took an arrow from his quiver and pulled it back in his bow.

He fired the arrow and it split into a dozen others as it arched through the air and took down a large group of the fighters. Some of the fighters realized what had happened and they started to charge toward them. Helaina flicked her wand and a dome formed around the fighters. They frantically hacked away at it with their weapons and tried to get out, but there was no way.

"They're under control. You may continue," said Helaina.

"I see!" he replied.

Helaina smiled and winked at him, then Archer

turned back to the undead and fired again. He took down a large part of the group that came toward them and as he was about to finish off the last of them, Herex placed his mace against his chest to stop him.

Herex turned to the rest of them, and he held his mace into the air. He whirled it in a circular motion and all the rubies lit up as a swirling dark hole formed below them and pulled them inside. They were swept away into oblivion then the hole dissipated.

"Why am I wasting arrows when you can do that?" Archer asked and Herex just looked back at him and shrugged.

Malcolm went into the center of the room so he could size up the enemy. They all went over to the ogre who was somehow still sleeping in the chair.

"Oh, no! Is that who I think it is?" asked Helaina.

"I believe. Yes. It is. It's Tonk," replied Malcolm. "That isn't good. When he sees me, he will be angry."

They continued closer to him. Helaina clapped her hands together and the dome that held the group of undead shrunk and vanished. It made a loud pop that woke Tonk from his sleep and he saw Malcolm standing in front of him. He quickly got up and went toward him as he tapped a large wooden club in his hand.

"Malcolm Cahpra, I hoped I'd get to see you. That's why I took this job," said Tonk in his goofy, scratchy voice. "Come to save your puny little friend? Well, this is as far as you'll get. I'm gonna pay you back for what you did to Tiny."

"Tiny?" asked Archer.

"Yea. It's his pet," Malcolm said. "It was more of a beast though, almost his size and it was hungry, for me!"

"So, what did you do?" asked Archer.

"I kind of tied his harness to an airship. I didn't know it was departing! It was on its way too, well, somewhere far," Malcolm said.

"That's enough talking. It's time to smash you and your little friends," said Tonk.

He took a handful of powder from a pouch, and he sprinkled it onto the floor beside him. Another ogre suddenly rose up from the ground just as big as him, but he was translucent.

"This time I have a little help," said Tonk.

They both picked up huge boulders from the ground and started to hurl them. Malcolm took out his sword and slashed through one of them, sending the pieces off to each side of the cave. Herex stopped another in midair and with a sweeping motion of his hand, he threw it away from the group.

The ogres charged and swung their clubs ferociously. Malcolm ran to Tonk and held up his sword to deflect the attacks. Wood chips flew off Tonk's club each time Malcolm blocked it with his sword.

Archer held off the other ogre as Herex formed a black hole behind it. He fired orbs as Archer fired arrows and each impact pushed the ogre back further and further until it fell inside. It rummaged around to try and find some solid ground to hold on to but there was nothing solid.

Malcolm and Tonk stopped fighting and they looked over to see the swirling wind pull the other ogre in and it closed behind him.

"Nooooo!" yelled Tonk as he swung his club wildly.

Archer was clipped by his swing, and it sent him flying across the cave. Helaina waved her wand and a glowing green moss formed below him. A bright sparkling aura surrounded his body to help heal his wounds. Herex quickly summoned a portal beside Tonk and inside it was a vision of Tiny in a dark forest.

"Is this some sort of trick?" asked Tonk. "Tiny is that you?"

Tiny let out a loud yelp.

"It is Tiny! Please, please. Can I go to him?"

"Yes. Yes, you can," said Malcolm.

Tonk squeezed his large body through the portal and ran to Tiny and embraced him tightly.

"Oh Tiny, Tiny, Tiny! I missed you so much!" He said joyously then Herex closed the portal behind him.

"Thank you, Herex. I wish you had done that in the first place. I kind of liked that Ogre. The problem was that beast didn't like me," said Malcolm.

Archer stood up and brushed himself off.

"Well, he's got it back now! Thank you, Helaina," he said as he came back over.

"Now it's time to finish this. There's only one more cave in this place and that's where Beck will be. Let's get him back and be finished here," said Malcolm.

They all went down a circular stairway that led to the cave below. It was dimly lit by small torches that hung every few feet along the walls. As they reached the bottom of the stairway it let out into a massive cave with an army of undead fighters that stood in a formation. The newest leaders of the depths were two much larger skeletal fighters with the same glowing red eyes as the rest of them.

At the far end of the cave was a tall fireplace that was lined with skulls and dangling from the ceiling not far away was Beck. He was entirely wrapped with rope and his hands and feet were bound behind him. His eyes were closed, and his head was slumped over to the side.

"There he is!" Malcolm said.

"I hope he's sleeping," Archer added.

"I think I can reach him from here," said Helaina.

She waved her wand over her head and the air around him began to glisten.

Immediately he awoke and eagerly looked around to see where it was coming from.

"It reached him! Gamon said it would cast further!" she said.

He looked toward the door and saw the light from the torches reflecting off the golden pattern on Helaina's gown.

"Let's start with the closest groups," said Malcolm.

Herex shook his head in agreement.

"There must be a few hundred of them," said Archer.

Herex went to the bottom step and pointed his mace into the air. He fired bright red orbs into the air and as they burst, dark clouds formed over their heads and began to rain fire on them. The undead scrambled and scanned the room to see where it came from. When they turned to the stairway, they saw Herex as everyone else walked out behind him. Some tried to attack, but they were quickly taken down by the fiery rain.

As the clouds receded, the remaining fighters made their charge. Archer took aim with his bow and fired at the closest ones. Malcolm's blade extended and the fiery aura intensified. He ran toward one of the groups and swung his sword right through them. The fiery aura now covered his whole body as he continued into the crowd. Soon after, the only thing everyone could see was the fiery glow from his blade as it swiped at the enemy fighters.

The two leaders moved toward them and drew their large bone axes. Helaina threw her arms over her head and a wall shot up between them to hold them back. The leaders pounded against it, but they were held there to watch as the rest of their fighters fell.

Beck started to cheer and holler.

"My friends are here! You two are in trouble now. You're lucky I'm tied up or else I'd give ya some trouble myself."

Archer continued firing arrows into the crowd, cutting down all the undead within reach with his bow. The fiery aura from Malcolm's sword and armor could still be seen in the middle of the undead. From where everyone stood, he seemed like a flaming propeller as he moved around the crowd. Archer turned back to Helaina and Herex.

"Do you see what I'm seeing?" he asked.

Helaina shook her head yes then she formed a green orb and fired it. It struck the ground at the feet of a dozen fighters. Moss began to cover the ground as the vine reached up and pulled them all down inside.

Archer noticed one of the fighters reaching into its pouch and he saw it pull out a small bomb and try to light the fuse. He quickly took aim and fired, but it was too late. The fighter tossed it into the air, and it exploded just over Malcolm's head.

A yellow poison cloud covered him and the fiery

aura from his armor dissipated. He immediately stopped fighting and fell to his knees as the undead fighters surrounded him. Helaina saw what happened and with a wave of her wand she lifted him high over the fighters' heads as the poison aura lingered around his body.

Herex fired a single black orb at the remaining fighters and when it exploded, the force shredded every fighter below him. Helaina swung her wand and cast a healing spell that glistened around his body to cure him of the poison. She placed him back down onto his feet and he was clearly disoriented as he turned back and nodded to thank her for the assistance.

The last group of undead fighters approached as they made their final stand. Helaina waved her wand and covered the ground with moss. As they walked over it, the vine shot up and held them all in place as Archer and Herex fired until they were gone.

The only thing left of them were chips of bone and the old torn robes. Everyone went over to Malcolm who was now standing in front of the leaders of the Everdark depths. They smashed against the wall to get to him, but they couldn't penetrate it. Helaina handed Malcolm a vial of clear liquid and he quickly drank it without hesitation.

"Thank you, Helaina. Your potions always seem to come in handy."

She looked up at him and shook her head in

agreement.

"You ready?" she asked.

"Yes. Let's go get Beck," he replied.

Helaina swiped her wand out in front of herself and the wall between them disappeared. The huge undead fighters charged toward them. Herex took aim and rapidly fired at their skeletal bodies. Malcolm's sword extended out as he deflected a powerful swing from one of the fighters.

Herex reached up toward Beck and with a flick of his wrist, the ropes that bound him began to loosen. He wiggled and kicked and tried to keep his balance as he slowly lowered to the ground. As soon as his feet were planted, he looked over at Herex with a grin of approval, then he turned back to the leaders and his expression changed to an angry snarl. He picked up stones and started to hurl them at the fighters. Herex giggled at Beck as he watched him. Archer fired arrows as fast as he could pull them from his quiver and Helaina fired a slew of orbs at their legs. Vine reached up and wrapped all around them as she whispered a spell onto them.

"Now they be cast in stone," she said.

With a wave of her wand, their bones began turning to stone, starting with their legs, then it went up their torsos and right to their skulls. Malcolm deflected its axe one last time before the fighter's arm became solid rock. Moss and vine wrapped around their skeletal bodies and as they cured, they looked like statues that had been there for some time. Everyone watched the red glow fade from their eyes then they turned to see Beck, now standing right next to them.

"If you would have just given me a few more minutes, I would have met ya's outside," he said with a giggle.

Everyone was thrilled that he was free, and they all gave him a warm welcome.

"It wasn't the same without you, Beck," Helaina said happily as she pulled him in and hugged him tight.

"It's good to be back," he replied.

After she let him go, he started to look around the room.

"Where's my backpack? I have something for this place!" He said as he saw it by the fireplace.

He went over and pulled out two small explosives and placed them by the leaders. He placed a few more of them in the corners then he ran back over. As he got back, the birds all flew in from the large hole in the ceiling that the water poured through.

"Herex, you know what I need you to do!" said Beck.

Herex nodded his head and reached into his satchel. He summoned his bird and jumped onto its back as the others climbed onto theirs.

"So, Beck. You wanna ride with me?" asked

Helaina.

"Absolutely! I'm not staying here any longer."

He jumped onto the back of her bird and all at once they leapt up into the air and flew off toward the ceiling. Herex flew around the room and fired burning orbs that lit the fuses of the bombs, then he followed everyone up into the next cave. They began to explode, and the stone skeletal fighters were blown to pieces as the walls crumbled and the cave filled up with water.

When they got into the cave above it, Beck lit half a dozen more and dropped them around the ground. As they exploded, the entire cave shook and started to collapse.

They flew swiftly toward the tunnel as the water followed behind them. They just made it inside as it poured into the tunnel. Beck lit another one and tossed it behind them. It exploded and the tunnel crumbled, making it impassable as they exited into the cave they arrived in.

Beck took out his last few bombs and hurled them toward Herex.

One by one he lit them with fiery orbs, and they landed all around the cave. As they flew toward the exit, they exploded and large chunks of rock fell from the ceiling. The cave fell around them and filled with water as they got into the exit tunnel. Beck took the last bomb from his backpack.

"Last one! Let's finish this," he hollered.

He lit the fuse and threw it just as they exited the depths. A few moments later, a hundred-foot geyser followed them out of the tunnel as they flew straight up and out of Sorrow Lake. The last explosion had closed the entrance to the Everdark Depths, forever.

Everyone cheered and congratulated each other as they leveled off and flew over the lake. One of the bird's talons skimmed through the water and made a fishtail behind them.

"We need to stop at my house. I need to feed the dog. It's been a whole day, and she gets grumpy when she's hungry, just like her dad," said Beck, jokingly.

"I was going to suggest that we stay at your place instead of traveling all the way back to the castle tonight," replied Helaina.

"Great idea!" said Malcolm and they adjusted their course and headed back to Beck's house.

CHAPTER 5
RIGHT IN TIME FOR SUPPER.

They flew over the dark forest and a tall mountain face at the edge of the Whispering plains. Behind it was a vast forest covered in luminous foliage with small bodies of water that glistened in the moonlight. Waterfalls fell from the tops of tall cliffs into sparkling pools. Iridescent water lilies lit the crystal-clear water for the fish and turtles that swam throughout. In the distance was the circular mountain range that surrounded the beautiful valley where Beck's cabin sat hidden inside.

"Ahhh, Home sweet home. Again!" said Beck.

They flew over the first range and dropped down into the sunken valley. A sparkling pond beside his cabin reflected into the trees above it as they swooped down and landed beside it. Beck hopped off the bird and walked toward the house. His dog suddenly crashed through the front door, entirely unhinging it from the frame. She was overjoyed to see him and charged toward him as fast as she could.

"Oh no. Easy, Mya. Daddy missed you too! Okay, slow down," said Beck as she knocked him to his back.

She licked his face with her saliva filled tongue.

"Blah! That's gross," he said.

Everyone laughed as he tried to get out from under

her. Malcolm patted her on the head as he walked past and into the house. She licked Beck's face once more then she followed everyone in the door. Beck got up and wiped his face as he followed them in.

"Make yourselves at home. I'll get the fire going and find something to cook," said Beck.

"We gathered some food yesterday. There's a turkey in the pen," said Archer.

"Great! I'll go get it ready," Beck said happily.

He took a match off the mantle and struck it against the hearth. Just as it ignited, Herex fired an orb into the fireplace, evaporating the match and scalding Beck's fingers as the fire began to burn at full force.

"Ahh! Alright you ambitious wanna be an undertaker! You don't like to do things the old fashion way, do ya?" hollered Beck as he shook his hand from the burn.

Herex giggled to himself, and everyone laughed along with him. Beck opened the back doors, and everyone went out onto the balcony. They looked around at the illuminated vegetation that grew throughout the hillside. A waterfall fell beside the cabin where a group of tiny purple dragons played in the falling water. Colorful lilies lit up the pond where schools of fish swam throughout.

"Would you mind helping me with this fire, Herex?" asked Beck.

Herex quickly fired another orb into the pit and

started a nice cozy fire for them out on the balcony.

"Thanks! I'll go get the turkey," he said as he went off down the stairs.

Everyone looked out at the valley and listened to the peaceful sound of nature and flowing water beside them. Suddenly an unpleasant squawk was heard from the turkey. Everyone turned to each other and laughed. Good old Beck was back. He came up a few minutes later with a plucked turkey and a barrel of brew on his shoulder.

"You know what we need?" asked Beck.

"Yes, I do!" replied Malcolm as he got up and went back into the cabin.

He went to the kitchen and took out five large steins from the cupboard and brought them back to the table. Beck jammed a tap into the top of the barrel, and he filled the steins till foam ran over the brims.

"It's time to celebrate and for me to thank you all for getting me out of there," said Beck. "Truth be told, it took a little longer than I hoped. I missed a few meals, but I'm back now! Right in time for supper!"

Everyone laughed at his comment since clearly his biggest upset throughout the whole ordeal was that he had missed a few meals.

"We were going to wait here for you, but we thought you might get hungry, so we came to get you," said Archer.

"Ha-ha! Really funny, Archie. I have your dinner here in this can along with the dog food. Would you like it warm or cold?" He asked.

Everyone laughed except Archer, but then he cracked a smile and began to laugh with everyone. Malcolm suddenly became quiet, and he sat back in his seat. Everyone noticed his silence and they gave him their attention. He held his stein up into the air.

"This is to the safe return of Beck and the journey ahead. May we all find our way home."

"To being home!" added Archer.

"To being together again!" said Helaina.

They all picked up their steins and clapped them together in a circle. They took a swig and slapped them back onto the table. Malcolm looked around at everyone.

"We have many things to do over the next few days. We leave for the ruined castle at sunrise. There's someone there I need to speak with, and we'll also be making our camp there to prepare for the battle. I'm hoping our old home hasn't been entirely claimed by nature over the years." he added.

"It was such a beautiful castle," said Helaina. "My favorite place in the world! I miss the shops and all the people who lived there."

"It was my favorite place too. We will see it again tomorrow by dusk. Tonight, we rest, and in the morning, we fly," said Malcolm.

They all sat around the table and talked for a little longer. Small animals ran across the valley as others climbed through the trees.

"This place really is something else at night," said Malcolm. "But I do think it's time to get some sleep. Thank you for dinner and the brew, Beck."

"Ahh, it was nothing. Least I could do after you all got me out of the Depths," he replied. "You all know where to crash. Make yourselves at home."

Everyone said goodnight and went inside. Helaina and Malcolm each took a bedroom and Archer and Herex stayed in the sitting room by the fire.

"You want the couch, Herex?" Archer asked.

Herex shook his head no and sat against the wall near the fireplace. Beck stayed outside and he dragged his seat over to the fire pit and sat down. His dog lay on the ground beside him, and Beck leaned the chair gently against her.

"It's good to be home, Mya. Really good to be home," he whispered as he fell asleep and began to snore.

The dog nestled in and took a deep breath before falling asleep too. In the morning, the sun peeked over the horizon and dimly lit the house, and everyone started to wake up. Archer opened his eyes to see Herex levitating in the corner of the room.

"Herex. That's just not normal!" said Archer.

Herex looked over at him and at the floor, then he

stepped down to it and shrugged at Archer. He saw that Beck was still sleeping in the chair outside with his dog and when he walked outside, he slammed the door to startle the dog. Mya quickly stood up and Beck fell over onto the floor.

"Oww! Darn it," said Beck. "Did you do that on purpose?" he asked.

Herex shook his head no and sat down at the table. Everyone came outside just as the sun began to rise over the valley.

"Well! Who wants some breakfast? I'll go and get some eggs," said Beck.

"Just don't go too far this time and don't talk to strangers," said Archer as he tried to hold back his laugh.

"Very funny, Archie. You're quite the morning person, aren't ya?" said Beck as he rolled his eyes.

Everyone laughed as Beck shook his head and walked down the steps. A few minutes later he came back up with a bowl of fresh eggs. Herex rekindled the fire and Beck cracked them into a large pan. In no time at all everyone had a healthy serving of eggs and a chunk of fresh bread.

"Herex, I need you to summon Gamon. I'm sure he's been waiting for us all night," said Malcolm.

"Oh! Little buddy! I'll go get him a plate," said Beck as he went back inside. Herex threw his arm up and the portal rose from the balcony. Inside the swirling cloud was a reflection of Gamon, looking around for any of Herex's tricks. He slowly walked through with Beck's new rifle on his shoulder.

"Where's Beck? You guys got him, right?" asked Gamon.

"He's here. He just went inside," replied Archer.

Beck came back out of the house excited to see Gamon.

"Hey, little buddy! How are ya?" he asked happily.

"I'm great! I'm glad you're back, I have something for you," replied Gamon.

"What in the world is that you have there on your shoulder, little buddy?" Beck asked.

"This here is my welcome home present. It's a four-barrel semi-automatic rifle. It's got a scope that will let ya see for miles and a launcher on the bottom that fires exploding orbs."

"Wow! She's a beauty. Thank you! I will cherish it always, for leisure and in battle, till death do us part!" he said as he took it in his hands and looked through the scope.

Helaina shook her head as everyone else laughed uncontrollably.

"When the battle is over, I'd like to do some fishing," added Beck.

"I thought you'd never ask," replied Gamon. "Just name the time and place!"

"I will, I'll think of somewhere good to go," said

70

Beck.

He handed Gamon a plate of eggs and Gamon sat down to eat with everyone else. He took a huge bite of bread and looked around at everyone at the table. Helaina laughed at his cheek full of food.

"Where are you all headed today?" Gamon asked.

"We're going back to the ruined castle," Helaina said.

"Really? I miss that old place. I wonder what's left of my shop. I haven't been back there since the battle," said Gamon

"It's been in ruin for ten years. Who knows what we will find inside those walls," replied Archer.

"We'll take care of anything unruly that we run into," said Beck.

"Yes, we will. We leave soon," added Malcolm.

Everyone finished their meals and looked out across the valley as they inhaled the fresh morning air. Their stomachs were full, and they were all ready for the journey. The sun peeked through the trees and the birds chirped harmoniously. A thin fog covered the base of the valley that made it seem as if the balcony sat high in the clouds.

Malcolm whistled for Star and the fog rolled around his wings as he flew in and landed. Malcolm greeted him warmly then climbed onto his back.

The rest of them called their birds as Herex released his orb. Everyone climbed on and prepared to leave. Beck's dog jumped on him and tucked her head into his neck to say goodbye. She licked his cheek then sat back down and gave her paw as she looked up at him.

"Hold down the fort, girl," said Beck softly and he climbed onto an older brown gryphon.

All at once they leapt into the air and flew straight up through the trees. Beck stopped and hovered for a moment to take one last look at his cabin.

"You'll be back before ya know it, Beck," Malcolm said. "Let's get going. We have a long way to go."

Everyone waved goodbye to Gamon, and they flew off in the direction of the ruined castle. Gamon went back though the portal then it sank down into the balcony behind him and disappeared Beck's dog went back inside and pushed the door closed behind herself.

They spent the entire day flying across the Isle and its many enchanting landscapes. Some areas had tall, jagged mountains and others were vast forests. Alluring green plains were filled with lakes and waterfalls and colorful foliage. Smoke rose from the chimneys of cabins that were built throughout the isle.

They noticed what looked like a large metal cage in the corner of one of the yards and they swooped down to investigate. As they got closer, they saw that it was holding a small group of skeletal fighters. They landed nearby and an older man in a black robe came outside.

"Lord Cahpra, I didn't expect to see you, but I'm glad you're here. My name is Gideon Marshall.

Malcolm was about to reply but the man interrupted.

"I know who all of you are, lord Cahpra. I am honored by your presence here at my home," he said respectfully.

"What is it you have here?" Malcolm asked.

"I came across these skeletal beings in the forest just east of here. I was unarmed or else I might have finished them off then, but I'm glad I didn't because now I've had a chance to study them. They gave me a run for my money. They chased me all the way back here and luckily, I was able to trick them into the cage. It's normally used to protect my livestock."

"What have you found?" asked Archer.

"Sadly, not so much. There's no getting through to them. It seems they only desire to cause harm to anything they meet, and they'll stop at nothing. It's their reason for being. They don't even have the cognition for self-preservation. There were three more, but they ravaged them the other night. They don't eat or sleep! They're still the tortured souls that old king Westmore cursed them to be."

Malcolm approached the cell, and they became angry and tried to grab him. He watched them for a moment and then he turned back to everyone.

73

"They've been subjected to their curse long enough. Someone please, relieve them of their misery," said Malcolm with remorse.

Everyone looked around for someone to volunteer but nobody did. Herex decided to take the task and he held out his mace as the ruby on top began to glow. A single red orb shot out and exploded inside the cage. When the cloud dissipated, they were gone.

"That was more humane than anything I could have done, so thank you," said Gideon. "I wish I could have found a way to change them, but it's not possible. There's just no way to help them. I'm afraid the coming battle is unavoidable."

"It's good that you tried. Now our task is clear," replied Malcolm.

"Best of luck to your journey. Thank you all for what you've done for the isle, and for all the things you're still, yet to do," he said.

"Our good people deserve to live in peace as we must leave you now to assure that. Nice to have met you, Gidion," said Malcolm.

"And you, my lord. Goodbye everyone," he said as they flew off over the trees.

In the last leg of the journey, they crossed over a part of the isle known as the Twilight Forest which would lead them to the plain at the foot of the ruined castle.

The forest was known for its brilliant vegetation

that illuminated when the sun set. At twilight, the forest would come to life and all the nocturnal animals that lived there would graze the land. There were flowers and plants there that only bloomed at twilight, then they would close back up before the sun rose in the morning. Most people had never seen the plant-life with their own eyes. Only a few of the isles botanists on expeditions were lucky enough to witness them.

As they passed over the last of the forest, Malcolm noticed a young boy running frantically through a trail as orbs deflected off the trees behind him. They quickly dropped below the canopy of the trees to see what was happening. To their surprise, an older man was chasing him. Everyone followed Malcolm to aid the boy.

Herex dropped straight to the ground and stirred up some dust as he landed in the man's path. He pulled out his mace and held it to his chest. His eyes began to glow red along with the rubies on top of his mace. The man immediately stopped and was shaken by him.

Malcolm and Helaina followed the boy further into the forest and stopped him. Malcolm hopped off his bird and went up to the boy who looked back up at him in awe. He had never seen armor like Malcolm's before. He looked up and down with wide eyes.

"Are you, Malcolm Cahpra?" asked the boy.

"Yes, I am," he replied.

"Then you must be Lady Helaina, Archer, and Beck! You're Herex! You're my favorite, Herex!" he said with excitement. "I thought you'd be taller though."

Herex looked around at everyone as he dropped his mace down to his side and shook his head. Malcolm laughed a bit and then he turned back to the boy.

"What's going on here, young man?"

"Umm, I, I was just trying to find food for my family," he said.

"Is that so?" asked Malcolm.

The man slowly walked toward them under heavy scrutiny from Herex. He pointed his finger at the boy.

"This little thief stole from me, and I want it back! I want it all back," he said angrily.

"I will pay you double for the food he took. He was trying to help his family," said Malcolm.

"I don't care what he was doing. Next time I catch him I'll teach him a lesson he'll never forget," replied the man.

"That won't be necessary," replied Malcolm firmly. "He won't be a problem to you anymore."

He reached into his pocket and handed the man three gold coins.

"This will cover it, and the rest is for your trouble."

"Don't let me catch you on my farm again boy," he yelled as he walked off into the forest.

"What is your name?" Malcolm asked.

"Marcus, sir."

"It's nice to meet you, Marcus. Why is it you had to steal from this man?

"My father lost his job at the docks, and I wanted to do something to help. The whole town has been very poor since the canal closed. There hasn't been any commerce in or out since those skeletons started showing up around the isle."

"It's wrong to steal, but it is honorable to help your family. Where is it, you're from, Marcus?"

"I'm from Watertown."

Malcolm thought of the times he traveled there as a child and the goods it brought to the isle. He took a sack of gold from his pocket and handed it to Marcus.

"This is to help the people of Watertown. Make sure nobody is left hungry there. You must promise me, Marcus."

Marcus looked up at him quite amazed by his kindness.

"I, I promise! Thank you. It will be used for only that. You have my word. My family and the people of Watertown, thank you," said Marcus as he bowed his head to him.

"You're welcome. Now run along and get back. Let the people know that we will bring stability back to the isle," said Malcolm.

"I will! Thank you, lord Cahpra. Bye everyone.

Bye, Herex!"

He smiled up at him then he ran off into the forest as the sack of gold coins jingled in his pocket. They all got back onto their birds and flew off toward the ruined castle.

CHAPTER 6
THE RUINED KINGDOM

They reached the edge of the forest and flew out over the plain as the ruined castle came into sight. It now seemed like part of the landscape with the ivy-covered walls that reached all the way up to the broken towers. It overgrew the roofs of the houses and most of the shops inside the town.

They circled the grounds to find a place to land and they swooped down to a large courtyard on the west side of the castle. An old fountain that was filled with murky water sat in the center of the overgrown grass and more ivy had claimed the steps that led to the castle door. They landed at the bottom and unmounted the birds then they drew their weapons and scanned the area.

"Helaina and Herex, I need you to scout the castle from top to bottom. Beck, Archer, search the town. I need to go and see an old friend. We'll meet in the old town square after all is clear," said Malcolm.

He made his way up the steps and shoved open the old ballroom doors. He went inside and looked around to see the once grand palace now resembled an overgrown cave. A large stairway on the far side of the hall was covered in moss and vines that climbed all the way up to the tall stained-glass windows at the top. He had a memory of his father walking down the steps in shining armor when left for battle long ago and as the door closed behind him in his thought, the wind slapped the door shut and it snapped him back into reality. He walked through a door to the side of the stairway, and it opened into a long dark corridor. At the end was a thick wooden door that creaked as it opened.

He took his sword out and the flame drifted up the blade to light his way down a dark spiral staircase. It led him into another long dark corridor and at the end was the heavy steel door of the dungeon. He pushed it open and slowly walked past all the cells in the block. When he got to the last one, he looked inside.

"Captain. Are you still here, old friend?"

He waited in silence for a response as he looked around at the other cells but saw nothing. He was disappointed not to see his old friend. Then suddenly a bright translucent ghost appeared lying on a cot with his feet against the wall. He wore a captain's hat with a black feather and a long leather trench coat with gold buttons.

"Malcolm, my boy. You have grown! You're not the same kid I remember, at all. I wondered if I'd ever see you again," said the ghost as he got up.

"It is good to see you too, Captain!" he replied with excitement. "You were thought of often when I made my hardest decisions. I always did what I thought you would have. You taught me a great deal while you shared your stories with me."

"That's good," replied the captain. "I don't get to do much else here in death."

"You know, you don't have to stay in this cell, right?"

"I know. It's just comfortable here and I get to rest for long periods of time. So, what brings you back here tonight, Malcolm?"

"The cursed army has risen into an army of the undead and they've been showing up all over the isle. I suspect their stronghold to be somewhere here in the north."

"How many of them are there?" asked the captain.

"It's unknown. Likely near a hundred thousand."

"And how many do you have?"

"We have twenty thousand brave men and women."

"Well, you're outnumbered, but the undead surely won't be a focused group of saps, so you will have that to your advantage. There is only one place I can think of that can hold that many of them and not be seen. The Old Gibb's mine. It's about a hundred miles east of here, below the Dyre Mountains," said the captain.

"The last time those mines were active was more than ten years ago, and it's not far from the gravesite of the cursed army," replied Malcolm.

"The tunnels connect to the Watertown corridor

south of here in the western Twilight Forest," added the captain.

"That has to be where their stronghold is," replied Malcolm.

"Thank you, old friend. You should go upstairs. We will be setting up camp here for a few days."

"Then I'll probably pop up and say, hello. There are some people that still live here. I see them from time to time, but they don't say much to me. Only a young boy named Lucas talks to me sometimes."

"There are people here. I must leave you now, Captain. I need to see what state they are in," said Malcolm as he quickly walked out of the dungeon and back out the way he came in.

Outside in the town, Beck walked around with his gun on his shoulder and Archer with his bow in hand as they searched the old, abandoned shops and houses in the town.

"I wish there were a few more of us to do this. This is not a small town," said Beck.

"Agreed," replied Archer. "This will take hours."

Just as he finished speaking, a small boy limped out the doorway of the old blacksmith shop. He had a piece of wood strapped to his leg that served as a brace and he slowly made his way to the middle of the road with a rock clinched in his hand. Beck and Archer watched him curiously.

"Uh, oh," said Beck as the boy lifted the rock.

He pulled it back over his shoulder and he whipped it at them. Beck was hit directly in the midsection, and he fell to the floor.

"Ooooooo. Oooooooooooooo, no he didn't!" grumbled Beck in pain.

He curled into a ball as Archer watched him in awe. The boy went to limp back into the shop, but Archer stopped him.

"No, dont go! We're not here to hurt you."

"Oh, yes we are," said Beck as he rolled around on the ground.

The boy slowly limped back over.

"You're the first then, mister. My name is Lucas."

"Hello, Lucas. I'm Archer and this is Beck. We're part of the king's army."

"Nice to meet you both," replied Lucas

"Not really," muttered Beck under his breath.

"There are three more of us here. I live in the old blacksmith shop with my family. We don't have much, but can I offer either of you a drink?"

"Is it a brew?" Beck asked as he opened an eye to look at him.

"No, but thank you, Lucas. We're both quenched," replied Archer.

"We need to let Malcolm know they are here. He'll want to get them somewhere safe. How many people live here in the town, Lucas?"

"There are four other families and then there's old

man Watson, but he's a little out of it lately. There's usually no trouble around here, but we do get some wanderers."

"We need you to give word to them. Have them come to the town square and we will give them food and supplies. We can have a doctor take a look at that leg too," said Archer.

"That would be great! It's been hurting me for weeks. I'll be sure to tell everyone, Archer. Thank you and I'm sorry about the rock, Mr. Beck."

"It was quite effective, wasn't it!" said Archer

"No. I just roll around the dirt because I like too, Archie," Beck replied sarcastically.

Archer laughed and turned back at Lucas.

"Okay, Lucas. You get everyone together and meet us in the square."

The boy shook his head yes and he limped back into the shop.

"BYE, LUCAS!" hollered Beck as he picked himself up off the ground with some help from Archer.

"Stop messing around, Beck. Let's get back and see what's going on."

"Messing around? Oh man, my stomach is starting to hurt," he said as he limped toward the castle.

"Well, at least we know who's in the town," said Archer.

Beck agreed as he slowly followed behind in pain.

Inside the castle, Helaina and Herex checked every room on every floor. Most of the castle's valuables were taken along to the new kingdom and anything left behind was looted. Broken pieces of vases were scattered over the floor. Windows were broken and the walls had holes from the fierce battle that was fought there long ago.

After they checked the last room on the highest floor and saw that it was clear, they made their way back down to the town square. When they got outside everyone else was just arriving.

"All is clear in the castle, Malcolm. We've checked every room, hall and corridor," said Helaina.

"Beck, what did you find in the town?"

"We found a young kid, and he threw a rock at me!"

Everyone turned to him and started laughing hysterically.

"Ha-ha. Laugh it up you guys," he said as he rolled his eyes.

Just then they saw Lucas and the other families coming toward them. There were a few small children and two babies in their mother's arms. Old man Watson followed behind with a suitcase that was filled with his belongings.

"Welcome friends! I'm Malcolm Cahpra and we are here to help. Herex, we need a portal to the new kingdom for supplies. Set it up in the ball room and summon Gamon, my father and a doctor to treat this boy's leg."

The adults in the families went up to Malcolm and dropped to a knee to show him their respect.

"Thank you, my lord. We always knew you would return," said one of the men.

"Please, follow me," said Malcolm.

They got up and followed him into the ballroom. Herex went to the center of the room, and he lifted his arms into the air. His portal rose from the floor and the blue cloud swirled inside. Gamon suddenly appeared and he walked through, followed by the king and a gnome in a white coat. He had a medical bag in his hand, and he quickly tended to Lucas's leg.

The portal lit up again and Monroe came through with a cornucopia that was full of fruit for the people. He gave it to them, and they hugged him in praise, before they sat down nearby and began to eat.

"Gamon, I need you to bring your tools down to the basement and get the power core up and running," said Malcolm.

"No problem! Will you help me with that, Herex? Maybe place my tools gently in front of me?"

Herex lifted his arms into the air and his tools appeared and floated through the portal. Gamon still covered his face, but Herex laid the toolbox down right in front of him like he asked.

"Thank you for not messing with me," said Gamon.

The sun began setting behind the ocean and a bright golden light shined through the ivy-covered windows.

"We will set up camp here in the ballroom," said Malcolm.

"Ladies, and gentleman. When you're finished eating and the doctor is done treating the boy, I ask that you follow my father back through the portal," said Malcolm. "On the other side is the new kingdom where you can join the rest of the people and start a new life for your families. This place is no longer safe. Please take your valuables with you."

"Our families are our valuables," said one of the men as he smiled back at them.

"Some would say we were rich for that reason alone," said another.

They finished eating and waited patiently for the king to guide them through to the new kingdom.

"Father, our old friend the captain believes the undead army could be using the Old Gibbs mine as a stronghold," said Malcolm.

"That's it! Why didn't I see that?" replied the king.

"Nobody's been in the mine for years. That would be the perfect place for them to regroup and not be seen. I'll take the families through now. If there is anything you require, please let me know. I'll have meals brought to you throughout the time you are here," said the king as he turned to the people from the ruined castle.

"Please, follow me. I will take you to the new kingdom now."

All the families along with old man Watson got up and followed him through the portal. Lucas walked behind them as he waved at Beck and Archer, now with a proper brace for his leg. He limped up to Beck and startled him again, but it was only to hug him.

"Thank you, Mr. Beck," said Lucas as he looked up with a smile.

Beck patted him on the head then Lucas followed his family through the portal and the bright aura around the frame dimmed back down.

"Let's set up camp and get the power back on. We need some light in this place."

Gamon and Herex headed to the basement where the power core was located. Malcolm and Beck collected firewood and started a strong fire in the corner of the ballroom just below a caved in part of the roof. A wave of Helaina's wand and a soft green moss grew over the fallen rock to make a comfortable sitting area around the fire.

"I'm going to check on Gamon and Herex to see how the repairs are going," Malcolm said.

He took a torch off the wall and lit it off a flame that sparked up on his forearm. His arm faded back to the blue aura, and he went down the stairs. The basement was a massive room with white stone walls.

In the center was a glass cylinder that stood from floor to ceiling and a large blue crystal laid on its side at the bottom.

Malcolm went in and watched quietly as Gamon studied the panel on the wall under a light orb that Herex had formed. He made some adjustments then flipped some switches and turned some dials.

"Alright, Herex. I'm gonna need you to align the crystal," said Gamon.

Herex went over to the cylinder and held his arms into the air. Slowly the crystal began to wiggle then it lifted into the air. It started to flicker as it neared the mounts that held it in place.

"Almost!" said Gamon.

With one last push the crystal was mounted between the coils, and they completed the circuit. It began glowing brightly as Gamon flipped a switch and the sound of the power winding up could be heard.

"We have power, folks!" Gamon said proudly.

The lanterns around the walls lit up along with the ones inside the ballroom.

"It seems they got it working," said Helaina.

"There's nothing he can't fix," replied Archer.

Malcolm went up to the power core and looked at the glowing crystal inside.

"Good job! I knew you could do it," said Malcolm.

"It's still in great shape! The crystal was just

knocked out of place. I'll give you a hundred-year warranty," said Gamon.

"I'll hold you to that, my friend."

"And I will honor it," added Gamon.

"Deal," said Malcolm.

They went back up into the ballroom and joined everyone around the fire.

"It's nice to be back here," said Helaina.

"Other than the hole in the roof, it's pretty cozy," added Beck.

As they sat around the fire, the portal lit up and Monroe emerged with a large platter of food. Two women followed him through with plates and drinks for the bunch. Beck excitedly stood up and watched as they placed all the trays down around them.

"Ahh, wow! Just what I was thinking. I'm starved!"

"Thank you, Monroe," said Malcolm.

"You're welcome, my lord."

"Did my mother have anything to do with this?"

"She had us make double, sir."

"I thought so. Thank you, and please tell her the same," said Malcolm.

"Gladly, sir. I bid you all a good night. May you rest comfortably," said Monroe then he went back through the portal, and it dimmed back down as they started to eat.

"This couldn't have come at a better time," said Beck before he bit into a chicken leg.

As everyone relaxed and talked together, the captain stood up inside the fire, startling Beck. He dropped the chicken leg on the ground and leaned forward with his eyes bright, amazed to see the man in the fire.

"Why in the world are ya in there, fella?"

The captain turned to him, and Beck leaned back as he raised his brow.

"This is my good friend, the captain," said Malcolm. "His real name is Jaxson Harlow. He had a short stay in the dungeon a hundred years ago, but he was proven innocent of the crime and released. He sailed the seas till he died, then he made his home here. He's sailed a million miles and fought a hundred battles on sea and land, but for some reason he finds comfort in the cell he occupied for those few days. He's been here fifty years now. I'd visit him in my youth, and he would tell me great stories of victory and heroism, even loss."

"There is loss in every victory and victory in every loss," said the captain. "Good evening, everyone. Please, just call me, Captain. The reason I stay here is because it's the only place I can materialize. Everywhere else, I'm just invisible. Something about this isle that's different from other places. Anyway, I thought I would float around tonight since there's finally some company here. I also wish to give you this, Malcolm."

He let a burning piece of paper out into the air and as it left the fire it extinguished and floated into Malcolm's hands.

"That's a map to the Brightwater Cavern on the west shore of the Twilight peninsula. You will find a gentleman inside one of the old shops. He sells goods of all sorts and he'll have something you will need for your journey. He won't be expecting you, so be careful when you run into him. He's quite crafty."

The captain turned and gazed at the plates of food and he started to lick his ghostly lips.

"Do you know how long it's been since I tasted a nice juicy steak?"

"Uh, let me guess. Fifty years?" said Beck.

The captain slowly turned to face him, and Beck leaned back again.

"You're smarter than you look, friend," said the captain.

"Yea, whatever. You just keep your little invisible fingers off the food."

The captain spitefully moved his hand through the platter.

"Ahh. Gross! I just lost my appetite," said Beck.

Everyone laughed at his reaction.

"Thank you, Captain. I will travel to the Brightwater Cavern at sunrise. It's good to have your company again," said Malcolm.

"You know where to find me if you're looking,"

replied the captain.

"Yes, I do."

"I'm not so sure this room will be to your liking if you're trying to rest," added the captain.

"Why do you say that?" asked Beck.

"What time is it?" asked the captain.

"It's almost nine thirty," replied Beck.

"Oh, you'll see," he said.

The captain dropped back out of sight into the flames. A moment later the room started to change. It became black and white as if it was a dream and the whole room was restored to the way it was before the battle. Everyone became on edge, unsure of what was happening.

Suddenly six robed fighters came crashing through the door. Everyone drew their weapons and prepared to defend themselves but then they noticed a strange glowing aura around them, much like the captain's. It seemed as if they were running from something and as they reached the stairway on the far side of the room, they ran halfway up, and another group burst through the doors. These were the king's fighters, and they shared the same aura as the others.

"They're ghosts," said Malcolm in amazement.

The fighters on the stairs fired bolts of purple thunder at the king's fighters. A woman in a red gown threw her arms into the air and formed a protective dome around her group. The bolts deflected in every direction and struck the walls.

Another one of the robbed fighters fired a flaming orb up to the ceiling and it started to rain fire down on top of them. The dome continued to hold as the fire rolled off onto the floor, forming a ring around them. When it stopped the woman dropped the dome and they advanced toward the stairway.

One of the king's fighters fired a bright blue orb back at them. It flew between two of the fighters and exploded in a flash, leaving no remains of the two fighters. A man with a bow fired an arrow and hit the third in the chest. The being's body ignited under the robe and crumbled to the floor.

The last three were now in the corridor that overlooked the ballroom. They noticed the robes of their comrades lying on the steps and they became furious. They fired down at the king's fighters, but a swipe of the woman's wand and she deflected all of it away.

A burly man with red hair and a beard pointed his rifle at the floor below them. He fired a shot and the ground under them collapsed. Two of them fell back down to ground and the armored man in the group charged toward them. His sword glowed bright red as he swung at the fighters. One was struck in the chest and his body burned away to ash. The other tried to flee but he kicked him back to the ground and plunged his sword into him.

A hooded man from the king's army fired a

burning orb that took the form of a fiery tiger. It ran up the stairs and chased the last fighter toward a stained-glass window at the end of the hall. It leapt in the air and dragged him through by his hood. The glass shredded them both and only bits and pieces of flaming robe fell to the ground outside.

The king's fighters were victorious and as they went to leave, the armored man peered back and stared at Malcolm with curiosity before he turned away and exited the hall. Cannon balls began to strike the hall and the ceiling above them collapsed. Everyone dove away from the falling stone. After a moment, they looked up and realized that the falling rocks were the same boulders they were sitting on, and it was only a part of the vision. They got back up and brushed themselves off. The room faded back to normal and none of them were sure what to make of it.

"What in the world was that?" asked Beck.

"I think it was a residual haunting of a battle that was fought here years ago," replied Malcolm.

"I feel like I've seen that woman before," said Helaina.

"Come to think of it, the man with the rifle looked strikingly handsome," added Beck.

"That man had my grandfather's bow. My bow," replied Archer as he looked down at it. "It was passed down through the generations. It had to be him."

"I've never seen anything like it. That man looked right at you, Malcolm," said Helaina.

"Could it be that our ancestors fought together, right here in this very room?" Malcolm asked as they all sat back down around the fire.

"The captain knew it would happen. Could this be an every night occurrence?" Archer pondered.

They picked on the food a little more as they looked around for any signs of the ghosts coming back. Beck finished the last of the food that he could manage.

"Belly is full," he said, and he took a gulp of his brew then slapped the stein down next to himself. "Is everybody finished eating?"

Moans and grunts came from everyone else.

"I am," replied Helaina.

"Okay! Then I know just the beast that's hungry right about now."

He reached for his necklace and pulled out a shiny dog whistle. He took a deep breath and huffed into it. A moment later his dog appeared out of thin air, wagging her tail and stretching her legs.

"Here, girl! I have something for ya."

He took one of the plates and put it on the ground. She happily trotted over and sniffed around, then she quickly dug in and devoured it all. She chewed the chicken right to the bone as everyone sat and watched.

"Waste not!" said Archer.

"Nope! Not with her around," replied Beck. "So, I hope nobody needs me tomorrow. I plan to visit a friend who lives nearby. Well, I'm hoping she still lives nearby."

"She? That's sweet, Beck. You going to see your crush!" said Archer.

"Ahh, don't break my chain, Archie. I'm on a full stomach here."

"I'm kidding ya, Beck. I hope she's there! I know she'll be happy to see you," replied Archer.

"She will be a lucky girl, Beck," added Helaina.

"Yea, good luck, Beck!" Added Gamon.

"I'll stay around here and prepare the town for the fighters and reminisce a little," said Archer.

"I'll join you. We must go to my old shop," said Gamon. "I have something to show you guys."

"Well, you have my interest," said Helaina.

"Sounds good to me," added Archer.

"What are you doing, Herex?" asked Gamon.

Herex slowly lifted his hand and pointed at him. Gamon paused and looked back at him.

"Do you really have to do that? It's just creepy," said Gamon.

Everybody laughed at how Herex always kidded with him.

"Nothing like a good campfire to strengthen the

spirit and ease some tension," said Helaina.

They all relaxed and enjoyed the warm fire. It wasn't long till each of them fell asleep nestled in the thick moss. It started to glow brighter, and pulses of energy sparkled into the air around them, replenishing everyone as they slept.

Beck's dog slept on the ground by the fire. She woke up and climbed onto the moss beside him and as she went to lie down but the sensation of the energy on her backside startled her. She quickly got up and turned to see what it was. When she didn't find anything, she went to sit back down and felt the same sensation, causing her to turn and sniff around some more. After finding nothing again, she gave up and laid back down on the ground. With one large exhale, she fell fast asleep along with everyone else.

CHAPTER 7
A DAY OF REST & RELAXATION.

A few hours later Malcolm awoke from his sleep. It was still dark, and crickets could be heard all around. A large moon shined down onto the castle and the overgrown moss inside the hall. He saw the fire was simmering down so he stirred the hot embers and added a few logs.

He took one last glance at everyone sleeping peacefully and he walked out the door. He examined the map that the captain gave him and he gazed in the direction he had to go. He whistled for Star who quickly landed beside him. Malcolm pets his head then hopped on his back and they flew off into the night to begin their journey to the Brightwater Cavern.

They sailed swiftly across the plain and shot up over the treetops. The sky was clear, and every star could be seen as they flew over the forest.

A short while later they reached a part of the land that was known as the Ancient Plains. It was a sandy wasteland and the only tree able to grow there was the Baobab tree since it was able to store water inside its trunk. They've grown there for hundreds of years. Some sprouted white flowers and others had thick green canopies that shaded the ground below and made it possible for other plants and flowers to grow.

They grew in groups all over the land except for a large circle in the center.

Two massive stone stages sat just high enough over the ground for the sandy terrain to not overcome them. It aroused his curiosity, but he continued along his path, and he soared up over the mountain range at the edge of the sandy basin.

Back at the castle Beck woke up feeling refreshed and he stretched his arms over his head.

"Today's the day. Here we go," he said under his breath.

Helaina pretended she was sleeping and watched as he began to fix his hair and straighten his beard. He brushed off his jacket and checked his breath. He looked up and saw her with a smile on her face.

"I'm flattered, Beck. For me?" She asked.

"How do I look?" he asked nervously.

"You look very handsome. She'll be very happy to see you."

"Thanks, Helaina. I needed that. I'm going for a tinkle." said Beck as he walked toward the doors.

"Thank you for sharing and ruining the moment. Typical," she replied as she shook her head and laughed.

"I'm gonna leave when I'm done, but I'll be back later tonight. Bye, Helaina," he said as he walked out.

"See you later, Beck. Good luck!" She replied as she sat up.

The door closed behind him and woke up everyone else. Gamon hopped right off the comfy green moss and roared as he stretched.

"I have something to show you guys. I need you to help me out at the old lab."

"Well, we have plenty of time to get the town in order before the fighters arrive. I'm with ya, Gamon," said Archer as he sat up.

"Me too," said Helaina.

Herex shook his head yes and they all got up and went out into the square. They made their way down the old broken steps, maneuvering between holes from cannon fire and the overgrown vine. As they got into the square, they looked around at the town they grew up in and how it now sat in ruin. The streets and shops were covered in brush. The benches and fountain were covered with ivy that grew right to the top of the lantern posts.

The carriage of a traveling salesman was covered in foliage as if the ground had reclaimed it for itself.

"This place is a mess, but we'll fix it when we're done," said Helaina.

"Good! Because boy do I want to show you guys something!" said Gamon with excitement.

He walked further into the square as everyone followed and observed all the shops along the road. Some of them collapsed and others had burned right to the ground. Beautiful plants and flowers grew wildly from an old flower shop, covering the charred remains of the shop next door.

The walls inside the flower shop were covered with every different color flower and large plants sprouted from all the seeds that were left behind. A bright green moss covered the ground and spilled out onto the road in front of it.

An old sign that once hung above the door read, 'Miss Carol's Wild Forest' and was now lying on the ground rotting.

"This was my favorite place in the world. It still has its beauty even though most of the shop isn't standing anymore," said Helaina.

Everyone continued down the road, and they went down an old vine covered alleyway. At the end, it opened into a small circular area with no ceiling. An old wooden door was covered with ivy and small blue flowers. Helaina waved her wand and it all pulled back, revealing a door with the engraving of gears and hand tools.

Gamon took out a key with the same engraving and he pushed it into the keyhole and turned it. There was a loud click and dust blew out from around the edges as the door popped open. Gamon and Archer pushed it open, and they peered into the old laboratory. The roof had caved in by the entrance and vegetation had grown throughout the lab.

"Oh, no!" said Gamon as he looked around at the damage.

He quickly made his way through to an old bookshelf. He looked through it frantically till he found what he was looking for. A sigh of relief came over his face as he took one of the books down and gently brushed off its cover.

"I've been wondering if I would ever see you again," he said as he blew the dust off the cover.

"What is it?" asked Archer.

"This is a journal my father and I made together. Inside are some of the greatest inventions we ever came up with. I wasn't sure if it was destroyed in the battle. Now that I have it back, I can continue our work."

"I can't wait to see the things you thought up when they're finished," replied Archer.

"We did finish one thing. You guys wanna see? I just hope it wasn't damaged."

Gamon went over to the far wall and reached through some vine to grab a lever. It was rusted and hard to pull so he hung onto it with all his weight and suddenly it broke free, and he fell to the ground. A door opened in the floor. Helaina waved her wand and the brush pulled back from the opening. Gamon crawled over on his hands and knees to look down inside then he looked up at everyone with a smile on his face.

"It's right down there," he said.

He got up and grabbed a torch off the wall.

"Herex, would you be so kind?"

Gamon held the torch far away from himself as he closed his eyes, thinking that Herex would certainly take the chance to mess with him again. He held up his mace and then a fireball shot out and lit the torch brightly. Gamon opened his eyes and realized that he wasn't even on fire.

"Ahh! Thank you, Herex," he said and Herex nodded back.

Gamon started down a stairway, and everyone followed right behind him. The bottom of the steps let out into a large circular room.

"This is the workshop!"

He flipped another lever and all the torches around the room lit up. As the room got brighter it revealed many seemingly unfinished inventions that Gamon and his father worked on long ago. There were gadgets all over the room. Small mechanical robots and a few rockets sat on the lab table. Along its side was a large device with wiring and coils sticking out of every side, but the most noticeable item in the lab was a beautiful black carriage that was the center piece of the room.

"This is one of our greatest inventions. It's impenetrable and it has everything you could ever need, right inside. My father and I were working on a teleportation device for it, but we never got to finish it," he said as he pointed to the device with all the wires and coils. "I'll have to figure a few things out and make some adjustments, but it'll be able to teleport us anywhere on the isle when it's done. I'm so happy to see that it wasn't damaged."

"It's beautiful," said Helaina.

"Thank you!" Gamon replied. "We never did get to take her out. What do you think? Wanna go for a ride?"

"What will pull the carriage?" asked Archer.

"Oh, you just leave that to me," Gamon said with a smirk.

He turned to Herex.

"That's an exterior wall of the town, right there. Can you help us with that, Herex?"

Herex pointed his mace and fired an orb that exploded and made a huge hole, plenty big enough for the carriage to pass through. Gamon climbed up to the seat on top of it.

"All aboard!" He hollered.

Herex climbed on top with him, and Helaina and Archer took a seat inside. Gamon took a handful of gray powder from his satchel, and he threw it out in front of the carriage. From out of the dust, two huge white tigers appeared in the reigns. Archer saw them through the front window and turned back to Helaina.

"I'm a little nervous about this," he said.

"Let's go!" yelled Gamon.

The tigers let out a fierce growl and they took off

running toward the hole. Archer was thrown back into the seat as they leapt through. Everyone held on tight as the carriage dropped down to the ground.

The tigers ran across the plain toward the forest with haste as they kicked up a cloud of dust behind them. Archer and Helaina held on for their lives as Helaina peeked out the window and hollered at Gamon.

"Can we slow down a bit?" she asked.

Gamon turned back to her and shook his head yes. He went back into his satchel and took out another handful of the powder. He threw it out in front of them as hard as he could, but the wind blew the dust back into their faces. Herex slowly turned to him as he shook his head. Gamon looked back with bright eyes and a face full of dust as he spat some of the powder from his mouth. The dust stuck to Herex and for a moment the silhouette of his face could be seen just before he waved his hand across himself, and the dust disappeared.

Gamon turned back to the tigers.

"Halt!" He yelled.

The tigers immediately slowed to a stop.

"Im sorry, Helaina," he said.

He reached back into the satchel and took some more powder out. He looked at Herex with a sigh and threw it out in front of them, transforming the tigers into two black stallions.

"Okay, let's go!" said Gamon and the horses began

to trot peacefully down the trail.

"This is better," said Helaina.

Archer shook his head in agreement but still held firmly to the armrest. Soon after, Gamon brought the carriage to a stop near a cliff that overlooked a large lake. They all looked out to see a place where they spent so many of their childhood summers. It was surrounded by tall redwood trees with vines that hung in the water. Colorful flowers and water lilies grew all around and huge lily pads floated on the surface. Bright colored fish and large turtles swam throughout the clear blue water.

"I know you all remember this place," said Gamon.

"Angel Lake! How could we forget? It's more beautiful than I remember," replied Helaina.

They all looked around and reminisced about the times they had there. None of them had seen it in years and it made them feel young again. After a few minutes, they all got back into the carriage and made their way further down the hill. When they reached the bottom, Gamon stopped near a small hidden pool that was separated from the rest of the lake by a glistening waterfall. Everyone got out and went to the shore.

"Who's hungry?" asked Gamon. "I'm gonna catch us some breakfast and we'll have a little barbecue."

He took a fishing pole and a tackle box from a trunk on the carriage and brought it over to the shore.

He opened it up and took out a shiny new lure.

"This is a little something that Beck and I made," said Gamon.

He tied it to the end of the pole, then pulled it back and cast it out into the pool.

"This one hasn't failed us yet," said Gamon.

Just as he said it the line became taut and Gamon started getting dragged toward the pool. A wave of Helaina's wand and he was lifted into the air and held above the water. The fish kept fighting and it pulled him further out as he tried to reel it in.

"Pull me back! Pull me back! We got a big one here!" he yelled.

Helaina pulled him back over the shore and Gamon reeled the fish in as it jumped out of the water. The fish was bright blue with a yellow stripe along its fin.

"Ahh! We got a yellow fin! You guys are in for a treat! Here we go!" he said with enthusiasm.

He reeled the fish out of the water and pulled it up onto the shore. Archer and Helaina cheered and even Herex threw his hands up from the excitement.

"Alright! Let's get a fire going. It's time to chow," said Gamon.

"There are plates and drinks in the cabinets under the seats and there are some chairs in the drawer on the underside of the carriage. I'll get the fish ready."

A short while later everyone rested comfortably as

the fish cooked over the fire.

"Now this is life! I wonder how Beck is doing," said Gamon.

"He'll be fine," replied Helaina. "She will be quite happy to see him again."

"Yea. Those two are perfect for each other," he said.

"I agree! They really are, perfect for each other!" Added Archer.

Somewhere west of the ruined castle, Beck soared over the treetops on his bird. He had a solemn look on his face as he looked out into the distance and saw a small puff of smoke rising from a chimney down inside a valley. He began to brush off his jacket and fix his hair, then he took a whiff of his underarm. He looked up and wrinkled his nose, but it wasn't so bad, so he shrugged and took a deep breath.

He swooped down and grabbed a handful of daisies from a field nearby and started toward the house, slowly navigating through the trees. He hovered for a moment and landed just in front of an old shabby white fence. He hopped off his bird and patted it gently on the head before it flew off into the trees. He slowly walked up to the house and looked around to see if anyone was there.

He saw a woman in the backyard with thick red hair and a rifle over her shoulder. He slowly walked toward her as he took off his hat, nervously crumpling it in his hands. A branch cracked under his foot and the woman immediately turned around and took aim. Beck stepped back nervously and held his hands in the air. She looked through the scope and saw that it was Beck, then she saw the flowers in his hand.

Suddenly she heard a noise in the woods, and she turned away and fired at a large turkey. Afterward she turned back to Beck with a gentle smile. He started to blush and crumple his hat some more as he twisted his foot in the grass.

"Hello, Rebecca," he said bashfully.

Rebecca smiled brightly at him.

"It's good to see you, Arthur. You're right in time for lunch," she said as she threw her rifle over her shoulder.

"Are you gonna get that?" She asked.

"Oh. Yes, of course! I'll pluck it too!" he replied.

He handed her the flowers and ran over to grab the turkey as she laughed and smelled their aroma. He brought the turkey over to the table in the backyard and began to pluck. Rebecca lit the fire then went over and joined him at the table.

"So, what brings you back this way, Arthur?"

"Ah, you can just call me Beck, like everyone else," he said.

"Well, I like Arthur better. So, I'll call you that," she said with a firm voice.

"Okay. Arthur works," replied Beck submissively.

After a brief pause.

"I came here for you, Rebecca."

They both gazed at each other for the first time in years.

"Can you stay this time, Arthur?"

Beck grabbed her hand and looked into her eyes.

"I always wanted to stay. I thought about you every day, but I had a duty to protect the kingdom with the rest of the fighters. Leaving was the hardest thing I ever had to do. For years I hoped the battles would end, but we kept finding more resistance."

"I thought you forgot about me," said Rebecca.

"I could never forget about you, Rebecca. The thought of you alone kept me going so that one day I could return, and you wouldn't be alone, because I would be here."

"I am so proud of you for the sacrifices you made for the kingdom and I'm so happy you're here now. I missed you very much, Arthur."

"I missed you too, Rebecca. There is one more thing that needs to be done though. The cursed army has risen on the isle, and I'll have to leave for a bit longer, but I will return to you after. I promise!"

"I understand, but you need to keep that promise, Arthur."

"I promise, the moment I can get back, I will," he replied.

"Well, I look forward to that. For now, let's enjoy this time we have together," she said.

Beck leaned into her, and they gave each other a warm hug. They sat down at the table and talked for a while longer.

"I'm finished with the bird. Let's cook it up and have a nice meal. The first of many to come," said Beck.

Rebecca skewered the bird and placed it onto a rotisserie over the fire. She slowly turned it as she looked at Beck and smiled awkwardly. Beck sat with his hands folded under his chin and he smiled back at her, then she turned away and hollered toward the house.

"Sammy! Come here, Sammy."

Just then, a huge dog came running out the door. It was the same breed as Beck's dog, only a male.

"Oh, you gotta be kidding me! I have the same kind of dog at home. Her name is Mya."

"Really? That's great! Sammy will have a new friend! I can't wait for them to meet."

"Actually, I can arrange that now!" Beck said happily.

He took out the whistle on his neck and blew into it. His dog appeared from thin air, wagging its tail and barking excitedly. She saw Sammy and quickly ran over. They sniffed each other for a few seconds and then they started to play. They ran all over the yard, chasing each other and roughhousing together. Rebecca sat back down beside Beck and started watching just in time to see them roll in some mud and make a complete mess of themselves.

"Oh, no! Those crazy dogs! Now they need a bath!"

"Don't worry about it. I'll wash them after lunch."

She reached over and held his hand firmly. Beck looked back at her and smiled as they sat together and looked out at the forest.

They talked and laughed together as they ate, and the dogs chewed some bones on the ground nearby. Beck suddenly became silent for a moment, and he looked back and forth at the table and Rebecca. He took a deep breath and was about to speak when Rebecca interrupted.

"I know what you're about to say, Arthur. You always take a deep breath just before you say that you have to leave."

"Yes, I do, don't I. I wish I could stay."

"You can, but I know you have a job to do. Please be careful and come back the moment that you can."

She put her hand over Beck's and looked in his eyes as he shyly stared back.

"I will return. I promise."

He stood up and called to his bird. It descended through the trees and landed beside him.

"Would you mind taking care of Mya while I'm

gone?"

"Of course. I hoped you would ask. We will all be here waiting for you," she said with a slight whimper.

The dogs got up and Sammy went to Rebecca's side. Mya went over to Beck, and she jumped up and tucked her head into his neck to say goodbye for a few moments. She licked his cheek and jumped down as he scratched her between the ears.

"Mya, you be good for Rebecca. I'll be back soon."

As he hopped onto his bird, Rebecca walked up and grabbed his hand.

"I'm with you everywhere you go, Arthur."

She handed him a small white orb and when he looked inside, he saw her face. He smiled and placed it into his pocket.

As they stood there, he thought he should kiss her goodbye, but he couldn't muster up the courage, even though it seemed like it was exactly what she wanted. She saw his shyness and backed off.

"Save it for when you get back," she said.

He blushed and giggled a bit. Completely bashful now, he took the reins of his bird.

"Bye, Rebecca."

"Bye, Arthur," she said as she smiled and backed away.

He turned and looked up to the sky. The bird leapt into the air, and they flew around Rebecca's house. Beck waved down to her, and she happily waved back before they turned toward the castle and disappeared into the distance.

"Why didn't you kiss her? She wanted to be kissed! I'm such a coward," he said to himself as he got out of sight.

He pouted for a few moments but then he regained his composure as they flew down into a valley and shot back up over a hillside on their way back to the ruined castle.

CHAPTER 8
THE BRIGHTWATER CAVERN.

Malcolm neared the west shore, and the white sand beach came into sight. They passed over the edge of the plain and Star perched himself onto a tree atop a cliff that overlooked the ocean.

He took out the map and studied it further. To his surprise there was a dotted line that led right from the tree to a red X just inside the shallows that marked the entrance into the Brightwater Cavern.

"It seems we're going swimming my friend," said Malcolm as he patted Star on the back.

Star acknowledged him then he leapt off the branch and soared down from the cliff. He leveled out over the beach and not far into the surf they flew straight up into the air then they plunged down into the water.

The entrance was just ahead of them, and their momentum let them descend right through an enormous, curved wall of water and they landed safely inside the cavern. When Malcolm looked back through the wall, he had a clear view into the ocean as schools of exotic fish swam around a coral reef not far from them. He climbed off Star and started to explore.

An old, abandoned town sat across from the wall of water and it looked as if nobody had been there in years. A dry fountain graced the center of the massive circular cavern.

"I need you to stay here, Star. I must go find someone," Malcolm said.

He walked along the store fronts and read all the signs that hung over the doors. The first sign he came to said, 'The Brightwater Cafe.' Inside there were old newspapers and plates still sitting on the tables. It looked as if everyone had just picked up and left and never came back.

He continued to the next shop and its sign said, 'Arlo's Gadgets and Doohickeys.'

The front window was shattered and when he looked inside, he noticed a strange green light that was shining from under a door in the back. He went to the front door and tried to turn the knob, but it was locked. He took his sword and with one strong swipe he knocked it off and the door popped open.

Suddenly a large beast came crashing through the door and knocked him on his back. He looked up to see the head of a dragon staring down at him from the doorway. He picked up his sword and shuffled back to his feet.

The dragon slowly walked toward him, tearing the door out of the wall as it pulled its body through the narrow opening. Its large yellow eyes were locked on Malcolm as it growled ferociously. The dragon stood ten feet tall, and its body was covered with impenetrable scales. Spikes filled its back from head to tail, but this wasn't an ordinary dragon. Its tail was

117

a large fin that was used for swimming. It was an aquatic dragon and unlike any other he's ever seen.

Malcolm backed into the center of the cavern as the dragon charged him and snapped its large teeth. The aura on Malcolm's armor stayed blue as he swung his sword and struck the dragon with the flat side of his blade. Its head was knocked to the side, and it quickly turned back to him, even more angry.

It lunged at Malcolm again and he swung his sword, this time chopping off the spike on top of its head. The dragon roared aloud as it hopped all around the cavern, then it jumped through the wall of water and swam off past the reef. A thin trail of blood drifted behind it from the severed spike. Malcolm put his sword back over his shoulder and caught his breath as he looked in the ocean to see that it wasn't coming back.

He made his way back over to the shop and went in. Inside there were shelves full of books all around the walls and broken gadgets spread over the floor. He went right to the back of the shop where the green light was glowing from under the door. As he got closer, he looked around to see that nothing else was there. The door and the floor below it was covered in deep scratches. He knocked gently on the door and leaned in to listen for an answer.

The door suddenly swung open, and the green light lit up a circular stairway that led down to the basement. He slowly walked down the steps and tried to look around the corner into the room. When he got to the bottom, he saw a large, hooded man sitting in front of a green flamed fire in the center of the room.

"Who dare invade my dungeon of horrors and, and really bad stuff you don't even wanna think about, because it's bad," said the robbed person.

"It's not so bad down here! Not quite a dungeon of horrors," replied Malcolm as he looked around the room.

Suddenly a small gnome no taller than two feet pulled open the chest of the robe and walked out yelling.

"You think it's nice down here. How would you like to be stuck down here with a huge sea dragon clawing at your door? And I'm almost out of food! How are two people gonna live down here? What are we gonna do now? You better not snore!" He said as he dimmed his eye and pointed at Malcolm.

"Wait! Take it easy, friend. The dragon is gone! It went back into the ocean."

"Are you messing with me?"

"No. It's gone! You will have no more trouble with it. A mutual friend has sent me here and said that you would have something that I need for my journey. Do you have any idea what that might be?"

"Well, I'm sure I have something you need," said the little man. All in good time, friend. All in good time. My name is Arlo. Welcome to my shop."

"I'm Malcolm Cahpra."

Arlo quickly turned back to look at him.

"You're the son of King William? Leader of the brave hundred?"

"Yes. The captain sent me here."

"The captain!"

"Yes. How do you know him?" asked Malcolm.

"I've traveled back to the castle in the north a few times. Then the power ran out over here about six months ago and the ground entrance wouldn't open. I've been stuck here ever since."

"Why don't you just swim out of here?" asked Malcolm.

"I can't swim. Even if I could, a huge man-eating sea creature has been waiting to make a snack of me for weeks!" Arlo replied.

"Oh, I see. If you'd like, you're welcome to leave with me and you can make a home in the new kingdom. You can open a new shop and live there in peace with the rest of the people."

"Is it nice there? asked Arlo.

"It is the most beautiful place in the land, and you are welcome to it," said Malcolm.

"Well in that case, let me grab a few things and we can get out of here!"

"I am still curious to know what it is that I need for my journey."

"Oh, yea," said Arlo as he walked over to a chain and pulled it. Three large trunks fell to the floor from what seemed to be out of thin air.

"I'm gonna go pack a few things."

He went up the stairs toward a small loft and turned back to Malcolm.

"Pick a trunk and open it. What's inside will be what you need!"

Malcolm went over to the trunks and looked at them all closely. He picked the one in the center and pushed the button on the lock. It slowly opened and let off a bright green light that dimmed out as the item floated into the air.

There in front of him was a large oval shield with a lion's head engraved in it and a shiny red ruby lodged in its fangs. He took it in his hands and the trunks disappeared in a puff of smoke. Arlo came back down the steps with a backpack over his shoulder and a black case in his hand.

"So. What do ya got there?"

"It's a shield," Malcolm replied.

Arlo walked up closer and took a better look. His eyes brightened as he reached out to touch it.

"Wow! This isn't just any shield. This is the King's Defender! This shield was used by every king on this isle for nearly three hundred years. Its last owner neglected to bring it into battle, and it ended up being the night that he died. It's been used by some of the most powerful leaders there ever were. Nobody's seen it in twenty years, which is a good thing because if king Westmore had this, he would have been virtually invincible. Nobody would have been able to banish him from the land. This is a powerful shield and there are many tales about it. If this is the item you need, then you must have a dangerous journey ahead," Arlo said. "Can we get out of here now?" he asked.

"Sure! Let's go," replied Malcolm.

They both walked up the stairs and back through the shop. Arlo saw the mangled front door and he was noticeably disturbed.

"What in the world happened here?"

"The dragon tore through it. There was nothing I could do," said Malcolm.

"Ah well," said Arlo.

He took his key and threw it into the mess of wood and then they went toward Malcolm's bird who was still waiting patiently. Arlo walked slowly behind him and peered nervously at the wall of water.

"You remember me saying I can't swim, right?"

"It will be fine. Just hang on and hold your breath for a few seconds."

Arlo now had a look of uneasiness on his face. Malcolm hopped on Star's back and put his hand out. Arlo grabbed on, and he pulled him onto the bird behind him. He held onto the shield now attached to

Malcolm's back as the bird started to run and jump into the air. They circled the cavern to pick up some speed and Arlo's cheeks were blown up from holding his breath as Star flew swiftly toward the wall of water.

Arlo closed his eyes and held on tight as they went through and with a flap of its wings they floated up to the surface. Another flap and they sailed off over the beach. Arlo let out his breath and he began to cheer.

"Yea! It's so good to be out of there! I missed the sun! Woooooohooooo!"

Malcolm laughed as they landed back up on top of the cliff. Arlo hopped off and took a deep breath of the fresh air.

"Wow! This is great! Thanks, Malcolm! I have a ride from here."

He placed the little black case on the ground, and it unfolded into a single seated flying device with a propeller on top. It suited Arlo perfectly so he jumped in and fired it up.

"I couldn't wait to use this little baby again," he said.

Malcolm was amazed by the contraption Arlo had created.

"I think I know someone you'd be very interested in meeting back at the castle. His name is Gamon and he's quite crafty, like yourself. You'll have a lot to talk about."

"Well, let's get going," said Arlo.

He put his goggles on and took off as his device let out a small stream of smoke and backfired a bit. Malcolm took off alongside and they headed back toward the castle. Soon after, they spotted someone in the distance, but Malcolm couldn't make out who it was.

"This way, Arlo."

As they neared the man, he saw a huge rifle on his back and a head of long red hair.

"That's Beck! Hey, Beck!"

Beck was startled and he turned around to see them closing in.

"Uh, oh," he said as he took the rifle off his back and held it in the air.

As they got closer, he realized who it was.

"Malcolm!" he said both surprised and happy to see him.

"You don't need that cannon my friend," replied Malcolm.

"I didn't know it was you. Who's this?" asked Beck.

"This is Arlo. He was the sheriff of the Brightwater Cavern for a while."

Arlo looked at him and rolled his eyes.

"Hey Beck! Nice to meet ya," he said.

"Likewise, friend. I like the, the. What is that?" asked Beck

"I call it a helichopper. The first time I used it, I

chopped down a tree with it. But I fixed it," replied Arlo.

"You need to meet our friend Gamon. You two have a lot in common!" said Beck.

"I told him that too! The two of them working together would be quite interesting," said Malcolm.

"Or dangerous," replied Beck with a giggle.

"We're burning daylight. Might as well get going," said Malcolm.

"Well, maybe not just yet. We need to travel into the Teardrop Forest and drop something off first," said Arlo.

He reached into his bag and pulled out a human skull.

"Whoa! What in the world? Your friends a little off, Malcolm," said Beck.

"This happens to be the skull of an old voodoo man who lived in the forest a hundred years ago. Somebody snuck into his hut in the middle of the night and beheaded him where he slept."

"It's kind of strange that you have it now," said Beck.

Arlo glared at him for a moment then continued his story.

"Anyway, since then, there's been a curse on the land, and nothing has grown there. It used to be the most beautiful forest you've ever laid your eyes on, but now it's just a wasteland. It's important that we do this, trust me!" said Arlo as he put the skull back into the bag.

"And how did you obtain this skull?" asked Malcolm.

"I was a traveling salesman for a long time."

"I guess we're gonna be late for supper, but let's go," said Malcolm.

Beck was reluctant after hearing that, but they all flew off toward the Teardrop Forest with Arlo in the lead and Beck and Malcolm following behind.

"So how did it go?" asked Malcolm.

"How did what go?" Beck replied with a bewildered expression.

"You don't have to be secretive about it."

Beck looked over and a big smile filled his face.

"She's still there. She was very happy to see me and now she's watching the dog. Oh, and she's a heck of a shot!"

"Sounds like you'll finally be able to settle down," said Malcolm.

"After this last battle is over, you'll know where to find me."

"I guess I will," replied Malcolm happily.

"So where did ya get the shiny new shield from?" asked Beck.

"I got it out of a trunk at Arlo's shop in the Brightwater cavern. Apparently, it's what I will need for our journey."

"It looks pretty fancy! I like it," said Beck.

They both laughed and followed Arlo as a little puff of smoke from the exhaust pipe dissipated between them. They flew over lakes and valleys and mountain ranges before they came up on the empty wasteland. There was nothing but sand for as far as the eye could see.

"I guess this is the place," said Malcolm.

"Yup! Just a bit further. There's only one tree that remains here. The tree where the voodoo man lived. It used to be in the center of a beautiful rainforest, but now it's all that remains. Now you see why we need to return the skull."

"If that's what needs to be done, then that's what we'll have to do," replied Malcolm.

"I'm with ya's on that," added Beck.

"Good because this freaks me out a little too much to do it by myself," said Arlo as they flew deeper into the wasteland.

CHAPTER 9
A CURSE THAT CAN BE BROKEN.

They flew for miles over the sandy terrain. In the distance, they saw a small hut that was built on a large elder tree in the center of the wasteland. A canopy of dead leaves shaded the hut and the ground below it. As they reached the tree, they circled around it to see that nobody was there.

The windows were so dirty that they couldn't be seen into. An old, rotted stairway led up to a porch in the front of the hut. Malcolm and Beck dropped in and landed nearby. Arlo landed his helichopper and shut down the engine. As he went to step out, he tripped and fell right onto his face. He quickly stood back up and pretended that nothing happened as he looked over at Malcolm and Beck.

They saw what happened to him but they turned away to hide any amusement so they wouldn't be rude. Arlo went into the back of his helichopper and took out a backpack. The wind suddenly picked up and it blew the branches of the old tree violently. Sand kicked up in their faces and every grain felt as if it were a needle.

A small tribe of pygmies popped out of the sand with pointy little spears and feathers in their headbands. They started creeping toward them and the birds jumped into the air and battled the wind to stay out of the pygmy's reach.

"Oh, no. Not again!" said Beck as he turned and ran for the stairs.

Arlo got there first, followed by Malcolm and as they ran up the steps, the old lanterns on the railing began to light. Beck got to the third step, and it broke under his feet. He fell through to a sitting position on the step below and his feet dangled just above the ground.

"Umm. A little help here!" He hollered nervously.

Malcolm saw him and ran down to help. The pygmies got closer and closer to him then one of them stabbed him in the behind from under the steps.

"Owwwww!" he yelled. "Are you kidding me! Okay! You wanna see what I have for you?"

He grabbed his gun and pointed it at the one who stabbed him. The four barrels were the same size as the little man and the rest of the pygmies watched motionlessly. Malcolm helped him back to his feet.

"So, you like stabbing people in the bum, do ya?" hollered Beck as he rubbed his backside.

He lifted the gun into the air and pulled one of the triggers. The gun fired from all four barrels at once and the recoil knocked him back into Malcolm. They both fell to the steps and the pygmies scattered.

"That was surprising! Now I know what that trigger does," said Beck.

They got up and went up the stairs as the wind

gusted around them. Arlo stood at the top with a curious look on his face.

"Why did you say, not again?" he asked.

"I don't wanna talk about it, Arlo," replied Beck.

"He hasn't had any good experiences with pygmies," said Malcolm.

Beck looked over and shook his head in agreement. Arlo shrugged his shoulders and went to the door. He gave the knob a turn and slowly went inside as Malcolm and Beck followed him in. The door slammed behind them, and Beck continued on rubbing his backside.

Everything was quiet and only the sound of the wind could be heard. The lanterns lit up around the walls and revealed the dusty contents of the hut. In the first room, there was a fireplace with old festive masks that hung above the mantle. A small banjo leaned against an armchair that sat beside it.

The next room was inside the tree where it had been hollowed out. There was a cot and a nightstand with a small circle rug on the floor. Below it was a stairway that led down to the base of the tree.

"Well, there's not much to see here. I guess there's only one place to go," said Malcolm.

They all started down the staircase that led deeper into the tree. More lanterns started to light on the walls as they made their way down. When they reached the bottom, the lanterns lit up what seemed to be an old laboratory. Potion vials were scattered on a table and there were shelves full of beacons with different color liquids. A cauldron hung in the center of the room by chains and on the far side of the lab was another cot. Only on top of this one was the remains of the voodoo man in an old torn robe.

"Okay. There he is! I think I just need to put the skull back for the curse to be lifted," said Arlo.

He took out the skull and looked at it nervously.

"I'm suddenly not feeling as motivated as I was. Here, Beck. You put it back!"

"Oh, no, no, no. This is your deal. I'm just here for support," said Beck.

Arlo turned back to the skeleton of the voodoo man and took a deep breath. He slowly went over and placed the head on the cot next to him and stepped back.

"No, no, no. That's not gonna work! You need to put it on his neck, like it was attached," said Beck.

"Do you wanna do this?" asked Arlo.

"Nope! Take your time," replied Beck as he held his hands out in front of himself.

Arlo picked the skull back up and placed it as if it were attached to the neck then he quickly pulled his hands away and wiped them on his pants.

"Well, that's it," said Arlo.

Just as he said it the lanterns inside the room started to brighten and the whole place began to shake. The lanterns dimmed back down, and everything went silent. They all paused and looked around the room.

"I guess that's it! All right! Let's get out of here and let nature take its course," said Arlo.

They all agreed and went back up the stairs and out the front door. When they got outside, they looked to see if the pygmies were still there. As they got to the bottom of the steps they checked under the hut and a small group was waiting for them as they exchanged dirty looks back and forth. The wind suddenly stopped, and everything became quiet and calm.

A huge bolt of lightning shot down from the sky and struck the tree, electrifying the whole house and shocking the pygmies below it. They all scattered, and Beck laughed hysterically as the last few ran away with the feathers smoking in their headbands. The sun began to set behind the horizon and the birds landed back on the ground.

Malcolm and Beck hopped on, and Arlo climbed back into his helichopper. He started the engine, and a little puff of smoke blew out of the tailpipe. They all soared into the air and flew off into a golden sunset as they made their way back to the ruined castle.

"We did our good deed for the day. I wonder what everyone else is up to," said Malcolm.

"I hope they had as much fun as we did," replied

Beck.

"I'm sure they kept busy," said Malcolm.

As they flew out of sight, all the lanterns outside of the hut lit up, flickering at first, but then they became fully illuminated. The fireplace ignited and smoke began to rise from the chimney.

On the cot where the bones were, now laid the body of the voodoo man. He was a dark-skinned man with an old worn robe. His eyes opened and he sat up but seemed to have trouble breathing. As he stood and tried to walk, he fell to his knees and crawled to a cabinet full of potions. He searched franticly through the shelves and broke some of the bottles as he did. He pulled one out with a green fluid inside and he ripped off the cap and took a swig. Seconds later, he was able to breathe. Just below the hut, water broke through the ground and a small plant leaf sprouted from the sand.

He looked around at how messy his lab had become. A wave of his hand in front of his torn clothing and it became a fresh black robe with small golden stars at the base. Another wave and the room lit up brightly and when it dimmed back down, it was clean and renewed.

The tree came back to life all at once. The leaves turned green and small red flowers began to bloom as a beautiful new canopy now covered the hut. He went upstairs to look outside, and he was stunned to see the baron wasteland around his home instead of the lush forest that he remembered. He went back down to the lab and took out a glass jar that was full of colorful seeds. He dumped them into his satchel and threw it over his shoulder, then he went back upstairs and out the door.

When he got down the steps the pygmies were there to greet him. They all got down on their knees and praised him, but he didn't pay them any mind since they've always been a nuisance. They only came around in hopes that he would show them magic, but he never did since he knew they would only use it in a mischievous way. He waved his hand in the air and a floating carpet appeared and rolled out in front of him. He hopped on and circled his hut while dropping the seeds all over the ground. They sank into the sand and with a slight glisten, it was changed back into rich, dark soil. He flew off into the wasteland and sprinkled the seeds all over the ground to bring back the Teardrop Forest that once covered the land.

A short while later everyone arrived at the ruined castle. They landed in the courtyard where Gamon's carriage sat outside by the steps. Malcolm and Beck fed their birds, and they flew off for the night. Arlo got out of his chopper, and it folded up into the black case as he ran up to the carriage.

"This thing's a beauty! Who made this?"

"I'm sure our friend Gamon built it," said Malcolm. The one I told you about. You both have very similar interests. I'd be excited to see what you two could think up together."

"I wonder what this carriage can do?" Arlo asked.

"You can ask him yourself. I'm sure he's here somewhere. Come inside and meet everyone. I'd imagine you both can eat?" asked Malcolm. "I know you ate not too long ago, Beck."

"Oh, I'll find the room, trust me," he replied as they went up the steps into the castle.

Everyone was sitting around the fire, and they greeted them warmly.

"I was wondering when you two were getting back. Where did you get the shield?" Helaina asked.

"We had an errand to run on the way back. The shield came from Arlo's shop in the Brightwater Cavern. It seems that it's what I need for our journey," replied Malcolm. "Everybody, this is Arlo. He's from the Brightwater Cavern."

Everyone introduced themselves and welcomed him.

"Hello everybody. It's nice to meet you all," Arlo said as he looked over at Gamon.

"Are you the one who built that carriage?"

"Yea. My father and I built it a long time ago. It's been sitting for years, but she's still a beauty, right?"

"That's what I said when I saw it!" replied Arlo.

"Arlo here built what he calls a helichopper, and he flew here in it. You should take a look," said

Malcolm.

"Yea! That's a great idea," said Arlo. "You can show me that carriage of yours too!"

"Sure! Let's go," replied Gamon.

They both turned away and walked out the door. It was as if they were already best buds.

"I have a feeling you just started something," said Archer.

"I can't wait to see," replied Malcolm as he placed the shield down by the fire.

Helaina leaned over to Archer.

"They can start by fixing the wall in Gamon's Laboratory," she whispered, and they started to laugh together.

"What do you mean fix the wall?" Malcolm asked with wonder.

"Well, we had to have Herex blow a hole in Gamon's lab to get the carriage outside."

Malcolm raised his brow and looked over at Herex as he shrugged his shoulders back at him.

"It doesn't really matter in this old place. I'm not surprised though. I could tell you some stories about Gamon and blowing things up!"

They all began laughing since Gamon was known for his share of inventions that went wrong.

"Have I ever told you how I met Gamon and his father?"

Everyone gestured no or said it.

"I was out in the Twilight Forest riding and suddenly a huge explosion knocked me off my horse and blew me clear into a pond. I got out soaked and wet and went to see what happened. About a quarter mile down the trail, it just ended and there was a huge crater a hundred feet wide. Who do I see crawling out of it, but Gamon and his father. They both had on the same circle goggles that kept their eyes clean, but the rest of them were covered in soot. They were actually working on what came to be the power source of this castle and the new kingdom."

"I guess it didn't work that time," said Beck.

"No, it didn't. At all! There's still a crater where the old laboratory was. He still goes there from time to time. I'm not sure why though."

Just then the portal lit up and Monroe came through with another feast of food and drinks.

Outside, Gamon showed Arlo the carriage and all its hidden gadgets.

"You could live in this thing if you had to. It's got everything you would need. The seats fold into a bed and there are window blinds for privacy. There's an overhang that pulls out to make some shade. It's all hand made from mahogany. The box in the back has all your camping, fishing, hunting, and cooking needs. I plan to install a teleportation device in it soon."

"How do you pull it?" asked Arlo.

"With magnets! There are two underneath the carriage and two behind the reigns of whatever animal you have. All they need to do is start moving and the carriage is weightless to them," said Gamon.

"So as fast as whatever's pulling it, is as fast as it's gonna go!" said Arlo.

"Yup. Exactly!" replied Gamon.

"This is great! I always wanted my own. I'll have to build one someday," said Arlo.

"I'd be happy to help when you do! So, what's this helichopper I hear about?" asked Gamon.

"Oh, it's right here!"

He pushed a button on the case, and it unfolded.

"Wow! That's amazing!" Gamon said.

"This is actually my prototype. I'd like to make a two-seater, but I can't seem to get the engine tuned right. I think I need a little more octane."

"Say no more!" Gamon said. "I have just the stuff you need to get her purring like a kitten. It's at my lab in town. We can go there in the morning. I'm thinking right now it's time to eat and I'm starving! This is a brilliant device though. I really like it," said Gamon.

"Thanks! I'm right behind ya," replied Arlo as he beamed from the complement.

They went back inside and filled their plates with food then they joined everyone else and found a comfy spot to sit in the moss beside the fire.

"So, what do ya think?" Malcolm asked.

"I think we need something to build!" Gamon replied.

"I'm sure you two will figure something out," Archer said.

As everyone sat around and ate, the captain rose up through the floor and looked around.

"Oh! Hello, Arlo! Good to see you again," he said.

"Hey, Cap! How's the afterlife?"

"It's peaceful. A little too peaceful at times."

"Well, I guess that's all part of resting in peace," replied Arlo with a giggle.

"I see you've been given the King's Defender," said the captain as he noticed the shining shield next to the fire.

"This will help you greatly in your journey, Malcolm. Well, what do ya know. It's already that time again," said the captain as he looked around the room.

Just then, the room turned black and white and the same hooded men bursted through the door and ran up the steps. Arlo jumped behind the rocks to hide and everyone else just sat and watched. When Arlo saw that nobody was panicking, he got back up and watched what was happening in disbelief.

The next group came in behind them and went to the center of the room. The same exact battle played out from the night before and again the man in the plate armor looked back at Malcolm before running out the door. The cannons struck the walls and the ceiling above them. As it collapsed, Arlo leapt onto the ground and covered his head. When the room faded back to normal, he stood up and looked around anxiously as he brushed himself off.

"That was strange!" said Arlo. "Actually! What was that?"

"I believe it was our ancestors who fought here many years ago.

"That man seemed like he was looking right at you," Arlo said.

"I know. He did the same thing last night," replied Malcolm. "I'm not sure what to make of it yet, but I'll find out. Let's all eat and relax. Tomorrow, we need to prepare the town for the arrival of the fighters."

"Herex and I will clear the town in the morning. It'll be ready by the time they arrive," Helaina replied.

"I bid you all a good night," said the captain. "It's time for me to rest."

"What do you mean, rest?" asked Beck. "You're already dead. That's all you do is rest."

"I'm trying to leave politely, if you wouldn't mind, Beck!"

"Okay, Captain. See ya in the morning, when you, wake up!" replied Beck as he rolled his eyes.

The captain disappeared into the floor, and everyone sat back in the plush moss. They all nestled in and talked for a while, until each of them drifted off to sleep, one by one.

CHAPTER 10
DEPARTURES AND ARRIVALS.

Night had fallen at the new kingdom in the south. The brave men and women of the king's army were ready to make their way north to the ruined castle and prepare for the coming battle. The town square was brightly lit and filled with the fighters and their families. Airships were docked around the grounds and birds hovered throughout the sky. The king's voice came over a gramophone and everyone quieted down to listen.

"Brave men and women of Cahpra isle. Tonight, you will travel to the old kingdom in the north to join my son. He will lead you through this battle, where you will be victorious!"

The fighters cheered and thrusted their glowing weapons into the air.

"Fly now brave souls. To the north. To victory!"

The fighters cheered and bowed to the king one last time as they called their birds. A few of them flew on beasts that they had tamed, and others flew on winged stallions called a Pegasus. The ground fighters boarded the airships and took off in a massive armada that filled the sky.

The roads and courtyards throughout the kingdom quickly became silent and secluded. The king and queen watched the sky as the last of the airships disappeared into the night.

Back at the old castle Malcolm awoke hours before sunrise. He saw that Herex was already up and around the room, so he leaned over and shook Helaina to wake her.

"It's time to prepare the town. The fighters will be arriving soon."

She slowly got up and followed Malcolm and Herex out into the square. They looked around at the old overgrown town that they knew as children. Herex lifted his arms up and a load of debris rose into the air. A swipe of his hand, it moved off and piled into a nearby shop that had collapsed.

Helaina waved her wand and all the brush and ivy receded back to the outer walls. Another wave and a layer of moss covered the debris as small blue flowers sprouted from it.

"That's a lot better. Let's clean up the shops that weren't destroyed so they can be occupied by the fighters," said Malcolm.

They all set out into the town and looked in the doors and windows to see which of the buildings were salvageable. The ones that were, *were* cleared of all the rubble. The ones that weren't, Helaina covered in a thick layer of moss and flowers to add a little beauty to the dreary remains of the town. As they got to the end of the road, they ended up at a familiar old shop called 'Wilson's Wonders.'

They all peeked into the window then went inside. The shop was mostly intact beside a few broken windows and some small debris on the floor. It only needed a good cleaning.

"Do you remember this shop?" Malcolm asked. "It was the most magical place to me when I was a child. I'd come here every Saturday morning to see what new tricks old man Wilson had up his sleeve."

"I remember them well," replied Helaina. "I would wait all week for his magic shows. I came here all the time to read his books. He would pretend to get upset that I never bought any, but then he would bring down cookies and apple cider that his wife made. He was such a nice old man. I wonder what happened to him. After his wife passed, he was never the same," said Helaina.

"The shop was never the same," added Malcolm.

She waved her wand around in a circle and all the dust and dirt flew out a broken window and landed in the wreckage of the shop next door. The vine began to pull back through the windows and the glass went back into place. The shop was restored to the way it was along with the home above it.

They looked around a bit more and Malcolm went up to one of the bookshelves. He looked over the titles on the spines then he pulled out a thick blue book to examine it more closely.

"He told me a story about this book a long time

ago," Malcolm said, "He said it was given to him by an old man who bought it from Merlin's bookstore many years ago who spoke of becoming part of the story, but I'm unsure of what he meant."

They all looked down at the book as Malcolm opened it. A bright yellow light suddenly shot from the pages and old man Wilson's head popped up.

"Get me out! Get me out!" yelled the old man.

Malcolm dropped the book onto the floor.

"Ouch! Don't drop me," he said.

Helaina and Archer were stunned by what was happening. Malcolm leaned down and grabbed the man by his arms and pulled him out onto the floor. The book began to bounce around the ground and the man jumped on top to close it and he quickly shoved it back onto the shelf. He leaned against the case and then he took a deep breath as he turned back to everyone.

"Thank you," said the man graciously.

"Old man Wilson?" Helaina asked.

He ran toward the door and started yelling.

"They're attacking! They're attacking! Get down in your cellars!"

He ran into the street and as he looked around, he began to realize the town wasn't what he had expected then he slowly walked back inside.

"How long have I been in there?" he asked with heavy eyes.

"About ten years, old friend," replied Malcolm.

"I'm Helaina. I used to come here to read, and you would bring me cookies and cider.

"Ahh, Helaina my child! It's so good to see you. You have grown!"

"I'm Malcolm Cahpra," he said.

"Malcolm? Good to see you too!"

"Same to you," replied Malcolm.

"Thank you for getting me out of there. You say it's been ten years? What happened here?"

"There was a battle fought here and the castle became unlivable, so the people moved south and rebuilt," said Malcolm.

"Are you the king?" he asked.

"No. My father is still the king. We have another battle in the days ahead. If I survive, then I will be his successor. Our army will be arriving here shortly so it will be a little busy around here," said Malcolm.

"I'm feeling a little hungry. I think I'll make something to eat," said old man Wilson as he walked upstairs to his home and opened the door.

A lamp suddenly flew from out of nowhere and hit him. He came sliding back down the stairs on his back and landed at everyone's feet. A ghostly figure of a woman stood angrily at the top of the stairs.

"Don't you dare come in here and try to steal from me. You came to the wrong place!" said the ghostly woman with ferocity.

She started looking closer at the man and realized that it was her husband. She quickly glided down to the bottom of the steps.

"My dear! Where did you go for so long?"

Old man Wilson looked up and saw the spirit of his beloved wife.

"My darling! I was stuck in a book, on the shelf."

"A book?" she asked.

"Yes. Right there on the shelf."

"I waited all this time wondering if you would ever return, and you were right there on the shelf?"

"I'm here now!" he replied as they smiled at each other lovingly.

"It seems you both have some catching up to do. We will leave you for now. If there is anything you need, we won't be far and if you're hungry, there's food in the great hall. Please, help yourself," said Malcolm.

"It was good to see you," said Helaina as they all went back to the door.

Old man Wilson looked at her and smiled, then he turned back to his wife. The three of them went out into the street and stood in front of the shop.

"I can't believe that just happened," said Malcolm.

"Well, he didn't age and she's already a ghost, so they really haven't lost any time," said Helaina. "They were so happy to see each other!"

"I guess this is the best the old town is gonna get,"

said Malcolm.

They walked back to the castle just as the sun rose and lit the horizon. Far off in the distance a dark shadow spanned across the dimly lit sky.

"Right in time for the fighters," said Malcolm as he pointed into the distance.

The armada filled the sky. Birds and airships flew in from over the trees and people on horses and tigers and huge mammoths exited the forest onto the plain. As the ships arrived, they tied them down all around the grounds as the men and women made their way off. Fighters landed their birds all around the plain and throughout the town. The crews on the ships set up large blue, green and purple tents all over the plain. They set bonfires and immediately began to cook. It was as if a festival had just landed in their front yard.

"It's nice to see some life at this place again," said Malcolm.

After everyone had arrived and the skies were clear, only a few fighters on horseback made their way out of the forest. Malcolm went back into the ballroom and woke everyone. They all sat up, yawning and wiping their eyes.

"The fighters are here. Everybody up," he said.

Everyone else got up and slowly followed them out onto an undamaged balcony that overlooked the grounds. Beck stretched his arms as he walked out and to his surprise, he saw the army now covering the land around the castle.

"Wow! When did they get here?" Beck asked.

"Only a few minutes ago," replied Helaina.

Malcolm looked out at them as they all started to notice his presence on the balcony. They turned to him and saluted. He saluted them back and looked out at all the faces of the brave men and women who were ready to lay down their lives. He had thoughts of how some would survive the battle and go on, but others would surely meet their demise. Helaina grabbed his shoulder and leaned onto him.

"Are you ready?" she asked.

He looked at her and took a deep breath, then he shook his head yes. She cast a spell to make his voice travel over the plain.

"Welcome brothers and sisters, brave fighters of Cahpra Isle. You all know what lies ahead. It will not be an easy journey, but this curse must end! Not only to maintain peace in our great kingdom, but to put these tortured souls to rest, once and for all. They have been burdened by their curse long enough. They now only exist to destroy us, but we will never let that happen."

Everyone began to clap in agreement.

"I am honored to fight beside all of you in this next theater of battle. The forsaken army is our last enemy here on the isle. After this fight, nothing will threaten our way of life. We will cleanse this land for our children's futures and restore its peace and prosperity. This kingdom will endure!"

All at once everyone cheered proudly.

"Please rest and enjoy yourselves. Tomorrow, we leave for the old Gibbs mine in the east."

Everyone cheered aloud again. The fighters saluted him as Malcolm saluted them. He turned back to everyone, and the fighters continued cooking and setting up their camps.

One last airship suddenly flew in from over the trees and descended to the balcony. It had a large white balloon with a yellow stripe. The ship was dark blue with beautifully crafted golden trim. A mermaid with a spear was carved into the bow and cannon ports filled the sides of the hull.

As the ship got closer, they saw that the entire crew was made up of women. The captain wore a large, brimmed hat with a feather and she peered down at Malcolm. He looked up and realized it was his sister.

"Jenny! I thought you were oversea?"

"I heard there was a lot happening around here so I came as soon as I could. Hi, Helaina!" she said as she waved down at her.

"Hey, Jenny!" replied Helaina with a smile.

"Hey, guys!" She said to the others, and they greeted her warmly.

"You're right on time," said Malcolm.

"Take a ride with me, Malcolm." she said.

She threw down a rope and Malcolm grabbed hold of it. The crew pulled him right up onto the deck.

"I'll have him back in a little bit everyone," said Jenny as she turned to the woman at the wheel.

"Take us up and circle the grounds, please. All hands! I introduce to you, my brother, Lord Malcolm Cahpra."

The entire crew took a knee.

"It's nice to make your acquaintance," he said.

"I didn't expect to see you, sis. This is a pleasant surprise," he said.

"Well, I couldn't let you go off without saying goodbye."

Malcolm smiled and leaned against the railing.

"This is quite the ship you have here."

"It's home for now. I'm looking for a change of scenery and I wanted to see what's become of our old home."

"There's not much left, but it still holds its beauty," he replied.

They both looked down at the castle and all the fighters and airships throughout the grounds. Fighters flew in the sky on patrols and others went down to the shore to set up camp along the beach.

"This place is nice, but it's a little too busy for me," she said with a smile.

"I agree," replied Malcolm as he laughed.

"There are a lot of brave people down there. This

will be the last night for some. Looking down, I wish I could see the ones who wouldn't make it and pluck them up," said Malcolm with sadness.

"Then others will be lost in their place," replied Jenny. "They choose to be here. They fight for their family's safety and their freedoms."

"I know, but it's hard being the one who has to lead them into the fight."

"They follow you for a reason, Malcolm. You've kept this isle at peace and given up years of your life to do it. You had a duty to the people and I'm proud of what you've done."

"Between the battles I dreamed of a time we wouldn't have to fight anymore. It's what kept me going at times," said Malcolm.

"I believe those dreams will play out soon," she replied.

"Someday sooner than later, I hope," replied Malcolm. "Will you be joining us for dinner? I know mom and dad would be happy to see you."

"Actually, I saw them yesterday, but yes, I'd love to! When and where?" she asked.

"Good! I'll see you at sundown, in the old ballroom."

"I will be there," she replied as she turned to the woman at the wheel. "Bring us back down, please."

The women turned the ship and descended right

down to the balcony.

"It's good to see you, Jenny."

"And you. I'll see you again at dinner," she replied happily.

He leapt over the railing and landed down on the balcony.

"Bring us up over the castle," said Jenny as she waved goodbye, and the ship rose back into the sky.

CHAPTER 11
THE FESTIVAL.

Malcolm went back into the ballroom where Gamon and Arlo were talking by the fire.

"Gamon, can you arrange a table for ten in the center of the room?" he asked.

"I have one right in the carriage that'll work perfectly! I'll take care of it," he replied. "Arlo, you mind giving me a hand?"

"Sure! I'm right behind ya," he said, and they both went out to the carriage.

Gamon climbed inside and pressed a button on the wall. A drawer folded down from the chassis and he pulled out a small wooden table.

"That's the size of a night table, Gamon. I'm not sure if that's gonna do it," said Arlo.

"Inside the trunk is a little red box. Can you get it and bring it inside, please?" Gamon asked.

As they stood there, the shade from Jenny's airship came over the carriage. They both looked up into the sky to see it hovering overhead.

"Wow! Look at that! I'd like to build one of those someday," said Arlo.

"A bigger one," replied Gamon. "A much bigger one!"

"The bigger, the better! What do you have in

mind?" Arlo asked.

"We'll talk about it again, soon. I think I have just what we need," said Gamon as he thought to himself.

He wrestled the table into the door and placed it in the center of the room by the portal. Arlo walked in with the red box and placed it down.

"If you can grab a hold of that side of the table, please," Gamon asked.

Arlo went over and grabbed the top of the table. Gamon started walking backward and the table stretched to about ten feet long.

"Wow! Wasn't expecting that," said Arlo.

"Okay. If you can go on the side now?"

He grabbed on the top again and Gamon pulled the table to about four feet wide, then its legs folded down to the ground.

"The seats are in the red box. The matching ones are for the heads of the table."

They pulled out all the chairs and set them up neatly around the table. Helaina came inside and with a wave of her wand, a flower bouquet and candles appeared in the center of the table. Gamon and Arlo gave her a funny look.

"What? It's a centerpiece," she said. "There will be ladies present and now it looks nice enough for the queen."

"The queen?" asked Arlo.

"Yes. It's tradition to share a meal before battle."

"Then I need to get cleaned up!" Arlo said.

He went over to his little black case and his helichopper unfolded. He went under the hood and took out a small luggage bag.

"I need to put on something nice if we're having dinner with the queen! I'm gonna find somewhere to get cleaned up," he said as the helichopper folded up and he walked out of the room.

Helaina, Gamon and Archer sat by the fire and Malcolm came back in to join them.

"Gamon, I'll need maps of the Old Gibbs Mine and the Dyre Mountains so I can prepare a battle plan," said Malcolm.

"I'll take care of it! The new tweeters are just about ready to go! I need to make a few final adjustments before we go, but I finished them the other day, just for that reason!"

"Great! Herex, I need you to take Gamon to do some reconnaissance tonight. I need to know every cliff and peak on that mountain. Every cave and shaft inside it and all the terrain around it."

Herex nodded his head to acknowledge his request.

"No problem! Piece of cake! The new tweeters are hummingbirds. They'll never even see them coming!" Gamon said.

"You never cease to amaze me. Your gadgets are always a great help. I don't know what we would do without them," said Malcolm.

"Well, you wouldn't be able to make a map of that place for starters! You must see what Arlo and I are planning to build. It's a surprise though."

"I can't imagine what you two thought up," replied Malcolm.

"It's gonna be really great!" said Gamon.

"I'm excited! I do need to ask something else of you. After the maps are done, I need you and maybe Arlo to check all the weapons to see that they're ready for battle."

"Sure thing! I planned to do that anyway."

"Thank you, Gamon. I'll have the armor and weapons brought to your shop."

"I'm not sure if Arlo will be dressed for it, but I'll ask him," Gamon said as he looked over at Helaina and Archer with a grin and they all started to laugh together.

"What do you mean, dressed for it?" Malcolm asked.

Just then Arlo walked through the door in a bright red tuxedo with a matching cloak and shiny black shoes. Helaina and Gamon could hardly contain themselves. Malcolm looked down at him in wonder.

"Aren't we dressed to impress! Looking good, Arlo!" he said.

"Thanks! I don't get to dress up for too many occasions, especially when royalty is present."

"I think the king and queen will be very pleased,"

added Malcolm.

"You think so? This is a nice tux, isn't it?" Arlo said as he spun around to show it off.

"You look very handsome, Arlo," said Helaina.

"Thanks!" he replied bashfully.

"I'd like for someone to walk the grounds and see if the fighters need anything. I'm going for a walk around the castle to gather my thoughts," said Malcolm.

"Sure! I'd be happy to," said Helaina.

She looked over at Archer and Arlo.

"Let's go you two. It's time to take a stroll," she said.

Malcolm went off into the castle and Gamon went to put the finishing touches on his gadget. Helaina, Archer, and Arlo went outside and made their way around the plain to see that all the fighters were taken care of. An older man, who clearly had a few drinks, approached them.

"Everyone is really good!" slurred the man. "We're cooking like crazy and drinking. Or are we drinking like crazy and cooking? I don't know. Hey that's a really nice tux!" he said to Arlo.

"Thanks!" Arlo replied.

"I'd like a tux like that," the man said just as he lost his footing and fell back into a tent.

It was wrapped around him and all that could be seen were his boots sticking out from under it. A woman climbed out and looked down at the drunken man. She threw her arms up in aggravation and walked off into the crowd.

They continued around the busy plain. People were singing and dancing while others had friendly duels between each other. People used magic all around them. Every group they went up to seemed to be content and enjoying themselves. A few people even asked Helaina if they were hungry and if they needed anything.

As they made their way toward the ocean side of the plain the people were racing on birds and other flying creatures. Two people lined up at the starting line and a dwarf fired an orb up into the sky. The riders crouched down and got ready. When the orb exploded the birds leapt into the air and flew straight out toward the water. When they reached the shoreline, they flew straight up till they lost their momentum, then they turned around as fast as they could and zipped back over the plain to cross the finish line first.

"I want to do that so much! What do you think, Archer? Want to give it a go?" Helaina asked.

"Umm. Yea, I guess so. I'm pretty fast though. Just want to let you know that now," he said confidently.

Helaina looked at him with a smirk and whistled for her bird. The bird flew in and landed beside her. She petted it gently on the head and climbed on.

"What are you waiting for?" she asked.

"Oh, you're in for it, Archer," said Arlo.

Archer looked back at him and whistled for his bird. It landed beside him, and he climbed on, then they both trotted over to the starting line. Everyone stopped to look at Helaina as she passed by on her snowy white bird. When they got closer, the dwarf saw them and stopped the next racers in line. Whispers were heard in the crowd as they passed.

"Hey! That's Lady Helaina," they whispered.

"Yea. That's her!" said someone in the crowd and they began to cheer for her.

"Go Helaina! You can do it!" they chanted.

Cheers of support were heard from all around for both of them.

They walked up to the line and looked over at the man to let him know they were ready. They crouched down and prepared themselves. The dwarf shot the orb into the sky and when it exploded, they both leapt into the air and flew out toward the ocean. They were neck and neck as they passed over the plains and flew out over the beach. As they reached the shore, they shot up into the air till they stopped, then they turned around and quickly flew back over the beach.

Helaina turned faster than Archer and she gained the lead. They crouched down and tore through the trees and out over the plain. Archer tried his hardest to catch up, but Helaina whipped past the finish line first and blew the dwarf's hat right off his head. He clicked his stopwatch and yelled out.

"That's a new record!"

Archer finished about four bird lengths behind, and the crowd cheered as they came in and landed nearby.

"Well, it seems you're even faster," said Archer, impressed with how fast she was.

Helaina smiled back at him then she continued around the grounds. A few hours later the sun went down behind the horizon. Hundreds of small fires lit the plain and many more lined the beach where some of the fighters chose to spend the night by the water.

Inside the castle everyone eagerly awaited the arrival of the king and queen. Malcolm walked into the ballroom wearing a red robe with a cloak that hung down to the floor.

He walked up to the portal as everyone else stood around the table and waited for the king and queen. A few moments later the portal lit up and Monroe came through with platters of food and others with refreshments. They placed it down and set the table, then they went back through the portal.

The outer doors of the ballroom suddenly opened and there was Jenny standing just outside in a light blue gown with a white ribbon around her waist. She wore a diamond tiara in her hair that sparkled in the light of the moon. Archer quickly went over to greet her. He put his arm out to guide her in and she

161

happily accepted. They walked to the table, and she greeted everyone kindly.

A moment later the frame around the portal lit up and the king walked through as he pulled the queen's hand. She unwillingly followed him with her eyes tightly shut. After she was through, she opened them up and was relieved to see that she made it through safely.

"She's actually squeezing my hand incredibly tight!" said the King. "We're here darling. You can let go," he said to her.

She noticed her firm grip and she let go.

"Sorry! I don't like portals very much. I feel like you never know where you'll end up," she said as she saw Malcolm and Jenny. "Hello, my children! Jennifer, I didn't know you were going to be here. You look so beautiful! I love that dress!"

"You both know everyone here except for our new friend, Arlo. He's from the Brightwater Cavern.

"Hello, Arlo. It's so nice to meet you," said the queen.

"Oh, it's so nice to meet you queen Talia. The honor is all mine!" Arlo replied dramatically.

He leaned over to bow, and he hit his head on the back of the chair.

"Ouch! I'm fine. Don't mind me," he said as he held his forehead.

"Shall we sit down and eat?" asked the king.

He sat with the queen and everyone else sat down after. In the center of the table was a grand feast. Everything from fruits and vegetables to chicken and steak. There was wine and water and even a barrel of brew for Beck.

"Please, don't wait for us. Help yourselves," said the king.

Everybody filled their plates and began to eat.

"Is everyone settled outside? Is there anything they need?" asked the queen.

"We walked the grounds earlier and everyone was surprisingly content, considering what lies ahead," replied Helaina.

"They are brave men and women," said king William. "I am proud to be their king and they will follow you now, son. Lead them well."

"I shall. I hope this will be the last time they are called to battle. Maps will be made of the Dyre Mountains tonight. I will know every way in and out of that mountain long before we arrive. Herex and Gamon will be seeing to that soon."

"Where you guys going? I wanna go too!" said Arlo.

"You can go with them if you'd like," replied Malcolm. "When this battle is over, we will build cities and towns across the Isle and protect it from shore to shore. I want this isle to be a safe haven for all who wish to live in peace," said Malcolm.

"Then that will be the future of this great isle," replied the king.

"We will not return until those poor souls are at rest," said Malcolm.

"It is terrible what was done to those people," said the king. "They weren't all bad, but nevertheless, they are still our enemy. If there were any other way, I would welcome it, but this is what needs to be done. I don't want to make this a solemn dinner. After all, this is supposed to be a celebration. I'd imagine I'm starting to sound like a bit of a drag," he said as he looked over at Helaina.

"Not at all! It's in the back of everyone's mind, anyway," she replied.

They all finished eating and talked for a while.

"I'd like to go outside and sit around a campfire," said the queen.

"I'd like that too! It's been a long time since we sat around a fire, especially one at this castle," replied the king.

"I loved it when we lived here. This ballroom, the town square and all the great shops. There's something I've always loved about the north. It's so beautiful here," said the queen.

"There is something about this ballroom that I want you both to see," said Malcolm. "What time is it, Gamon?"

Gamon looked down at his watch.

"Oh, it's time to go! We only have a minute, and I don't wanna see that show again. Herex, Arlo. You ready?

"What show?" asked the king.

"You'll see shortly, father."

The three of them stood up from the table and bowed to the king and queen. Gamon went over and took his backpack off the moss covered stone by the fire.

"Okay. Let's hit the road!" he said as he looked down at his watch. "Thirty seconds. Let's go!"

Herex waved his hand in front of the portal and changed its destination to the Dyre Mountains. The frame around it glowed brightly as the cloud inside began to churn and the smoky aura rose off the top. Gamon put his backpack on and followed Herex inside.

"I don't really like these things unless I made it myself, but here goes nothing!" said Arlo as he took a running jump.

His cape floated behind him, and he disappeared inside. Almost immediately the room began to change.

"Don't be worried. They won't harm us," said Malcolm.

"Who?" asked the king.

Just then the room turned black and white as all the cloaked fighters ran through the door. The same scenario played out and the king and queen couldn't believe their eyes. Once again, the man in the plate armor looked back at Malcolm, and this time he also looked at the king before he ran out the door. The cannons began to hit the walls and the ceiling. The roof collapsed over the fireplace, then the room faded back to the broken and overgrown walls.

"What was that?" the king asked. "Was that? No, it couldn't have been."

"I think it was grandfather. I think it was all our elders," said Malcolm.

"That's what I thought. This happens every night?" asked the king.

"Every night so far. I don't know what to make of it yet, but we will study it further," replied Malcolm.

"That was the strangest thing I've ever seen," said Jenny.

"Well, I don't ever need to see that again," said the queen. "That's enough for me. Is everyone finished? I'd like to go outside for some fresh air."

"Sure! Let's go," said Jenny.

They all got up and walked toward the door.

"We must find out what's happening here. You don't think he's stuck repeating that battle, do you?" asked the king with concern. "Do you think he's aware of us?"

"I'm not sure what to think, but we'll get to the

bottom of it," replied Malcolm.

The king agreed and he took the queen's hand. Jenny took Archer by the arm, and they followed everyone outside.

The square was dimly lit by campfires. There was only a small crowd inside the town, but everyone seemed to be enjoying themselves. As more and more people saw the king and queen they started to cheer and clap for them.

The king and queen waved back to them, and they walked down the stairs to sit by an empty campfire at the bottom.

"It seems so dark and dreary out here, doesn't it?" asked the queen.

"I can fix that," replied Helaina.

She took her wand and waved it overhead. Suddenly the vines started to grow up the walls and they reached high up over the square. They met in the middle and formed a huge canopy of bright green foliage. White luminescent orchids bloomed all around it and lit up the square brightly. Strands of vine stretched down the roads and smaller orchids bloomed along them to light up the rest of the town.

The people around the plain saw the bright dome Helaina created and they headed over to come inside. Immediately everyone seemed happier, and they began to fill the roads throughout the town.

It was like old times when the north kingdom was full of life. People sang and danced, and others made a comfortable place to rest or sleep. A tall man in a black overcoat stood by the old fountain and played a song on his banjo. Everyone sat around the fire and enjoyed the festival.

CHAPTER 12
RECONNAISSANCE.

Herex, Gamon, and Arlo exited the portal onto a windy dune where wild animals could be heard calling out in the darkness. The land was lit by the moon, but it became so dark when the clouds passed in front, it made it hard to see any distance at all. During a break in the clouds everything lit up and they turned to see the Dyre Mountains.

"I'm starting to think I should have stayed at the castle. This place is no fun at all!" said Arlo.

"It's certainly no picnic," replied Gamon. "We don't have to go any closer though. Look at this!"

He took a small box out of his backpack and opened it. Three small hummingbirds flew into the air and hovered close in front of them. He pulled out a pair of goggles and a remote-control panel.

"These are my little buddies! They'll make us an exact map of this whole place," he said.

"That's good thinking. I like it!" said Arlo.

"Thanks!" replied Gamon. "It took me a little time to fine tune them, but I got em just right. Now I can send them wherever I need them to go. They have a range of about five miles so we can stay right here and let them do the rest."

Herex gestured to continue.

"Alright, keep your pants on," said Gamon. "You

fly around the perimeter," he said as he pushed a button and one of the birds flew off into the darkness around the dune.

"You head up to the peak," he said, and the second bird flew off to the top of the mountain.

"And you my friend will explore the mine."

The last bird took off directly toward the entrance.

"Now we wait," said Gamon as he put the goggles on.

"Through the goggles I can see what the birds see. Okay, I see. Wow! That's a lot of undead inside the mine. There are huge caves full of them. It's like an ant hole!" said Gamon.

"Can I see?" Arlo asked.

"Sure. Take a look. I'm gonna switch it to the mountains," said Gamon.

He handed Arlo the goggles and he put them on.

"I see a huge camp with a bonfire in the center. There must be a few thousand of them up there," said Arlo.

"All right. Let me see. I'll make you another pair when I get a chance."

Arlo handed them to Gamon, and he put them back on.

"Wow. They have camps down here, and not too far from, from here! This might not have been the best place to do this," said Gamon nervously.

"What do you mean? How far?" asked Arlo.

"Only about a hundred yards, by these calculations," Gamon said.

"That's too close!" said Arlo with concern.

Herex scanned the grounds around them. Suddenly a dozen orbs of light came floating down from the mountain and lit up the grounds. They flew all around and moved closer and closer to them.

Arlo squatted so he wouldn't be seen and Gamon just stood there, unaware that the orbs of light were coming. One of the orbs spotted them and a bright beam of light shined down on them. Herex pointed his mace and fired an orb that shattered it to pieces.

All the other orbs quickly moved toward their last position and in no time at all, a dozen were overhead. Herex rapidly fired on them and destroyed the rest. The dune went quiet, and the clouds covered the moonlight again. Gamon stood there with his goggles on, still oblivious to what was going on around him.

"I think we need to get out of here," said Arlo. "It seems a little too quiet now."

Moments later undead fighters came running toward them from a trail nearby. Their carriages were made of bone and pulled by skeletal horses with red eyes.

"There are undead everywhere around here," said Gamon as he lifted the goggles.

He saw them running toward him and he pulled them back down, then up again to see if it was real.

"Wait a second. There here! Herex! Do something!" Gamon yelled in a panic.

Herex glanced over and shook his head since it was only now that Gamon realized what was happening. He turned to a pack of the undead fighters and fired on them. He waved his mace in a circle and a swirling hole formed below the closest ones.

Dozens of them fell in or were pulled into the funnel. The others stopped and growled angrily while some ran around the perimeter to get to them. As they closed in, Herex fired a ball of energy over them. After a bright flash, a cloud formed, and lightning began to strike down on them.

Dozens of undead fighters fell with each bolt along with some of their carriages.

"We just need another minute. They're almost back," said Gamon as he peeked into the goggles.

Herex began to guide the bolts with his mace, and they tore through the fighters in blinding strikes.

"Almost here!" said Gamon.

The bolts died down the undead started to advance. Herex glided over the ground as if he were sliding on ice. The ruby on the top of his mace glowed brightly and he fired a dozen orbs. Large groups of undead were taken down by them as a red haze filled the air around their remains.

Herex looked back to check on Gamon and Arlo and he noticed a strange black fog above the portal. With a sweeping motion of his arm the wind picked up and created a sandstorm. The undead were swept up and tossed a hundred yards, but the fog remained above the portal.

Gamon looked into his goggles again and quickly opened the box. All the birds arrived at the same time and landed inside.

"Herex! It's time to go! We're ready!" hollered Arlo.

"Stop playing around, Herex. Let's go!" said Gamon.

Herex turned away and as he made his way back to the portal, one of the undead managed to reach him and they stood face to face. Herex stared into the fighter's eyes as his own began to glow inside his dark hood. The fighter lifted its sword to take a swing and Herex bashed its arm clean off its body and the sword fell to the ground.

He formed a small red orb in his hand and shoved it into the chest of the fighter, then he went on and made his way back to the portal. The fighter looked down at the orb now glowing inside its chest. He tried to get it out, but it exploded and its bones flew in every direction.

Herex fired orbs all around them and with a sweeping motion of his hand, a gust of wind blew Gamon and Arlo right back through the portal. They slid along the floor in the castle and came to a stop.

"He could've given us a little warning before he went and did all that," said Arlo.

"Welcome to my world!" replied Gamon as he dusted himself off.

As Herex got closer to the portal, two of the undead fighters snuck around the back and leapt into the castle. They charged toward Gamon and Arlo who were still sitting on the floor. Herex fired an orb into the portal and they both watched as it came through and blew one of the fighters to pieces. At the same time, Beck was coming back inside to get another brew and he saw the last fighter. He dropped the stein and took aim with his rifle and fired, reducing the last fighter to chips of bone that scattered across the floor.

Gamon and Arlo got up and watched Herex still inside the dune. He stood beside the portal and formed a large smoky black orb in his hands. The undead charged and they were almost on top of him. They leapt into the air and prepared their weapons. He took one last look up at the black fog, then he dropped the orb and stepped backward through the portal. It quickly sank into the sand and bolts pulsed through the ground from where it stood.

The undead fighters collided together where Herex was, and they growled angrily. When they realized he was gone they became infuriated as some of the others poked at the smoky orb that was left on the ground.

Herex stepped back into the castle and the portal disappeared behind him. Malcolm and Helaina came running inside after they heard the shot. Herex placed his mace back over his shoulder and put his hand to his ear to signal for everyone to listen.

In the dune, the undead fighters surrounded the orb. The black fog that sat above the portal quickly departed. A moment later it exploded and all the fighters in the vicinity were blown to shreds. None of them were left standing. The black fog barely escaped the blast as it flew off.

Everyone in the castle listened quietly. Suddenly, the echo of a huge explosion rumbled over the castle, and they all looked over at Herex.

"I guess that was you?" Malcolm asked.

Herex shrugged his shoulders as he went over to the fire and sat down.

"The undead army knows we were there," said Gamon.

"Then we can't waste any time. I'll need those maps as soon as possible," replied Malcolm.

"There's an incredible amount of undead there! They're up in the mountains and all around it. The mines are filled. There must be a hundred thousand of them! I'll go to my lab now and make the maps for you. Arlo, you wanna help me out?"

"I'd be happy to! Let's get to it."

"Very good. I'll be there shortly to get them," replied Malcolm.

They both walked toward the door and Arlo turned to Herex as he passed.

"That was impressive out there. You're okay in my book, Herex."

Herex lifted his head to acknowledge him, and they went out into the square where everyone was still enjoying themselves.

"Wow! There's a party out here," said Arlo as they made their way through the crowd.

"This place looks great!" said Gamon as he looked up at the dome of vine and bright flowers that Helaina made.

They went down the alley and navigated through a group of people.

"Excuse me, coming through. Thank you," said Gamon.

They happily moved aside to let them by.

They went in and right down to the lab. As they got inside Gamon was reminded of the huge hole they made in the wall.

"Oh man! I forgot about that," he said.

"I'll take care of it," replied Arlo. "Do what you have to do. I'll close this up in a jiffy!"

Gamon went over to his desk and put his backpack down. He pulled the box out and opened it up. The birds flew into the air and hovered in front of him. He laid three pieces of parchment on the desk and each one went to its own piece and started to peck away. They printed every place they traveled in detail with ink from their beaks. Each area on the map was labeled and a head count was taken of how many undead fighters there were in each place. All the entrances and exits in and out of every camp, cave and tunnel were drawn out perfectly. A red X marked the spot where they stood in the dune.

When they were finished with the maps, the birds perched themselves on a shelf above the desk and became motionless. Arlo had the hole in the wall just about sealed when they heard a knock at the door followed by the creak of it opening.

"It must be Malcolm. He's right on time," said Gamon.

Malcolm came walking down into the lab.

"So, what do you have for me, Gamon? Did everything turn out well?" he asked.

"Yup! They're right here. The ink is still a little wet so be careful."

Malcolm breezed over them, then he gently rolled them up and placed them into a protective tube.

"Good work, you two. Thank you. I'll be in the old library putting together a battle plan if you need me," he said as he walked away.

"We'll be right here if you need us," replied Gamon.

Malcolm went back up the stairs and exited the shop.

"Hey Arlo, you wanna see something cool?"

"I sure do! What do ya got?"

"Follow me. There's another room below the lab

that nobody knows about. It holds quite an inventory of items. I'll show ya!"

CHAPTER 13
THE HIDDEN WORKSHOP

Gamon went to a bundle of chains that held a large steel chandelier over the center of the room. He pulled one that was slightly off to the side of the rest and a clicking noise was heard, followed by a puff of dust that blew up from the floor. Slowly the stones lowered and slid to the side to reveal a spiral staircase that led down to another room.

They started down the steps and the only light in the room shined down from the lab above. Gamon walked into the darkness, and he flipped a lever. Torches began to flicker around the outer walls. They burned stronger and stronger until they illuminated a dirty old workshop atop a large stone mezzanine. It overlooked an enormous room that was built below the entire town.

There were ground moving machines for mining and a fleet of carriages. Large ocean ships sat on planks to keep their hulls from rotting on the ground. Across the room was a large object under a tarp that spanned four lengths across the room.

"This is my kind of place, but why is all this stuff just sitting here?"

"This is what I used to do here. We built vehicles for transportation and machines for working in the mine. When the battles started it was basically forgotten about. I'm glad to see that nothing was damaged!"

"Gamon, what's under the cover?" asked Arlo.

"That is my crown jewel. I built it years ago."

They walked down a stairway to the ground level, and they went over to it. Gamon grabbed hold of the cover.

"I could use some help pulling this down, Arlo. It's a little heavy."

"Sure! Let's do it!"

They both yanked the huge cover off to reveal a shiny black locomotive with golden trim around the engine and the cab.

"It was a steam engine, but I redesigned it to use an alternate power source. Now it uses the same crystals that we use to power the castle. It was almost finished. Just a little more tinkering and a few more tweaks and I could have tested it, but then everything started blowing up around here."

"She's a beauty! Show me what's under the hood," said Arlo.

"Sure! Climb aboard!"

They climbed onto the walkway along the side of the engine. When they got to the center, Gamon opened a panel and inside was a glass cylinder. There were two mounting brackets to hold a crystal in place, but there were no wires to connect it.

"I'm sure you can see what's missing. Everything

else is done! It took months to get the gearing right to accept the extra power. All we need to do is make the wires and find a crystal, then it's ready to hit the track! That, well, still has to be built. You know what I'm thinking we should do tonight. I think we should make that big ship over there, fly!" said Gamon.

"You know something. I think you're right!" replied Arlo.

"I'm pretty sure we have just what we need too!" said Gamon as he went over to a large crate and pried it open with a bar.

Inside was a massive black canvas balloon that was folded up neatly.

"This balloon was made for one of the troop ships. It's huge! If we can fill this baby with helium, it should be able to lift that ship with no problem, and I have just the thing to push it. We will have to take some stuff out of the locomotive, but we can fix that later," said Gamon.

"I like this idea! What do you have to push it?" Arlo asked.

"Rockets! Powerful rockets! We'll mount them in the back and take the crystal core from the locomotive. I'll make the coils now and we'll be flying!" said Gamon with excitement.

"Hit me down low," said Arlo.

Since they're only about two feet tall, they gave each other a high five.

"Yea! This should be fairly easy. Let's do it," Gamon said as he cracked his knuckles, and they walked toward the ship.

Directly above them in the square, the fighters still celebrated as everyone else sat around the fire with the king and queen.

"William, my dear. It is nearly midnight so we should get back. Tomorrow's an important day," said the queen.

"You're right. We've had our fun for tonight. It was nice being back here again," replied the king.

He stood up and reached for the queen's hand and she happily accepted.

"Make sure you all get proper rest tonight," said the queen. "It was nice spending time with all of you. Goodnight, everyone!"

They all wished each other a good night and the king and queen went back into the castle. Again, she was hesitant to walk through the portal, but the king took her by the waist and pulled her through. She squeezed her eyes shut as the portal lit up and they disappeared inside.

In the castle library, Malcolm sat at a table with candles burning all around him. The room was in disarray and books were scattered all over the floor as he studied the map. The others walked in and gathered around the table.

"What do you have so far?" Helaina asked.

"We will need to split our fighters into four groups. One will take out the camps on the outskirts and one will head into the mountains. The last two will infiltrate the mine. After we take out the camps outside, those groups will come to the mine to keep all the undead inside. That will give us the upper hand. I count a little over a hundred thousand undead fighters. We will break the mine up into four parts and keep each one separated from each other. What's strange is that I don't think the undead could have coordinated something like this on their own. I suspect there may be a puppet master."

"But who would ever go through all of this?" asked Archer.

"I'm not sure," replied Malcolm. "We need to watch for anything that's going on behind the scenes. They will have no place to hide. This is our most important battle yet. We need to rid the land of this foe, once and for all. This time tomorrow, we will be at war."

Back inside the workshop, Gamon was below deck bolting the rocket engines into place. Arlo cut out two panels on the back of the ship that would open when the engines were in use. The large glass cylinder from the train engine was now mounted in between them and Gamon was finishing up the wires that would connect the power crystal.

Outside the front of the castle, the black fog from the dune floated out of the forest and up to one of the castle's chimneys. It drifted down inside and exited the massive fireplace in the center of the shop, not far from Gamon and Arlo. They both could be heard hard at work inside the ship. The fog floated up and over the deck and down a stairway into what was now the engine room. It silently hovered over them as they worked.

"Okay! The wires are finished. I put a braided mesh sleeve over them that will help to keep the heat down," said Gamon

"It looks great! I think that'll work perfectly. Now all we need is a power crystal and we're finished down here. Let's go work on the balloon and get it secured in place," said Arlo.

They turned to walk up the stairs and they noticed the black fog floating near the ceiling of the room. They both stopped and stood motionless. They looked at each other nervously, then slowly back up at the fog.

"What in the world is that?" Gamon asked.

"I have no idea, but I'm thinking we should get out of here," replied Arlo.

Just then the fog began to take form and it changed into the voodoo man on his floating carpet. Gamon and Arlo quickly jumped behind the engines and hid.

"Do not fear me," said the man. "My name is Jacob Vondoo and I'm here for you, Arlo."

"What do you mean you're here for me? How do

you know my name? I'm not interested! No, thank you. Please don't come again." said Arlo as he crouched down behind the engine.

"I'm here because you lifted my curse and gave me back my life."

"Oh. You're the voodoo man?" asked Arlo.

"I am here to repay you for the great deed that you have done for me. Anything you may need. It will be my duty to help you in any way necessary."

"Okay. So, you're not gonna kill us?" asked Arlo.

"Just the opposite, friend."

"Well, that's good to know. So, Jacob Vondoo?" he asked. "Is it okay to call you, Voodoo?"

"As you wish," he said. "I heard you say that you need a crystal to power your device?"

"Hello! I'm Gamon, and yes, we do!" he replied.

"Greetings, Gamon."

Voodoo reached into his satchel and pulled out a box. He opened it up and inside was a large blue crystal in the shape of a teardrop.

"This is the most powerful crystal you'll find in the land. It came from the bottom of Teardrop Lake. I give it to you as a token of my gratitude," said Voodoo as he happily handed the box to Arlo.

"Would ya look at that," said Arlo as he looked over at Gamon.

"This will be perfect! Thank you, Voodoo!"

"You are welcome," he replied.

He put on a pair of thick gloves and picked up the crystal, then he placed the mounts inside the cylinder. He plugged in the wires and the crystal began to glow bright blue as the energy flowed through the wires into the rockets.

"You can hear them powering up!" said Arlo.

"That did it! We have power," replied Gamon.

"I guess we're finished down here, but maybe you can give us a hand with mounting the balloon over the ship?" asked Arlo.

"I'd be happy to help," replied Voodoo.

They all headed out of the ship, and they went over to the crate. Gamon moved it to the side and revealed another box below it that was filled with thick braided steel cables.

"We need to clip these wires onto all the loops you see around the balloon." said Gamon. "We'll keep the front and rear sails so we can still turn the ship. The balloon will sit between them, and the center mast will go right through the tunnel of the balloon. Then we'll secure the cables to the main beams of the ship."

"That will work! It's almost like it was meant to be," said Arlo. "I'll bring those helium tanks aboard and mount them below so we can inflate and deflate the balloon at will."

"Great!" Gamon replied.

Gamon and Voodoo went to work connecting the

thick steel chords to the balloon. Arlo took the tanks below deck and secured them to the center mast.

"I think we're done. We just have to get the balloon up there."

Voodoo jumped back onto his carpet and grabbed hold of the huge balloon. He flew up over the ship and gently slid the tunnel right over the center mast. The top of the balloon sat below the crow's nest and just above the sails in the bow and stern. Arlo plugged in the hoses for the helium tanks as Voodoo landed back on the ship. They secured the cables to the beams below the deck, then they all stood back and observed what they created.

"I think we're finished!" said Gamon. "The only thing left to do is to get it outside and inflate it."

"And clean it," added Arlo.

Voodoo waved his hand across the railing and all at once the dust from the ship disappeared, leaving it shiny and new.

"That will do it!" said Gamon. "Thank you, Voodoo! Now we only need to get it out of here."

"How do we get it outside?" asked Arlo.

"There's a large hidden door in the wall over there. So, we'll need to get the ship over there, somehow."

Voodoo threw his arms over his head and the ship lifted into the air. Gamon and Arlo lost their balance for a moment as it slowly moved in front of the door. With another wave of his hand, a stack of logs flew over and landed below, then he gently lowered the ship down on top of them.

"And that takes care of that. Thank you! You're quite helpful, Voodoo!" said Arlo.

"I'm honored to help in any way I can. You've done a much greater deed for me, Arlo," replied Voodoo.

"I'm glad we could help you. You're a good guy, but I really don't want you to just wait around for me to need something. I do appreciate it though," replied Arlo.

"Then I'll only help when it's needed," said Voodoo.

"Isn't that the same thing?" Arlo asked.

"I guess our work is done for tonight," Gamon interrupted. "I think it's time go and get some rest. We can get the ship out in the morning."

"I will travel home for the night and return in the morning to assist you," said Voodoo as his carpet appeared under him. "I bid you both a good night and thank you again for your deed, Arlo."

He changed back into the fog, and he floated up and out of the chimney.

"That was interesting!" said Gamon.

"Agreed!" Arlo replied. "But I like him!"

"Me too! He seems like a nice fella."

They both went back up the staircase and out of the lab into the alleyway. They made their way through the crowd that had quieted down since earlier. Most of the fighters were sitting and talking quietly with one other. Even the light from the orchids dimmed down so the people could rest. They walked thought the square and back into the castle. Everyone was fast asleep around the fire except for Herex, and they both went over and picked a comfy spot in the moss.

"We have a huge surprise for everyone in the morning. Herex, you're gonna love it!" Gamon said.

Herex shook his head to acknowledge him as Gamon and Arlo nestled in. Seconds later they both fell asleep and snored in harmony with each other in the glistening moss. Herex shook his head, displeased that he would have to listen to them all night.

In the morning, all the men and women around the castle were awoken by the sun as it rose up over the trees. Some of the early birds were up and already preparing food for the rest of the army. The castle was filled with the smell of breakfast. Beck woke up wrinkling his nose as he sniffed the pleasant aroma.

"Oh, I know what that is," he said.

He stood straight up and was about to walk outside when the portal lit up and Monroe came through with trays of food and he placed them down on the table in front of him.

"Perfect timing!" said Beck.

Everyone slowly got up and went to the table. They all had tired looks on their faces, but then there was Gamon and Arlo who could barely contain themselves.

"Tell him, tell him!" said Arlo.

"Okay, okay!" Gamon replied. "Arlo and I and the Voodoo man were down in the shop last night and we made something."

"And who? The Voodoo man?" Malcolm asked.

"Yea. He showed up and said he was indebted to Arlo for making it so he can live again. He helped us in the shop last night," said Gamon.

"The Voodoo man," Malcolm replied as he looked over at Beck. "How did he get into the castle?"

"I think he was in the form of a black fog that came down the chimney in the shop, because that's how he left when we were done," replied Gamon.

Herex looked over at them, realizing now what the black fog above the portal in the dune was in fact the Voodoo man.

"I see. What is it that you all did in the shop last night?" Malcolm asked with curiosity.

"That's a surprise for after breakfast," replied Gamon.

"Voodoo said he would return in the morning so he may pop up anytime now, so don't be alarmed if you see a man in a black robe on a floating carpet. He's a friend," said Arlo.

"I'll keep that in mind. I'm wondering what it is you two are up too," said Malcolm.

"You're really gonna like it!" said Arlo.

Everyone started eating but their attention stayed

on Gamon and Arlo as they shoveled down their food. When they were finished, they stood up on the chairs and looked around to see if everyone else was done.

"Okay, gentlemen," said Malcolm. I'm interested to know just what it is that you two and the voodoo man did last night."

"Meet us on the north lawn in twenty minutes and you'll see," said Gamon.

"I'll see you in nineteen minutes and fifty-nine seconds," replied Malcolm.

"Starting now!" said Arlo.

"Let's go!" said Gamon as they ran out of the room and to the shop.

"I can't even imagine what they thought up," said Malcolm.

As Gamon and Arlo made their way into the workshop, they saw that Voodoo was already there with the ship.

"Right on time! We will need your help," said Arlo.

"I have an easy way to do this. If you could just get the door open, I can handle the rest," said Voodoo.

"Sure thing," replied Gamon as he ran over to a lever on the wall and pulled it.

He had to use all his weight to pull it down, but it gave. The door that opened in the wall was huge. Plenty large enough to get the ship out.

"Okay. My turn," said Voodoo.

He held his arms up over his head and the ship lifted off the timber and floated out the door. The center mast cleared the massive door by only a foot and as they got it outside, the sunlight shined down onto the fresh black paint. The golden trim gleamed and it reflected onto the ground below.

The ship was magnificent. It stood a hundred feet long and thirty feet wide and it would now be the biggest airship in the sky. The door closed behind them, and Voodoo placed the ship gently onto the grass.

"Quite impressive, Voodoo!" said Arlo.

Voodoo's carpet appeared below their feet and it flew them all up to the deck, then they headed down below to the helium tanks.

"Let's open them up and get this balloon filled. Everyone will be here soon," said Gamon.

They turned the valves all the way open, and the balloon began to rise up over the ship. A few minutes later it was filled and Gamon shut off the valve.

"We only used a third of what we have in the tanks to fill the balloon," said Gamon.

"There's no doubt that this thing's gonna fly!" replied Arlo.

"It sure will," said Voodoo. "You two really did something great here," Voodoo said.

They all went back on deck and waited for everyone else to come outside.

CHAPTER 14
NEW MEANS OF TRANSPORTATION.

Gamon and Arlo glanced over at the castle just as everyone was walking out the door. They anxiously watched as they all stood in awe at the sight of the massive ship.

"This is the most beautiful airship I've ever seen," said Helaina.

"Truly amazing. They've really outdone themselves, and this is only their first day," said Archer.

They all went over to the ship and climbed aboard to take a closer look.

"Everyone, this is Voodoo," said Arlo.

Voodoo went right over to Malcolm and Beck.

"You both assisted Arlo in lifting my curse. I am grateful and indebted to you both."

"I'm Malcolm Cahpra. This is Beck, Helaina, Archer, and Herex."

Everyone greeted him kindly.

"It is nice to meet you all. Herex, you almost sent me back to my maker with that orb you left in the dune last night. You did however wipe out all the undead fighters around, with style if I may say," said Voodoo.

Herex just looked over at him and shrugged.

"Herex doesn't speak, but I'm sure he didn't realize," said Helaina.

"So! Now you're a captain, Malcolm," said Beck.

"No, I'm no captain. But I do know a captain!"

"You're gonna let that crazy ghost from the fire, fly this thing?" Beck asked nervously.

"That crazy ghost happens to be a legend. I know he'll be happy to tell you some stories," said Malcolm. "He's sailed around the world many times and now I think we can give him something to keep him busy."

"He was saying how there's nothing for him to do around here. We should go get him and take her out for a ride," said Helaina.

"Okay. I'll go and get him," Beck said as he climbed off the ship and headed back to the castle.

"When we get back, Arlo and I will install a device that will form a shield around the balloon, and we'll upgrade the weapons a bit too! Cannon balls are just too heavy. We'll put in a plasma conduit that will feed the cannons with powerful orbs instead. That'll do more damage than any old cannon ball ever could, and it can be set for single or rapid-fire burst! Whatever the situation calls for!" said Gamon.

When Beck got into the dungeon, he walked along the cells and looked in each one. The last one was a little brighter than all the others and he went over. The captain was lying on his back with his feet up against the wall.

"Hey Captain. We have a surprise for ya. I need ya to come with me. You're always complaining about how there's nothing to do around here. Well, now we have something for ya to do," said Beck.

The captain stood up from the bench.

"You know, Beck. If I had solid hands, I think I would choke you," said the captain.

"Ahh, whatever. Come outside and see. Maybe you'll get a tan! Trust me, you'll be happy ya did," said Beck as he walked away.

"Well, this should be interesting," said the captain and he followed him up through the castle. When they got out of the dungeon and into a bright room Beck looked back for the captain, but he didn't see him. He stopped and called out to him.

"Hey, Captain! Where did ya go?"

"I'm still here," he replied. "You just can't see me in the daylight. I'm kind of, a nocturnal being these days."

"Oh, okay. Thought I lost ya. Just outside these doors, Cap."

They exited the castle and to the captain's surprise was the massive shining airship in the center of the lawn.

"I've never seen anything like it," he said.

"Well, come aboard and get a closer look," said Beck.

He climbed aboard and the captain floated up to the deck.

"The captain's here, Malcolm, but we can't see him during the day. I'm not too upset about it," said Beck with a chuckle.

"Welcome aboard, Captain. I trust you can get us underway," said Malcolm.

"You want me to Captain the ship?" he asked.

"I can't think of anyone better for the job. With all your experience and to have a captain that never needs to sleep can be an advantage," said Malcolm.

"I'm honored that you would entrust this beautiful vessel to me," said the captain gratefully. "I will treat her like the lady she is, Lord Cahpra."

"We are honored to have such a legendary captain at the helm," Malcolm replied.

Everyone aboard began to clap.

"What shall we call her?" Malcolm asked.

"I'd like to call her, Auburn," the captain replied.

"Auburn it is," said Malcolm as everyone clapped again and Gamon broke a bottle against the bow.

"Even though we can't see you, please take the wheel and bring us out for a ride," said Malcolm.

The wheel turned slightly from side to side, showing that the captain was holding it.

"I'll go put some more helium in the balloon and we'll be off. I have a remote that I'll bring up and I'll show you how to use it, Cap. This is gonna be great!" said Arlo as he ran down below.

A minute later he came back up with a small remote control and he screwed it to a panel in front of the wheel.

"Captain if you push this button, the ship will ascend. If you press this button, it will descend. It fills up and releases fast, so you'll be able to maneuver quickly when you get used to it."

"Thank you. I think we'll head up then," said the captain.

He pressed the button to fill the balloon and the Auburn lifted into the sky. Before they knew it, they were a hundred feet above the castle. Everyone looked down at the fighters as they all looked back up at the mighty airship now hovering in the sky.

Jenny's ship came up alongside so she could see it for herself. The sky began to fill with more ships and people on their birds to see the Auburn. Everyone saw it as the flagship, and they celebrated the new and greatest symbol of their kingdom.

Gamon went down into the engine room and looked over the wiring on the engines to see that all the connections were tight. When he was done, he went up to the wheel with another remote and mounted it beside the other.

"This one makes you go, Captain! This dial has three positions. Forward, neutral and there is no reverse, yet. Turn it to the right and you go forward, there's quarter power, half power, three-quarter and full power. Easy, right?"

"Yes. Simple enough! I'll take her out," said the captain.

He turned the knob slowly to one quarter of its power and the engines fired up in the stern. Flames from the rockets shot out of the back and the ship soared out toward the ocean. Nobody could see it, but the captain had a bright smile across his face.

"This is incredible. No more dark and dirty, dungeon. This could be a whole new start for me," said the captain joyfully.

"I'm glad you like it," said Malcolm. "Take us around the grounds. Let's test her out."

The captain turned the dial to half power and the ship started to make way. As he turned the wheel, the sails shifted and turned the ship effortlessly to follow the shoreline.

"Take us out to Coral Island," said Malcolm.

"As you wish," replied the captain.

He turned the wheel, and they headed out to sea. Everyone stood by the railings and enjoyed the fresh air that flowed across the deck.

"Let's open her up a bit," said Gamon. "Give her full power, Captain!"

The captain turned the dial to full power and everyone was pushed back from the acceleration. The ship reached full speed and they darted through the sky. Gamon and Arlo went around and inspected the engines and the cables as they sailed along. After a few minutes Coral Island was coming up fast.

"Okay, Cap. Back off on the throttle a bit," Arlo said.

The captain turned the dial back slowly to one quarter power and the ship fell forward from the wind resistance.

"Well, it moves alright, Gamon. I think we need something on the front of the balloon to deflect the wind and maybe some engines in the bow to help slow us down because for a second there, I almost lost my breakfast," Arlo said.

"I agree! We'll have to make some adjustments before we leave tonight," replied Gamon.

"We're on approach," said Malcolm. "Put us down in the water at the east end of the island, please."

"Yes sir! Down we go," replied the captain.

He lowered the speed dial to minimal power and held down the button that deflated the balloon. They began losing altitude and as they got closer the captain let off the button to level out and take some momentum off of their descent. He placed the ship gently into the water just off the east side of the island.

All the other ships and birds filled the sky above them. Some people even dove their bird's right into the water for a little refreshment.

The sun shined on the deck and a gentle crosswind blew past. They all gathered at the stern and looked out at the island. The water was clear and full of fish and turtles and other creatures that swam in a colorful reef below the ship.

"I wish we had some fishing poles," said Beck.

"I knew I forgot something!" Gamon replied.

"We can't stay long anyway, but soon we will spend the day here, doing just that," said Malcolm.

A cloud moved in front of the sun and gave some shade to the deck of the ship. The captain could faintly be seen grasping the wheel in his hands.

"Hey, Captain. I'll need you to take us back now," said Malcolm.

The captain lifted his hat to him, then he inflated the balloon and turned the ship. The engines fired and pushed them through the water toward the castle. As the balloon filled, the ship slowly lifted out of the water and soared up into the sky.

When they reached the castle, the captain brought the Auburn safely back down to the lawn. Everyone thanked him for the ride, and they slid down some ropes to the grass.

"Arlo, we have some work to do," said Gamon. "Hey, Voodoo. Would you happen to have another one of those crystals for the cause?"

"I do. I will travel to Teardrop Lake now and be

back by the time you're ready for it," said Voodoo.

"Great! Thanks, Voodoo," Gamon said appreciatively.

His carpet appeared under him, and he flew out of sight toward the Teardrop Forest as Gamon and Arlo headed back into the shop. The captain stayed aboard and went below to explore the lower decks of the ship.

By the afternoon, Gamon and Arlo had the two engines aboard and mounted in the front of the ship. They connected all the wiring and checked everything twice.

"Finished! All that's left is to connect the crystal and I have the perfect thing to use as a nosecone for the balloon. It's back in the shop," said Gamon.

They went back inside to the stack of wooden crates. Gamon climbed around on top of them and looked around for a particular one.

"I got it! It's this one, right here," he said, and he hopped up and down on it. Suddenly the crate crumbled below him, and he fell inside. Arlo climbed up to help him and he looked down to see Gamon sitting inside a large cup.

"You, okay?" asked Arlo.

"Yup! I'm alright. This is the one. I'm glad the other side wasn't facing up," he replied with a chuckle.

Arlo pulled him back out of it.

"Well, that was fun!" said Gamon.

"Let's get it outside," said Arlo. "What is this thing anyway?"

"It was supposed to be mounted on the peak of the tower, but since there are no more towers, this will work just fine for what we need it for. It's made from copper that was dug from the Old Gibbs mine."

"Now it will be part of the greatest airship in the sky," replied Arlo.

"That it will," said Gamon. "And the fastest!"

"I guess this is that something big you were talking about. There's not much left to do here so we'll have to figure out something else to keep us busy," said Arlo.

"After this battle, there will be plenty of things for us to do," replied Gamon.

"I hope you're right."

"For now, let's get the cannons in order and the shield device for the balloon. That should keep us busy till Voodoo gets back," said Gamon.

"Let's do it!" Arlo replied.

As Voodoo reached the border of Teardrop Forest, he saw saplings and fields of grass that formed from the seeds he had spread. Life had returned to the forest and the start of a whole new eco system was in motion. He was happy to see his home returning to the way it was. When he reached his hut, he landed on the front porch and looked out at the newly formed landscape around his home. Thick trees with lush foliage surrounded it now. Green moss covered the ground and flowers bloomed all over the ground.

He walked in the door and exhaled a breath of relief as he saw that everything was back in order. He went down to his lab and took out an old trunk. Inside was a long wooden staff with a crystal ball entwined in branches at the top. As he took it out it began to let off a bright purple glow. He placed it over his shoulder and went back up the stairs. He took one last look around his home then he headed out the door.

A crow was perched on the railing, and he went over and petted it gently on the head.

"My friend. It is good to see you!"

He took some seed from his satchel and poured it onto the railing.

"I will need you to fly to the old Gibbs mine below the Dyre Mountains and be my eyes," said Voodoo as the bird ate the seed.

The bird finished and bowed its head to him, then it leapt into the air and flew off in the direction of the mine. Voodoo hopped onto his carpet and flew toward Teardrop Lake.

When he arrived, the lake hadn't fully developed and it was smaller than he remembered, but the deepest part of it was already filled with water. He stopped over the center then he waved his staff in a circular motion and formed a bubble around himself. After it sealed around him, he jumped in and sank all the way to the bottom. As he settled there, he scanned the area to see that nothing saw him. Fish and turtles swam around as he pushed his hands through the bubble and sifted through the lakebed.

After a few minutes, he found a crystal. He grabbed it with both hands and gave it a pull. Out came a bright blue crystal. He pulled it into the bubble and placed it in his satchel, then he went looking for more. Soon after, he found another, and he yanked it out. This one was significantly bigger than the last and he had to hold it in his arms as the bubble rose back up to the surface.

When he was halfway up a huge alligator spotted him. Voodoo tried to rise faster but it came right for him. It struck its body against the bubble repeatedly, but the bubble held up against its powerful blows. He held the crystal tight as it tried numerous more times but failed. He reached the surface and floated up over the water. The bubble popped just above the carpet and dropped him right back on top. The alligator glared up at him then it turned away and sank back down into the lake. Voodoo flew away and back to the castle as fast as possible.

A short time later, he arrived and flew right to the north lawn. Gamon and Arlo were aboard the ship as he landed on the deck. He put the large crystal down and Arlo and Gamon came over to see it.

"Wow, that one's huge! I think it will be more than enough to power the cannons," said Gamon.

"I also have a smaller one for the bow engines," replied Voodoo.

"This ship is ready for action!" cheered Arlo.

"Yea. Let's go see how it fits," said Gamon.

They all went down into the cannon room in the center of the ship. There was a large glass cylinder where the plasma would build up before getting pushed through the conduits and out to the cannons on each side of the ship.

They picked up the huge crystal and placed it between the mounts inside the cylinder. The conduit immediately began to power up.

"Unfortunately, we can't test it yet, but I know it's gonna work," said Arlo.

"Let's get the last crystal in the bow engines, then we only have to mount the nosecone," said Gamon.

"I'll take care of the last crystal and meet you both outside in a few minutes," said Arlo.

He took the crystal and headed to the bow engine room. He mounted the crystal, and it began glowing bright as the bow engines powered up. He tested them out for a moment to see they were in working order then he shut them down and swiped his hands together. He went outside to see Gamon squeezing a large tube of permanent cement into the cone.

"This glue means what it says. We gotta get this right the first time because as soon as it contacts the balloon, it'll never move again," Gamon's said.

Voodoo held up his staff and the crystal on top began to glow. The cone lifted into the air and floated toward the ship. Slowly it pressed against the front of the balloon, then he lowered his staff and placed it back over his shoulder.

"Well, that's it! It's in place forever. That should cut the wind nicely," said Gamon. "Good job everyone! I couldn't have done it without you guys. Let's go tell Malcolm that it's ready."

He put his hand up and Arlo gave him a high five and Voodoo gave him a low five as they all walked back to the castle.

As they got into the ballroom, the door on the other side of the room flew open as some of the fighters came running in with a young boy.

"This kid came running up to us in the forest speaking of the undead in the mine near his town. He said he needed to speak to you, so we brought him here," said one of the men.

Malcolm recognized him and quickly went over.

"Marcus, what's the matter?"

"Dead, skeletons, mine," said Marcus frantically, still out of breath from running.

"Get this boy some water, please," said Malcolm. "Take it easy. You're safe now. Breathe and tell me what's wrong."

Marcus took a deep breath and exhaled.

"I was in the mine with some friends. I know we're

not supposed to be in there, but we went deeper in than ever before. This time there were skeletons. Lots of them! They were making their way to the Watertown corridor. I didn't know what to do, so I came here!"

"You did the right thing, Marcus," replied Malcolm as he looked at Helaina.

"Round up two ships and twenty fighters that are ready to depart immediately and alert the medical ship, please."

She quickly ran out the door onto the square and started rounding up the fighters.

"Gamon, prepare the Auburn for departure."

"We were actually just coming in to tell you it was ready," replied Gamon.

"Ready! Good. Then we leave now. Tell the rest of the fighters to prepare for our return."

Just as he stood up, Jenny walked into the room to see what the commotion was.

"Marcus here said that the undead are on their way to Watertown. We will be leaving momentarily," said Malcolm.

"Please be careful, Malcolm," said Jenny. "Come with me, Marcus. We'll get you something to eat."

Jenny took Marcus out into the square as everyone else went out to the north lawn. Two ships sat overhead waiting for the Auburn to lead their way. Malcolm boarded the ship and went to the stern.

"Captain, Take us up! Destination Watertown, three quarter power," he said.

The captain inflated the balloon and the ship rose into the sky. He turned around in place and pointed it in the direction of Watertown, then he turned the throttle to three-quarter power, and they flew swiftly off over the castle. The two other ships trailed behind alongside the medical ship.

Malcolm stared anxiously into the distance.

"Full power, Captain."

The captain turned the dial, and everyone held on as the ship darted through the sky. The other Captain's realized that the Auburn was pulling away.

"Bring us to full power!" They spoke.

The ships started moving faster, but their propeller power was no match for Gamon's rockets, and they quickly fell behind. Not long after, Merchant Lake was coming up in the distance.

"Gamon, ready the cannons," said Malcolm.

"Yes sir," he replied.

He went below deck with Arlo to the control panel and he flipped the power on. The crystal lit up so brightly that they could barely look at it. Green balls of plasma formed and started flowing through the glass conduits on both sides of the ship.

"They're ready to go. All we must do is aim and fire. I'll have to make another pair of goggles for you, Arlo. I only have one pair again, sorry. Let's go topside. Everything is ready down here."

They went back up and joined everyone on deck.

"The cannons are ready," said Gamon.

"Very good," Malcolm replied. "Bring us over the town."

CHAPTER 15
THE RAID OF WATERTOWN.

They arrived at a large town that was built on Merchant Lake. It was abandoned by most of the people, but some stayed in the town they adored so much. At one time Watertown was filled with life and a scene that you could place on a postcard.

Attached two story homes made of brick and stone lined the canals throughout the town. Their doors opened onto stone footpaths and bridges crossed over the waterways. A massive square dock in the center of town was a well-known fishing spot and the Watertown flag still waved high above.

The town was connected to the shore by long wooden docks that could hold dozens of ships, but they were all empty. Only canoes filled a small corner for traveling inside the town. A large canal on the far side of the lake led to the ocean and was frequently used for commerce, but it hasn't been traveled in some time.

As they got closer, they noticed a group of people who were running from something on the ground. Malcolm looked through his spyglass and saw the undead fighters crawling from the corridor like an infestation.

"Come about, Captain. Show them the port side. Put some cannon fire between the people and the undead, Gamon."

Gamon hastily ran down to the cannon room. He put his goggles on and took the trigger, then aimed and fired. The plasma balls shot from the cannons and struck the ground in large green explosions that wiped out the fighters nearby.

"Let's get down there! Protect the town!" Malcolm hollered.

He leapt overboard and everyone else followed. Their birds snatched them up and they all soared down to the ground. The corridor was a long stone walkway that led to a tunnel in the hillside where the undead swarmed from like a hive. The other ships arrived and joined Gamon in firing their cannons on the entrance.

The undead filled the hills around them and Malcolm's armor turned fiery red as he pulled out his sword. Everyone stood alongside with their weapons ready as the undead fighters crawled closer. They all spread out and started to fight. Bright colored orbs began ripping through the trees and exploding on their targets. The sound of clashing steel now filled the corridor.

More and more fighters crawled from the tunnel. Helaina waved her wand and formed a wall of bright moss and vine to hold them inside. Archer fired his arrows into the hills and Beck took down any of the fighters that got to close.

Herex walked toward the entrance and the undead

fighters leapt at him. A toss of his arm they stopped midair, then with a slight wave of his hand they were flung back into the hill. He continued forward and formed a dark smoky orb in his hands then he placed it on the ground and casually walked away as he fired on some fighters that dared to attack him.

A group of undead tried to sneak up on some of the king's fighters and Herex thrusted his mace into the air. The rubies lit up brightly and a cloud formed over their heads that poured a fiery rain, melting their bones in a blaze of fire.

The undead inside the tunnel had almost chopped their way through the vine as the ones the hillside lessened by the second. Herex looked over at Helaina and pointed to the orb he left on the ground. Just as the undead started piling out of the entrance she threw her arms into the air and an invisible wall rose up between them.

The eyes of the undead glowed red and they growled viciously as they tried to get through it. A wave of Herex's mace and the orb exploded. The undead fighters were incinerated, and a cloud of dust rose up behind the wall. There was silence after the explosion. When the dust settled, they could see the entrance to the tunnel was now empty. Helaina lowered the wall and the dust wafted toward them.

"Let's finish this! said Malcolm. "Two groups join us in the cave and two, stay out to protect the town."

As they entered the tunnel, the undead were making their way in at the other end. A wave of Herex's arm and they were all thrown back out. The rubies on his mace lit up and he fired an orb down the tunnel. In a bright red flash, the way into the next cave was clear. Malcolm charged inside into a mass of undead fighters. He swung his sword ferociously as his armor turned fiery and his blade extended.

Beck fired his orb launcher and took down groups of the undead in large green explosions. Herex formed more of his whirling black holes and dozens of them were pulled inside. He placed his mace back over his shoulder and his eyes turned bright red under his hood. He lifted his arms into the air and the black hole rose off the ground and engulfed all the undead around them. He levitated into the next tunnel and pushed the whirling hole through it as everyone else made their way in behind him. As they got inside, they could barely see Herex at the other end and they ran to catch up with him.

When they reached the next cave, they saw him hovering in the air over a hundred undead fighters. He turned in a circle and fired his orbs rapidly. Everyone else entered the cave and started to fight. The undead climbed on top of each other to try and reach Herex, then he suddenly crouched down, and a dark cloudy aura began to radiate all around him. He threw his arms into the air and the cloud spread across the cave as thunder began to strike down in every direction. Helaina quickly formed a dome over everyone so they wouldn't be struck. The bolts only lasted a short time, but they cleared out the entire cave.

Herex slowly dropped down to the ground and stumbled to a knee. Everyone ran over to see what happened and they tried to help but he just gestured for them to stop. He slowly stood up and waved to show that he was okay.

The cave behind them flashed as the other groups held off the fighters that piled out of three more tunnels that led further into the mine.

"You ready to go, friend?" Malcolm asked.

Herex looked up at him and shook his head yes. He stood up and held his arms out to the sides. A black fog formed around him, and a small white orb appeared. It circled his feet then it went up and around his head and disappeared into the air. Everyone else looked around at each other in wonder of what happened as Herex took his mace out and signaled that he was ready.

"Okay! Let's finish this. Two groups take the left and right tunnels, and we'll take the center," said Malcolm as they walked toward them.

Archer fired his arrows and pushed the fighters back inside. They all entered together and noticed a dim purple glow at the other end. When they took down the last of the fighters in the tunnel, they all walked out onto a ledge that overlooked a massive cave.

Everything was silent and the only thing that could be heard was a small waterfall that flowed down a moss-covered wall into a sparkling pool. Purple lilies floated on the surface, and it was surrounded by a thick bed of green moss with colorful flowers.

They all looked around the cave, but the undead fighters were nowhere to be found. Suddenly the pool began to brighten. The flowers and moss started to glow and bloom as a large white orb rose from the water. It moved in a circular motion and a woman fairy appeared as the orb fizzled out over her head. She had long black hair and sparkling wings that flapped rapidly to hold her above the water. She abruptly turned her head to look at everyone on the ledge.

"Do not be fooled. They are still here," she said in a calm, angelic voice.

All at once the floor of the cave became foggy and moved as if there was a current of water, then it dissipated to reveal hundreds of undead fighters. Some had robes and others wore old, tarnished armor.

They quickly began to fire up at the ledge and it blasted away at the cave around them. The king's fighters fired blue and yellow orbs back and turned their targets into dust that spread across the floor.

The undead fighters leapt up toward the ledge, but a wave of Herex's mace swept back into the crowd.

Archer fired his arrows and pierced the old armor of the undead. They stopped attacking and looked down at the arrows just in time to see them explode.

Beck perched his rifle on the ledge and fired his orb launcher all around the cave. Large groups of the undead were taken down in bright green bursts that sent glimmering clouds up to the ceiling.

On the far side of the cave there was a bright flash of light, and a swirling portal began to form inside another tunnel. A hundred more undead fighters came crawling through it and entirely filled the cave. Everyone watched as the light dimmed back out behind them. Malcolm looked at everyone to see if they were ready.

"Attack!" he yelled as he leapt down off the ledge.

He landed with so much force that it shattered the bones of the undead fighters near him. Everyone else landed right beside him and readied their weapons. The fairy waved her wand and a clear wall formed around the pool to protect it from harm.

Malcolm's armor turned fiery red as he began to fight. One of the groups jumped down to join them and the second stayed on the ledge so they could fire on the undead from above. The whole cave lit up bright from the orbs that ripped through the air. The tunnel on the far side of the cave began to light up again and more of the undead started to come through. Helaina waved her wand and formed a clear wall in front of it that quickly filled up with the undead fighters.

The undead inside the cave lessened with each swing of their swords or burst of their orbs. Every arrow fired or flick of a wand was a crucial blow to the undead. Some of them tried to sneak past the fairy as she watched them in pity while they scurried past.

"You poor souls. May you now be free," she said as she flicked her wand.

A glistening light formed around them and the moss below them lit up brightly. The fighters both collapsed as their bones crumbled away and left only the ghost of the person they were before. They looked around for a moment in confusion but then they walked off through the wall of the cave.

Three of the undead fighters stood in a circle with their arms above their heads as a large red orb began to form over them. Archer and Beck tried to take them out, but they couldn't penetrate a shield that surrounded them. The orb turned solid red, and smoke lingered off the top, then they fired it up at the ledge.

"Incoming!" hollered Beck at the top of his lungs.

Everyone tried to deflect it away, but it stayed its course. A woman on the ledge began to form a dome around her group, but it was too late. The orb exploded against the ceiling of the cave above them, and large chunks of rock came crashing down. The entire group was devastated. Everyone watched in awe as the dust cloud rolled off the ledge.

They all became angered by the loss of their comrades and turned back to the undead with renewed animosity. They attacked the undead with everything they had. Malcolm leapt into the air and landed on the three fighters with so much force that it penetrated their shield. A bright flash of energy exploded in every direction and the fighters disintegrated.

Herex shot a black orb into the air and a dark cloud formed over the army. Bolts of thunder pounded down on the undead fighters. Helaina quickly fired a green orb at their feet and vine grew around their legs to keep them from moving. The bolts struck down on them until they were gone.

The undead fell further and further back into the cave. They were cut down to a quarter of what they were and the rest of them retreated into a dark corner. All that could be seen was the red glow of their eyes.

Everyone prepared for the final attack when suddenly the sound of cracking bones began to echo through the cave. Helaina fired a light orb into the air, and they saw the remaining undead fighters mending together to form a large skeletal dragon. Its eyes lit up the same glowing red and their swords became razor sharp claws.

It charged out of the dark and trampled one of the king's fighters as it breathed a large stream of fire. Helaina quickly formed a dome to protect everyone from it. When it was out of flame, she lowered it and

Beck fired back at it.

Herex fired orbs that exploded all over its body, severing the tail and shattering its ribs. It went to blow another stream of fire, but Helaina formed a dome around the dragon to keep it inside. The flame covered its body, and it roared loudly as its bones started to burn away. She dropped the dome and Beck fired his launcher at the ceiling repeatedly. As the orbs exploded large boulders began to fall on top of the dragon and pin it to the ground. When the falling rocks stopped it could only lie on the ground and growl viciously as it stared at them with its glowing red eyes.

Beck fired another orb beside its head, and it exploded, severing the dragon's head and the red glow faded from its eyes. The few remaining undead fighters stared out at the remains of the dragon. Malcolm walked toward them, but he was stopped by Beck.

"I'll take care of the rest," he said then he fired three more orbs from his launcher.

The undead tried to retreat but the orbs exploded and left no remains.

The fairy dropped the wall around the pool and looked over at the man who was trampled by the dragon.

"Bring him to me," she said as she pointed to him.

His friends picked him up and brought him over to the pool. The fairy dropped down into the water and laid his head on her lap. The pool suddenly lit up and the water began to bubble. The air glistened around them as the moss and flowers illuminated brightly, then it dimmed back down, and the man opened his eyes.

She smiled down at him, and he smiled right back as he slowly sat up and looked around at everyone in the pool. They helped him to his feet, and he examined his body that was now healed of the injury.

"Thank you," he said as he dropped to his knee in praise of her.

She bowed her head, and he left the pool to rejoin his group who welcomed him warmly.

Malcolm quickly made his way up to the ledge where the fighters were still trapped under the rock. He frantically moved the large boulders away to get to them. Helaina went over and grabbed his shoulder.

"It's too late, Malcolm. There's nothing we can do."

He threw the stone he was holding and dropped his head in sadness as the rest of the group joined them up on the ledge.

"We must do something with the rest of the undead. That wall won't hold forever," said Helaina.

"You and Herex, seal it up," said Malcolm in a solemn tone.

They both went over to the wall as Herex formed a large red orb in his hands. Helaina threw her arms into the air and the wall exploded into the tunnel.

Herex fired the orb, and it disappeared in the darkness. A few moments later it exploded, and a huge flame blew out of it. The explosion collapsed the tunnel and entirely cut off the old Gibbs mine from the Watertown corridor. Inside the undead stronghold they angrily crawled around to find a way through, but there was none. The tunnel was now sealed.

The fairy watched Helaina and Herex as they walked past.

"Thank you for ridding my cave of those tortured souls."

"You're welcome," Helaina replied. "Thank you for helping our friend."

The fairy bowed her head as the white orb rose up and circled around her again till she disappeared, then the pool dimmed down, and they made their way back up to the ledge.

"Let's get them back to the ship," said Malcolm as he headed back the way they came in.

Herex waved his mace and moved all the rocks away from the fallen fighters. Helaina formed a green orb that broke into five smaller ones that floated to a fighter and gently lifted them into the air. They folded their arms onto their chests and their weapons were placed back into their holsters. Everyone walked out of the cave as the fallen fighters slowly floated behind.

When they reached the exit of the mine the townspeople cheered and offered food and drink as they walked back out of the corridor. The cheering stopped as the fallen fighters made their way out. Everyone went silent. The men took off their hats and the whole town bowed their heads. An older woman placed a flower in each of their hands as they passed.

The medical ship was docked nearby, and everyone watched as they were brought aboard and laid gently on the deck beside two other fighters that fell before the corridor was breeched.

Malcolm and Helaina stood on the dock and looked out at Watertown, both pleased that it was now safe. The mayor of the town ran up to them.

"Thank you for protecting our home," he said. "We are forever in your debt. We wish to build a memorial for those who were lost here today. We will never forget the sacrifice they made for us. They will be spoken of often and proudly honored here, forever."

"Thank you," Malcolm replied. "Their families will appreciate that."

"Thank you, Lord Cahpra," said the mayor. "I'm sure I speak for the whole town when I say, best wishes to you all in your journey ahead."

"Thank you," Malcolm replied gratefully.

Moments later a group of women from the town went out to the dock with large flower assortments. They boarded the ship and placed them all around the fallen fighters. It looked as if they were sleeping in a colorful bed of flowers. Everyone watched as the ship prepared to make way. A man stood at the edge of the lake and played the bagpipes for the lost souls. The captain of the medical ship could be heard calling out.

"Take us up. It's time to bring these brave soul's home."

The ship slowly rose out of the water and set course to head back to the castle. Everyone saluted them as they flew off into the sky. Malcolm peered up at the Auburn as it circled overhead. Everyone called their birds, and they flew back up to the ship.

When they landed back on deck, they saw Gamon and Arlo waving their hands in front of Voodoo, but he wasn't responding. He seemed to be in a trance. Malcolm went over to see what was happening.

"What's going on here?" he asked.

"He just started staring off into nowhere. I'm not sure what's going on," Arlo replied.

A second later Voodoo snapped out of it and noticed everyone was staring at him.

"The undead are staying put for now but something's happening inside that mine. The last explosion disturbed the whole lot of them."

"How do you know this?" Malcolm asked.

"I have a friend who's a crow. It's a lot like Gamon's hummingbirds. I can see whatever he sees. I sent him to the old Gibbs mine to watch the undead. I thought it would be wise to keep an eye on the area," he said.

"I agree. Please keep me informed of any changes."

"Yes. Of course," he replied.

Malcolm looked over at the captain.

"Take us back, please. Three quarter power."

The captain adjusted course as the ship sailed off and the people of Watertown waved to them as they flew out of sight.

CHAPTER 16
JOURNEY TO THE TWILIGHT FOREST.

They arrived back at the castle as the rest of the king's ships prepared for departure to the Twilight Forest. The captain brought the Auburn down to the lawn and everyone zipped down the ropes to the ground.

Voodoo went up to Malcolm with a concerned look on his face.

"The undead are gathering outside the mine. There are many of them. They board a fleet of airships that are rising from the sea and the rest cover the land around the mountain. Some on foot, others atop skeletal creatures. They even fly on skeletal birds."

"Thank you, Voodoo," he replied, seeming as concerned as Voodoo now while he turned to Helaina.

"We leave now," he said, and she nodded back to him.

He went into the ballroom just as his father was pulling his mother through the portal. On her other hand was Jenny, laughing at her as she checked herself over to see that she was okay.

"We will be leaving soon," said Malcolm. "The undead army has left the mine, making our maps useless. We will have to fight them in the open."

"Oh dear! I can't bear to watch you leave again,"

said the queen.

She touched his cheek and gazed up at him in his armor.

"I will return from this mother, and we shall see each other often."

The king grabbed him by his shoulder.

"I look forward to those days, son. I'm so very proud of you. You're braver than I had ever hoped," he said.

"I won't let you down. After this battle, the undead will be at rest and never again will they threaten the sanctity of this isle."

"My brave brother, going to save the isle again," Jenny said. "You watch yourself! I don't want to have to come out there and get you."

"Maybe we'll all just stay here, and you can go by yourself! But I wouldn't do that to the undead. They've been through enough," he replied as everyone began laughing together.

Jenny hit him on the arm in response.

"Good Luck," she said with a worried smile.

"Thanks. I will return," said Malcolm.

He hugged his mother and kissed her cheek. As they stared at each other, Malcolm smiled brightly and it caused her to crack a smile for a moment, but then it brought her to tears and she hugged him tight. He kissed her cheek and turned to his father. They grabbed each other's forearms and gazed proudly at one another.

"My son. Be well. Be focused. Be victorious!"

"I shall father."

Malcolm turned and walked away, and his family watched as the ballroom doors closed behind him.

He trekked across the lawn as the ships took on their supplies. Medics in white coats consulted each other beside the medical ship. They were mostly gnomes, but a few dwarves were among their group. They all boarded the ship with medical bags in hand as cases of supplies were hoisted aboard.

The sky began to fill with ships and fighters on birds. In the center of it all was the Auburn in all its beauty, dwarfing all the ships around it. The only bigger ships were the two enormous soldier transport ships that sat off to the side of the plain and began to fill with fighters. They were so large it took a dozen balloons the size of the Auburn's to lift them. Massive props mounted at the sterns of each one spun slowly as they warmed up for the trip. Fighters began to fill the benches across the decks, and some manned the cannons that were mounted all around the perimeter of the ships. Malcolm made his way to the Auburn and went aboard.

"Preparations are going well. We will be ready to depart soon," Helaina said.

"Good. Thank you," Malcolm replied as he looked over at Gamon nearby. "Gamon, do you have the maps for the eastern Twilight Forest?"

"I sure do! They're in your ready room."

"Then you know where I'll be. Thank you, Gamon."

He went into the room just off the deck and unrolled the map onto a large wooden table. With an old copper compass, he measured the distance between them and the undead army.

Helaina went to the railing and looked out at all the other ships. She saw Arlo flying slowly through the crowd with Voodoo beside him on his carpet. As they got closer, she noticed that Arlo was dressed in camouflage. His face was painted, and he wore a bandana on his head.

They landed on deck and Arlo turned off the engine. He climbed out of it, then it folded up and he shoved it under a bench. He strutted by Helaina like he was a force to be reckoned with as he nodded and winked at her. She couldn't help smiling back at him.

"Hi Arlo," she replied as he walked past.

Gamon met him at the top of the steps, and he looked him up and down.

"Hey Arlo!" said Gamon as he looked over at Helaina.

"What's up, Gamon?"

Before he could even answer, Arlo strutted right past.

"I'm going below to get ready," he said.

"You actually look like you're, pretty ready to go!"

Gamon replied.

Arlo went down to the deck below. Helaina and Gamon could barely contain themselves, but they did since they've become quite fond of Arlo and all his surprise wardrobe changes.

Gamon went into the ready room to join Malcolm and go over the map. He turned the knob to go in, but the door stuck so he bumped into it twice to get it open.

"I'll have to fix this," he muttered to himself as he went inside.

Voodoo and Helaina laughed, and she looked back out at the plain again. This time she spotted Beck, Archer and Herex coming toward the ship.

When they got nearby, she waved her wand and three ropes dropped down from the mast.

"Not sure if this is a good idea," said Beck.

Herex and Archer were pulled aboard, and they landed safely on deck. Beck closed his eyes and held on tight as he was suddenly yanked off the ground. He yelled aloud as he sailed through the air and couldn't quite keep a hold on to the rope. It slipped through his hands, and he dropped back down on the deck and crushed some wooden barrels.

"Owww! How did I know something bad was gonna happen!" he said as he rolled around.

"Well, you're aboard," replied Helaina as she burst into laughter that she couldn't hold back any longer.

"Next time I'll use the ladder, thank you."

He got up and sat down on one of the other barrels. He placed his rifle against the railing and looked up to see everyone was still staring at him.

"What? The new rifles a little heavy."

Everyone insincerely agreed then they went back to what they were doing. Most of the ships were loaded now and hovering over the plain. Two small gunships were still taking on their gunners. When the last of them were aboard, they pulled the ramps and the ships rose up to join the rest of the armada.

Malcolm walked out of his ready room and went over to Helaina as the last ship rose into the air.

"We're ready to depart," she said.

"Have the Captain take us out, please."

She went up the stairway to the wheel.

"Please take us up, Captain. Destination, Twilight Forest."

The captain complied and the Auburn rose through all the other ships and turned halfway around. The engines fired and thrusted them forward as all the other ships took formation.

The Auburn led the way and was followed by four large gunships. Behind them were the two massive troopships that were surrounded by the smaller gunships. Six long-ships followed them, and the medical ship sailed safely in between. Fighters on birds and other creatures were scattered throughout.

After a few hours, they reached an old port that was known as Pirates Cove. Years ago, it was the life of the Isle. The dock was a mile long and filled with old taverns and shops. The mast from a wrecked ship stuck out of the water in the middle of the abandoned harbor.

Built inside a tall cliff at the east end of the docks was the 'Stones Throw Inn.' It had thirty floors with a dozen rooms on each. They all had balconies that overlooked the cove, and an old torn blue flag still blew in the wind at the top of the cliff.

Beck looked closely at the dock and noticed a bunch of ropes that were hanging into the air.

"Helaina. Do you see the way those ropes are hanging there? Or is it just me?"

She looked down and saw the same thing.

"I do! They look like they're tied to something, but there's nothing there. We'll have to investigate that further."

"I'm not looking into anything further. Nope, not me," said Beck.

"You know you'll be right there when we are," she replied.

"We'll see," he added.

He turned back and looked down at the cove.

"Not this guy," he whispered to himself.

They continued and the cove drifted out of sight. Malcolm called everyone into his ready room. They all gathered around the table and started to study the map. Gamon climbed up on the edge of the table with a long wooden pointer.

"I believe at our current speed we will meet the undead army here, a few miles north of the Twilight Plateau. We will arrive in about three hours, so it'll be dark when we get there," said Gamon.

"We will use the Starlite Valley and its old, abandoned town as our stronghold," said Malcolm. "If we can lead the undead fighters into the valley and keep them there, we will be able to finish this once and for all."

He pointed to the valley on the map and showed where they needed to go.

"The town of Andromeda."

"Andromeda?" asked Arlo.

"Yea. It was built by a group of astronomers," replied Gamon.

"They named it after their favorite constellation along with the lake nearby which they call Orion Lake. There's an abandoned observatory at the top of the hill on the east side of the valley, but it's been vacant for years."

"We need to set a pace that will get us there with some time to spare," said Malcolm.

"Forty-five knots to be exact," said Arlo.

Helaina went out and relayed it to the captain. A few moments later the ship started moving noticeably faster and all the other ships kept pace to stay in formation. Everyone settled into a spot on the deck and looked out at the beautiful scenery on the isle.

Arlo and Helaina sat on the bench that was just beside the ready room door.

"So! How did you all meet?" he asked.

"We were childhood friends, and we grew up in the town inside the old kingdom that we just departed. We spent our childhoods learning our powers and just trying to be kids. We had to learn how to defend ourselves at a young age since the isle wasn't always a safe place back then. I guess it wasn't much of a childhood at all, but sometimes it's just the hand that you're dealt."

"What happened to that castle?" Arlo asked.

"Just over ten years ago, the cursed army attacked, and it was destroyed beyond repair. It also held painful memories for many so King William made the decision to move south. They rebuilt a new kingdom, and we went off to fight the remaining enemy that spread throughout Halicon."

"So. What about Herex? Is he, ya know, dead?"

"Herex is very much alive, but it's his spirit that's with us here."

"How did it happen?" Arlo asked.

"About five years ago he was crossed by the banished king's son, Morgan. During battle in Halicon, he betrayed and cursed Herex with a foul potion. His spirit was separated from his body which is now being kept in a hidden location until he finds the antidote."

"Lately he's been fading from being out of his body for so long. He was a kind and gentle and a man who would do anything for you, and he still is, but there are times when he's not himself. He's a little reckless sometimes and since he is so powerful, that can be dangerous, but we understand his frustration."

"Wow, that's a lot to deal with," replied Arlo.

"Yes. It is. So, we give him his space."

"How does he make the portals?" Arlo asked.

"He's a warlock! A warlock portal is like a fisherman's fishing pole. He's just always had it. If you ever see him, drop a stone on the ground, it means he's marking a spot he'll be able to port to later. Warlock's can only port to places they have already been or somewhere that they can see. If he's never ported to a particular place, he'll drop a stone to mark a location," said Helaina.

"That's amazing!" Arlo replied.

"So. How about you, Arlo? Where are you from?" Helaina asked.

"I'm from the Gnomelands, west of here. I lived in a city called New Salem. It was the greatest place in the world. It was as beautiful as the places here. Anyway, we were a very technological community, always building and experimenting."

"I used to be my father's assistant. We did everything together! Then the people my father worked for wanted to build a reactor that would power the whole city, which was great, but my father found a flaw in the plans. He tried to tell them, but it would have set them back years to fix it. So instead, they built in anyway. It ended up melting down and making the city unlivable. It's more of a ghost city now."

"Everybody was forced to leave and find new homes. I set out for the Brightwater Cavern. My father was supposed to meet me there, but he hasn't made it yet. That was a year ago. I hope to find him someday and I hope he's well."

"I'm sorry to hear this, Arlo. I hope that one day you are both reunited and that he is well too."

"Thank you, Helaina. I hope so."

Suddenly a cloud of smoke streamed across the sky, and everyone got up to see where it came from. One of the small ships had an engine on fire and it was losing altitude quickly. When Herex saw it, he ran to the stern and dove off the Auburn toward the falling ship. When he reached it, he landed firmly on the bow. He held his arms into the air and a bright energy formed around him. The ship's descent slowed, and he brought the ship safely down to the ground.

The armada stopped above them and waited.

Malcolm and Helaina called their birds, and they quickly flew down to the disabled ship.

"What's happened here? Can it be fixed?" asked Malcolm.

"I think we blew our engine. She's not gonna go any further today, but we didn't crash, so we can fix it! Thank you, Herex. That would have been the end of my ship. I too, to follow the code," said the captain.

Herex bowed his head to acknowledge him and then he let his orb into the air. His bird appeared and he made his way back up to the ship.

Two other ships descended to the ground to take on their passengers.

"Okay, Ladies and gentlemen. Split up evenly and board these ships. We're all going to the same place anyway," said their captain.

The men and women split up and boarded the ships as Malcolm and Helaina got on their birds and flew back up to the Auburn.

"Let's continue on, Captain," said Malcolm.

The large armada of ships sailed off through the sky as the disabled ship sat smoking on the ground.

"We're still ahead of schedule, Malcolm. No worries," said Gamon.

"Good! Voodoo, what is the undead army doing now?" Malcolm asked.

"They are just walking. They seem to be letting the

airships get further ahead of their ground force. They're like ants covering the ground," replied Voodoo. "It's sad what those people were cursed to become."

"Yes. Yes, it is," Malcolm said as he shook his head in agreement. "Please keep me updated on their movements."

"As you wish," Voodoo replied.

"Now entering Twilight Forest airspace," said the captain.

Everyone went to the railings and looked out at the vast forest. All the trees and plant life shared a dim glow. A gust of wind blew some of the colorful leaves through the air.

"It's amazing," said Arlo.

"It's even more beautiful at night," said Helaina. "When the sun goes down the rest of the forest illuminates and it fills with wildlife. Most of the plants and animals that live here are nocturnal. They only bloom and graze at night. At twilight, it does something even more amazing, but I'll let you see that for yourself."

"Really? I'm kind of excited now, even though we're headed to war," Arlo replied.

"Do you know that this forest is still home to a pygmy tribe? There's a village we will be passing over soon," said Helaina.

"Those wretched little devils," said Beck.

"Had a run in with them before, Beck?" asked Arlo.

"I don't want to talk about it, Arlo," he replied.

"They're best to be left alone," said Malcolm with a smirk on his face. "But they really don't harm anyone, unless provoked," he added as he looked over at Beck.

"Me? I didn't provoke anyone. They had it out for me the moment I stepped on their little leader," replied Beck, defensively.

Everyone laughed at the exchange.

"Well, you don't have to worry about them anymore," Malcolm said.

"No, no, no. It's the other way around. They don't have to worry about me," Beck replied firmly as he pointed to himself.

Malcolm walked away laughing, knowing that he was sensitive about the topic. Beck stood up seeming aggravated now.

"Darn those little devils. Twice they stabbed me in me bum!" he muttered in dismay.

"Oh! So that wasn't the first time that happened to you at Voodoo's house?" asked Arlo.

"I don't wanna talk about it, Arlo."

"That's some bad luck," he replied.

"Thank you, Arlo!" Beck grumbled.

Everyone began to laugh uncontrollably.

"Ha-ha. Real funny," he said.

He turned away and went below deck into one of the rooms. He closed the door and looked around to see that nobody could see him. He took out the orb that Rebecca gave him, and he let it float out in front of him. A vision of Rebecca's house suddenly appeared, and he could see her sitting in the kitchen. She got up and ran over to the orb as the dogs both sat beside her, swiping their paws through the reflection of Beck.

"It's so good to see you, Arthur. I was hoping you would use the orb soon."

"Hello, Rebecca. It's good to see you. How are the pups?"

"They're great! We took a long walk through the forest today and I gave them each a bone for being so good. They miss you Arthur, and so do I."

"I miss you too, Rebecca. I'm on the ship now and we'll be there soon. I'm not sure what it will be like yet."

"Please be safe, Arthur. I can't lose you again," she said.

"You're not gonna lose me, Rebecca. It would take more than a bunch of bone bags to stop me."

"Oh, like a tribe of pygmies," she replied with a giggle.

"Ha-ha. Very funny! Everyone's a comedian today!"

Rebecca laughed humbly at Beck, and he smiled

bashfully back at her.

"I have to get back now but I'll be home as soon as I can, Rebecca."

"Arthur, we are all here waiting for you. Please be careful."

"I will. I'll be in touch soon. I can't wait to get home to all of you."

"Me too," she replied.

Mya suddenly turned and licked her face.

"Us too! Get home to us!" she said laughing as she wiped the saliva from her cheek.

Beck smiled and stared happily at the vision of his family. He reached his hand into the reflection, and she did the same.

"Bye, for now, Rebecca."

"Bye, Arthur."

The hologram disappeared and the orb dimmed back down. He took it and placed it safely back into his pocket then he went back up on deck.

"We're getting close now. We will arrive in the town within the hour. Gamon, are the cannons ready?" asked Malcolm.

"They're set to go, but I'll go down and check anyway," he replied.

He went down below, and Arlo followed him.

"Let's keep an eye out for any undead scouts from here on out," said Malcolm.

Everyone looked out at the land as they sailed

deeper into the forest.

Down below in the cannon room, Gamon checked the gauges on the wall and adjusted some dials.

"I'm gonna power it up. Let me know if there are any fluctuations in the crystal. Here we go. Powering up!" said Gamon as he flipped the switch.

The crystal lit up bright as the machine energized and a green ball of plasma started to form inside the glass conduit.

"All is well from what the gauges say," said Gamon.

"The crystal looks stable. All is well over here too," replied Arlo.

"Okay, shutting down!" Gamon called out.

He flipped the switch and the system wound down and began to cool.

"It's gonna work like a charm. We should check all the piping again to see that it's tight, then the cannons will be ready."

They both walked around the room and checked all the connections along the walls and back up to the core.

"It all seems good to go," said Arlo.

"I agree. I put my seal of approval on it," replied Gamon.

"Good! Let's go see if there's anything else we can do," said Arlo.

They went back on deck and joined everyone at the

bow. They climbed up on a barrel to look out at the scenery. The sun was setting, and the sky was getting darker by the minute. The glowing canopies of the trees and bright vegetation lit up the thick forest now. It was as if it was coming to life. Everyone watched in amazement as they stared out at the beauty of the Twilight Forest.

"Look at the sparkling water rolling down that waterfall," said Arlo.

"It's quite beautiful isn't it," replied Helaina.

"It's incredible!"

Voodoo's crow suddenly landed on the railing and started to squawk at him. He reached over and pet it gently on its head.

"This is Edgar. He's my eyes and ears."

Helaina happily went over to pet him too.

"The undead are still a few miles from the valley. We will have time to prepare when we arrive," said Voodoo.

He gave the bird a chunk of bread then it flew off and landed above the sail in the stern of the ship.

"Everybody, look! It's the pygmy camp," said Archer as he pointed down at them. "Look! You can see them all sitting around the fire!"

Beck went over to the railing and looked down as they all looked up at the ship. They lifted their spears and shook them in the air.

"They're shaking their little spears at me! Those

little devils," said Beck.

He quietly laid his rifle on the railing and pointed it down at the camp.

"Beck! Don't you dare!" said Helaina sternly.

"Oh, come on! Just one orb!" Beck pleaded.

Helaina stared back at him with a disgruntled look on her face and when he noticed, he quickly took his rifle down off the railing.

"Oh, fine!" he said as he placed it back against the barrels.

"I'm sure they're not shaking them at you, Beck," Malcolm said.

"I feel like they're looking right at me. Can we just drop one orb down there?" Beck asked.

Malcolm shook his head and laughed as Helaina smirked at him again.

"Oh, I was just kidding! It would be funny though," said Beck as he looked back down there.

He waved his arm in the air, and they all went into a frenzy, then Beck shook his head and walked away laughing.

"Little devils," he added.

The sun set behind the horizon and the crews lit all the lanterns on the decks of the ships. The pygmy camp fell further and further into the distance as everyone looked out at the landscape.

"I see Orion Lake in the distance and there's Andromeda. We're here!" said Archer.

"Signal to the troop ships to drop into this clearing," said Malcolm. "It's only a half mile or so from the town. Have some people stay back to guard them. I need the fighters from one troopship in the town. Have them light the torches at the main gate to attract the undead army. The other ship I'll need to split in two and flank the undead from the east and west hills when they enter the valley. There will be undead fighters in the air so alert the ships to protect their decks. Gamon, we'll need air support until there's any risk of hitting our own people."

As the ships reached the valley, they hovered over to see that it was clear. The fighters from the first troop ship piled into the town and searched all over to assure that it was vacant. Some of them lit the two huge torches at the front gate which was the only way in and out of the town. They all hunkered down and took positions on the rooftops, and some went inside the old abandon shops.

"There's no way they won't see that. It's lit up like it were daytime," said Archer.

"All the ships behind the trees! Douse the lamps," ordered Malcolm.

CHAPTER 17
BATTLE IN THE SKY.

A dark silhouette from a fleet of airships filled the sky and slowly moved in over Starlite Valley. Everyone looked out into the distance and prepared for the arrival of the undead armada.

"Rise up on my command. Ready the cannons," said Malcolm as their ships came into view.

Gamon ran down and put on his goggles. He powered up the cannons and waited for Malcolm's order to go to war.

The ships sat below the thick canopy of the trees as the undead armada entered the valley. Their ships were old and decrepit as if they too were dead. The sails were torn, and the wood was weathered and rotting. Undead fighters climbed the masts and hung from the lines as they moved in above the town. Long-ships with hulls full of cannons led dozens of smaller gunships. An airship far in the distance rose into the clouds unnoticed.

The king's army silently stared up at all the ships now overhead. They saw the red glow of the undead eyes looking down from the nearest one. The ship began to descend toward the ground, and everyone became on edge as it dropped, knowing they would be seen as it got below the trees. Malcolm held his hand into the air.

"Captain. On my order, take us up," he said.

The captain gripped the wheel tight and watched the enemy ships above. As they got below the tree line, the undead scanned the forest. Some of them made out the king's ships and they growled viciously, alerting the others on board.

Malcolm threw down his arm and the war-horn sounded. Gamon pulled the trigger and fired a single green orb from the cannons. It left the hull of the Auburn and crashed into the side of the enemy ship. In a bright flash, it exploded and shredded the hull. The straps that held the balloon snapped and the bow came crashing down on the ground. Undead fighters rolled off the front of the ship and charged toward the Auburn.

"Take us up!" said Malcolm.

Immediately the Captain filled the balloon and lifted the ship into the air. The undead climbed into the trees and leapt from the branches to get at them but the ship rose too fast, and they fell back down to the ground. All the king's ships rose into the air and began to fire. Gamon rained the orbs onto the crippled ship until he was sure it wouldn't fly again, then the captain brought the Auburn to a higher altitude and joined the others.

The undead ships broke their formation and the king's ships gave chase. Vessels from both sides began to fall in blazes of fire as others had clouds of smoke trailing behind them. Some crashed and burned but a lucky few glided in and landed before their balloons had completely deflated.

The undead crawled out of the wrecks and frantically searched for someone to attack. A group of the King's fighters exited the gate of the town and the undead charged at them. One of the men from the king's army fired a blue orb that struck the undead fighters and froze them in place, then a gnome lit the fuse of a small bomb and rolled it up to their feet. It exploded in a bright flash and when the dust cleared, it was gone.

Undead fighters on skeletal birds filled the sky and started to storm the king's ships. Orb fire began to light up the decks as they fought with the crews. Everyone watched from the railing of the Auburn as Gamon fired bright green orbs from the cannons below. A brave captain sailed his ship right through the center of the undead armada. The cannons burst from both sides of its hull as the gunners crippled multiple ships while he navigated through.

The medical ship sat high in the sky and was protected on all sides by the smaller gunships. The medics leapt overboard and skydived down to help the injured fighters. They released their parachutes and quietly floated in. As they reached the wounded fighters, they formed a dome around themselves so they could treat the injured safely.

Everyone watched as the battle unfolded and Malcolm noticed a group of the undead fighters had turned their sights on the Auburn.

"Incoming," he yelled.

Beck fired his gun and knocked one of them right to pieces. Another tried to fire on the balloon, but it was deflected away by Gamon's shield device.

Archer fired back and impaled it with an arrow that exploded and left no remains. As the last two were closing in everyone prepared to defend the ship when suddenly Gamon took them out with a short burst from the cannons.

The moonlight lit the entire valley as numerous ships burned across the grounds. The beautiful Starlite valley had become a war zone.

Everyone watched as a group of the king's fighters boarded one of the undead ships. Each of them lit the fuse on a small black bomb then they threw it down a stairway into the base of the ship. One by one they all jumped off the stern of the ship and their birds swept them back up. When the bombs exploded it tore large holes in the deck. The cables ripped through the balloon, and it fell toward Orion Lake. When the ship landed it hit the water with so much force that it submerged but then it popped back up and floated on the surface.

A group of the king's fighters surrounded the lake and began to fire on it. A man on the shore formed a bright white orb and fired it out over the ship. A cloud formed above the ship and bolts of thunder began to strike down violently until it sank.

Suddenly there was a bright flash in the sky and an explosion was heard. One of the king's ships was hit and it began to fall as a trail of smoke billowed behind them. The crew abandoned the ship and parachuted down into the valley. Everyone on the Auburn watched while they fought small pockets of undead fighters as they helped each other to the town. The large torches at the main gate lit their way through the thick vegetation. Malcolm noticed that one of the undead long ships had started to line their cannons up with the Auburn.

"Come about, Captain. Parallel that long-ship! Gamon, fire full effect!" he hollered.

Gamon shot a dozen orbs with each pull of the trigger. Each one ripped through the side of the long-ship and exploded. The deck ripped away from the rest of the hull, and it floated off into the sky. The hull dropped into the hillside and disappeared into the luminous foliage. A few moments later it ignited, and a huge fireball burst into the air.

A group of undead fighters on the ground made their way to the entrance of the town and went inside. All the king's fighters were on watch and began to fire. All at once their orbs collided into a bright ball of energy that caused a massive explosion. The undead fighters disappeared, and a powerful shockwave blew through the town. The king's fighters braced themselves, but the wave was so strong that it knocked many of them to the ground.

"Let's try not to do that again," said a voice from out of the darkness as another one answered.

"Agreed!"

Small battles were being fought all over at the base of the valley so some of the king's fighters decided to go off and seek out the wandering undead that survived the shipwrecks. They put together a few small groups and went off through the front gate of the town.

In the center of the valley a bird from the king's army began to fight with one of the undead birds. They both slashed at each other with their claws as they flew erratically into the air. Then they locked their talons and began to fall back toward the ground. They spun out of control but just before they hit, they broke apart and landed a few meters apart.

They leapt back into the air and flew higher and higher as the bird from the king's army overpowered the skeletal bird, and again they dropped straight back down to the ground. This time the live bird landed on top of the skeletal bird with such force that its bones scattered in every direction. Everyone watched from the deck of the Auburn as the bird went back over to its fallen master. It nudged her cheek, but there was no response, so it laid down beside her and spread its wing to cover her body.

Back on the ship, everyone looked around at each other as they became anxious and could not stand to watch any longer.

"Captain, keep her out of harm's way. Gamon, target those long-ships. They've claimed too many of our ships," said Malcolm. "Signal to the Captain's to focus their attacks on them. We need them out of the sky."

Helaina went to the bow and signaled to the other ships. They immediately changed course and started to fire on the long ships. Another one of the king's ships was hit, but as it fell it dragged one of the undead ships down with it. The king's fighters leapt off their ship and parachuted to the ground. The undead, with no thought of self-preservation, went down with their ships and crumbled in a blazing fire. Two burning undead fighters crawled from the wreckage and tried to attack, but they collapsed and burned away to ash.

Everyone called to their birds, and they landed on the deck. They all jumped on and one by one they leapt overboard. Malcolm pulled out his sword as his armor turned fiery. One of the undead fighters attacked him but he dodged the swing and counter swung, cutting its upper body right off. The lower half of it tipped off the bird and fell to the ground.

Helaina watched how animalistic the undead fighters were, and she noticed a group of them that was flanking her from the side. She calmly waved her wand around herself to form a wall. As the undead leaned in with their weapons drawn, they crashed right into it. Their bones shattered and dropped into the valley below. Beck saw what she did, and he started to laugh hysterically.

"Ha-ha. That was great!" he said.

Archer had now cleared their path to the first long ship. Malcolm reached it first and he chopped through one of the thick cables that held the balloon and the corner of the ship dropped. He made his way to the next cable but as he pulled his sword back an undead fighter leapt at him. He impaled it through the chest, and it became stuck halfway down his blade. Another fighter attacked but he knocked it away with a swipe of his sword. It kicked and growled all the way down to the ground. Malcolm turned back to the fighter on his blade as it stared back at him and growled. The blade flared up and burned its bones to dust that blew away in the wind.

Malcolm flew back around and severed the cable, causing the back of the ship to fall. The weight was too much for the remaining cables and the third cable snapped. Moments later, the fourth and balloon floated off into the clouds as the rest of the ship fell from the sky.

They all continued the next long ship. Beck fired a dozen orbs down a stairwell that led into the base of the ship. As they flew over, it exploded, and the hull split in two. Cannons fell from each side along with the crew. They scratched and clawed to hold on, but the falling cannons and debris dragged them from the ship.

As everyone set their sights on the next ship, they saw it fire on one of the king's ships. The cannons struck the stern and destroyed its engine. Another hit the balloon and the ship started to fall. The captain fought to regain control as the crew ran up on deck.

"Abandon ship!" yelled the captain.

They all saluted him, then they quickly jumped overboard. One by one their parachutes deployed, and they floated safely into the valley. Their captain turned the ship on a collision course with the long ship that took him down and he crashed right into the side of it. Both ships exploded in a ball of fire, and they scattered across the ground.

Everyone watched the burning remains in awe after witnessing the captain's bravery.

"Let's move on," said Malcolm.

They turned to the next long ship but before they could attack, three gunships dropped down in front of them and began to fire. Everyone maneuvered away as the ships gave chase.

They flew along the hillside as the undead cannons tore up the land below them.

Herex was in the back of the group, and he leveled off with one of the perusing ships. He faded out and became invisible as it flew up behind him. His bird flew off and he disappeared into the bow.

He stood motionless as he floated past the undead crew. When he reached the stern, he stopped inside the captain and possessed him. For a moment, it was as if he had a body again. He took the captain's skeletal hands off the wheel and held them into the air. The crew watched as a red orb formed between the captain's hands, then he released it into the center of the ship.

Herex separated from the captain, and he slipped through the back wall. His bird reappeared under him and flew him out of harm's way as he faded back in.

The captain of the ship was unaware of what had happened. He lowered his hands back down to the wheel and gazed at the orb that was now floating in front of him. A moment later it exploded, and the ship was enveloped in flame. It dropped from the sky and crashed into the hillside.

Herex got behind the next ship and started to fire orbs from his mace. It flew evasively but he struck it repeatedly till it exploded. It dropped to the ground except for a small part of the bow that stayed attached to the balloon. A single undead fighter could be seen inside as it floated off into the sky.

He caught up to the last ship and was about to attack when a burst of green orbs suddenly ripped past him from the cannons on the Auburn. The ship was hit a dozen times and it crashed inside the valley beside the other smoldering wrecks.

He looked back up at the Auburn and saw the cannons turn directly at him, making him slightly uneasy. Gamon watched through his goggles and laughed, then he turned the cannons away and began firing on the other ships. Everyone else caught back up with Herex.

"You thought you were going to be on the receiving end of those cannons for a moment, didn't you?" Malcolm asked.

"It's about time he got you back," he added as Herex shook his head in agreement.

Arlo watched the battle from the deck of the ship, and he noticed a group of undead fighters were heading right for him. He ran away just as they landed on the deck with their skeletal birds. They charged toward the captain and swung their weapons at him, but he just stood there and laughed.

"Sorry. You're a little late! Took care of that years ago!" he said with a grin.

Arlo ran to the bow where Voodoo was randomly firing on the undead that neared the ship. The fighters noticed Arlo and they began chasing him.

"Voodoo! This is one of those times! I need ya!" he yelled nervously.

Voodoo turned around and saw him running from the fighters. He pointed to his staff and the crystal on top began to glow. He fired a single orb that knocked all the fighters right off the ship.

"Thank you, Voodoo," said Arlo.

"No problem," he replied.

Malcolm and the rest of the group were now closing in on the remaining long ships.

"Two more to go," said Malcolm. "Let's take them down!"

They all came up behind the next ship and everyone began to fire. Herex took out some of the cables and the ship started to teeter out of control. Everyone fired relentlessly till the deck couldn't be seen through the explosions. Then suddenly the ship dropped and sent a large fireball into the air as it crashed at the base of the valley.

The last long-ship began to line up their cannons with them, but they quickly flew out of its reach.

"Follow me," said Malcolm.

He flew up to the stern of the ship and landed on deck then he drew his sword and made his way down into the cabin. When he reached the bottom of the steps he looked around at the undead crew. They noticed his presence as the others came in behind him.

"Oh boy! This is just uncomfortable," said Beck.

Malcolm's armor turned fiery as the crew charged them. They began to cut the undead down, one by one as they made their way across the ship.

When they got to the wheel, Herex fired an orb that blew their captain to pieces. The wheel suddenly turned abruptly, and everyone was tossed to the ground. Malcolm quickly grabbed it and got the ship back under control as everyone finished off the last of the crew. When the cabin was clear, they all looked around.

"This is an ugly ship. What do you wanna do with it?" Beck asked.

"Mann the cannons," replied Malcolm.

Everyone loaded the cannons as the other undead ships flew alongside, unaware that they were in their crosshairs.

"Fire at will," Malcolm said.

He lined the cannons up with the ships and they fired as fast as they could load them. They managed to bring down half a dozen of the undead vessels, sending them to what had become a ship graveyard inside the hills of Starlite Valley.

When the undead caught on, they turned their guns on them. Cannon balls began to rip through the hull. An unmanned cannon took a direct hit and after a loud metal clang, it flew across the cabin and ripped through a support in the center of the ship. They kept on firing and took down four more ships before the long ship took a crippling blow to its center mast and began to fall out of the sky.

"Time to go!" said Malcolm.

Everyone tried to run up the stairs, but they were tossed around by the rapid descent. They helped each other up to the deck then they all leapt off the ship. Their birds quickly plucked them out of the sky as it crashed into the valley floor, and they flew back up to the Auburn.

"The ground forces are near. They'll be arriving soon," said Voodoo as they arrived.

"Do we send ships to head them off?" asked Helaina.

"No. We fight them here. There's a reason I chose this valley, and they can't miss it now. We need to keep them together as they enter, then we'll close them inside. There may be eighty to a hundred thousand of them, but I have a plan, and it seems we will be winning the battle in the sky."

The rest of king's ships split into groups and ran down the last of the undead ships. As one of the last ones fell, an undead gunner took their last shot. The cannon ball ripped through the hull of a king's ship and struck the center mast. It tore a hole in the balloon, and it began to fall toward the town.

"Oh, no! Not good!" said Helaina. "It's going to hit Andromeda! Herex, I need a portal to the lake!"

He threw his arms into the air and his portal rose from the deck.

"Why haven't they abandoned the ship?" Malcolm asked.

"They might land in the water," said Beck, skeptically.

Helaina ran into the portal and came out by the shore of Orion Lake. The ship was losing altitude quickly and falling right toward the town. She raised her wand into the air as a bright aura formed around her. The crew was about to jump ship into the water but one of them saw her on the shore.

"Hey, wait! I think that's lady Helaina down there! Don't jump yet!" hollered the man.

The ship dropped closer and closer, and she held the bright aura out in front of her. She pulled her arms back to her chest and the ship was pulled down toward her. She dropped her arms to her sides, and it soared down over the water. Everyone else could only watch as the ship barreled toward her. The crew yelled out as a small gnome hung over the railing and prepared to jump.

"I'm jumping! We're gonna crash!" he said.

Helaina seemed as if she had the entire weight of the ship on her as it began to push her back. The aura around her became brighter as she pushed forward with all her might. Slowly the ship shuddered to a stop no more than a foot away from her with its stern high up in the air. The crew cheered as Helaina released the vessel down into the water. It swayed side to side and the gnome fell off the railing into the lake. The crew laughed at him, but then they went right back to praising Helaina.

"I told you she had it," said one of the crew.

"That's lady Helaina down there. I wish I knew how to get her to fall for me," said another man on the crew.

Helaina heard what he said and looked away

bashfully. She noticed that everyone was standing on shore with stunned looks on their faces. She looked around herself and realized that she was levitating over the water, and just as she did, she fell right in. When she came back up it was clear to see that she wasn't happy. She spat out some water and looked over at the gnome swimming nearby. He smiled at her and waved.

"I knew you had it the whole time," he said.

She turned away and swam back to shore. Archer helped her out of the water, and it seemed as if she wanted to scream as she rung out her gown, then she quickly went back through the portal.

"That's not good," said Beck.

"No. Definitely, not good," replied Malcolm as he walked into the portal.

Everyone followed them through and went back up to the Auburn. They all gathered by the railing just in time to see Gamon finish off the last undead ship with impressive accuracy. Helaina came back out a few minutes later in a fresh white gown as she strained the dampness from her hair. She went to the railing and looked out to see the last of the king's ships returning.

"We won the battle in the sky, but we still have a long fight ahead of us," said Malcolm. "Tell the men to hunker down and have the ships drop out of sight. Captain, take us back behind the trees. The smoke from the burning ships will provide us cover."

The captain lowered the ship into the darkness and the others dropped down nearby and they quietly waited for the undead ground force to arrive.

"Can you see where they are, Voodoo?" Malcolm asked.

"They're here," he replied in a somber tone.

CHAPTER 18
BATTLE IN STARLITE VALLEY.

In the distance, a blanket of darkness covered the luminescent landscape. The king's fighters looked out at Starlite valley as it was overcome by the forsaken army. Torn black flags waved in the air and the footsteps of skeletal beasts could be heard as they dragged their cannons and catapults across the terrain. The undead fighters lashed the beasts with long leather whips. The weapons they had were old and corroded but the blades were razor sharp. Their glowing red eyes became brighter and brighter as they marched closer to the town.

The king's fighters moved into position at the top of the hills and the ones in the town quietly watched as the undead crept toward the flaming torches at the gate. They became riled when they saw the wreckage of their ships and the bones of the others spread across the ground. Their growls and cries became louder and louder till the entire valley was filled with the sound of the undead's torment.

Malcolm looked out at the sea of evil red eyes that seemed as if they were staring right back at him. He looked over to see that everyone was ready, then he turned back to the undead.

"Attack!" he hollered.

The war-horn sounded, and the ships rose from the

trees. The king's fighters charged down the hills and collided with the undead army. They poured out of the town and fearlessly fought their way into the massive army of skeletal fighters.

Malcolm peered out at the battlefield.

"Time to go," he said as he leapt over the railing and soared down to the ground.

He landed with so much force it tore the nearby undead apart and threw others to the floor. As the dust cleared, everyone landed behind him. They drew their weapons and prepared to fight.

The captain turned the Auburn to face the cannons at the army and Gamon fired on them. A group of the king's ships moved in over the back of the valley to close the undead inside. Two others took positions over the old observatory platform and the rest of them circled the hilltops.

The undead army was surrounded but they still largely outnumbered the king's fighters. The entire valley began to light up from thousands of colorful orbs that ripped through the landscape and exploded on their targets.

The medical ship took position high above the center of the valley, far out of reach of the forsaken army's cannons. Medics have already dived in to assist the injured. A catapult had damaged one of the king's long-ships and a plume of smoke billowed from the engine. They fired again and blew a large hole in its hull, but still, it didn't take them down.

A few moments later they fired again, and the ship took a solid hit. It swayed violently and the crew was thrown across the cabin. They tried to get back up, but more blasts were heard, so they braced themselves for the impacts. The cannons struck the side of the ship and snapped all the cables along the starboard side. The right side of the ship dropped, and the crew fell to the lowest point. They attempted to get back to their stations, but the ship swayed as more of the cables started to fail.

After a short silence, a single cannon blast was heard. It was a direct hit to the balloon and the ship fell from the sky. It tore the branches off the trees as it dropped. It suddenly turned right side up and the crew was tossed back to the floor. They all waited to crash but suddenly it stopped, and the ship was held in place. The crew got up and looked out the portholes to see what saved them and they saw the thick branches of an elder tree held them high above the valley. The cannons still faced the undead and the captain yelled out to the crew.

"Mann the guns! Take out those cannons! We're not finished here," he ordered then he looked through his scope.

The crew quickly ran to the cannons and loaded them. They took aim and fired on the cannons that brought them down. After a slight adjustment, they destroyed them all.

The undead noticed the long ship in the trees and

they made their way up the hill to it. The crew watched as their glowing red eyes got closer and closer. A group of the king's fighters saw them approaching the long-ship and they went to head them off. The undead fighters leapt up into the trees and climbed toward it.

"Uhh. We have company!" said a man on the crew, nervously.

They came over to the top of the deck and started to attack them. A robed man rapidly fired yellow orbs from his mace and knocked them right back off the ship. The king's fighters reached the base of the tree and fired a slew of orbs and arrows up at the undead. A tall burly man fired his rifle as a shorter man no taller than a foot stood on his left shoulder and fired his own tiny rifle which seemed to have a powerful recoil. After a few shots, they took down the rest of the fighters just before they reached the ship.

The crew finished off the ones on deck then they waved down to thank the fighters at the base of the tree. The others waved back up then continued pushing the undead back into the valley as two ships moved in above to help defend the fallen long-ship.

Back on the ground, Malcolm fought his way into the undead army. Beck fired his rifle and bashed them with the butt of it. He fired his orb launcher, and they landed throughout the crowd. Seconds later they exploded in bright green flashes that took out dozens of them.

Malcolm continued further in, and he swung his fiery blade through numerous fighters at a time. Herex followed as he fired orbs in every direction. He lifted his mace into the air and a dark ball of energy shot into the sky. A cloud formed above the undead and thunder began to strike down, tearing through dozens of them with every bolt.

Archer fired his arrows as fast as he could load them. Each one split into a dozen more arrows as they arched through the air. They pinned the fighters to the ground, then the arrows ignited, and their bones turned to ash.

Helaina followed behind them and cast glimmering spells that healed any of the fighters that needed. A bright aura followed her as she made her way across the battlefield. Even the ground lit up from her energy as she walked along. A group of the undead charged toward her but with a wave of her wand, vine reached up from the ground and pulled them down into the dirt.

Another group tried to attack her from behind, but they ran into clear wall that she had in place. They growled and smashed their weapons against it to get to her as she slowly turned and stood face to face with them. As she gazed down at them, they started to lower their weapons for a moment but then they quickly became angered again. She twirled her wand in a circle and the wall wrapped around them to form a ball. They were lifted into the air and one of the fighters shook its head side to side as if it were pleading with her not to do what she was planning. A flick of her wand and the ball shot high into the sky, then she turned away and followed everyone further into the battle.

The undead catapults fired and another one of the king's ships was hit. A fire broke out on the deck and the captain was forced to bring it down in the middle of the enemy fighters.

Helaina watched as it went down, then she saw the ball of undead fighters falling back out of the sky. With a wave of her wand the ball disappeared and left them falling to the ground where they shattered to pieces. She quickly turned back to the fallen ship and reformed the dome around it to protect the crew from the undead that were now surrounding them.

Moments later the crew exited as the undead tried to penetrate the dome. They covered it to a point the ship couldn't be seen below them. Everyone made their way over as Beck fired his launcher to clear their way. When they arrived, Helaina exploded the dome outward and cleared the undead from around the ship, then everyone else helped the crew.

Herex glided into the air and levitated over the ship as he fired his red orbs in every direction. He placed his mace over his shoulder and formed a large black orb with a smoky aura that lingered off the top.

He looked over at Helaina and she knew exactly what he wanted her to do. She shook her head to acknowledge him and then he threw the orb into the air. He dropped down to the deck and Helaina quickly reformed the dome over the ship. The orb fell on top, and it slowly rolled down the side. In a flash, it exploded, and nothing could be seen from inside. It lit the valley so brightly that all the other fighters couldn't even look in the direction.

Every undead fighter in a hundred feet of the ship turned to dust along with the vegetation. The force knocked over a tall tree that also fell on undead fighters. Helaina lowered the dome, and they helped the crew to the ground.

"Let's get them to the town," said Malcolm.

Gamon saw them leaving the ship and he fired down to clear a route. They dodged the craters and ran through the green clouds that his cannons left behind.

They all reached the entrance of the town, and they went inside. Beck saw an abandoned distillery and he led everyone down a stairway on the side that brought them into its basement. Large wooden barrels filled the room and an old copper still sat in the center.

Herex formed a portal to the medical ship above, but when it rose from the deck, the medics ran from it. One of the more curious ones went up and stuck her head through to see where it was. She saw Malcolm and quickly came through with a bag of supplies.

Beck went through some cabinets and found an old stein, then he went over to one of the barrels and pulled the lever. To his pleasant surprise the stein filled up with thick golden brew.

"We've got suds here folks!" he said happily.

He took a healthy swig and slapped the stein down.

"Ahh. Refreshing!" he said as he wiped his mouth with his sleeve.

"Okay. I'm ready," he said.

Everyone hurried back out into the center of town. Herex took out a few undead fighters that were wandering by the old fountain. They made their way through the town and searched the old shops and alleyways. Bright flashes of light and the clang of steel got louder as they went further down the road.

Gamon watched the battlefield, but he couldn't fire since the king's fighters were now spread throughout. The undead army turned their catapults on the Auburn and fired. The captain dropped the bow just as two fiery balls passed over the deck.

"That was close," he muttered to himself.

Arlo came up on deck and went over to him.

"Hey, Cap! Gamon needs you to take us behind those catapults. He's gonna blow em up!"

"Happy to oblige," the captain replied.

He turned the ship and coasted along the hilltop to get behind them. The undead saw what they were doing, and they started to turn them as Gamon watched through his goggles.

"I'm gonna have to put it on single fire," he said as he turned a dial on the panel.

"They've almost got the catapults turned all the way around!" said Arlo nervously as he looked out a porthole.

"Just a moment more," replied Gamon.

Just as they were turned to face them, Gamon slowly pulled the trigger five times. With each pull a bright green orb fired from the hull of the Auburn and demolished each one along with all the undead fighters around them.

"We now have air superiority," said Gamon confidently.

He stood up with his chest out and his chin high.

"Good work! I'll never question your cannon firing ability," replied Arlo.

Gamon hung the goggles on the hook and went back up to the deck.

"You can take us back now, Captain," Gamon said.

The captain turned the ship and headed back. When they reached the town, they had a bird's eye view of Malcolm and everyone else walking down the road toward a flashing light. It suddenly died out and left the road in darkness. An undead fighter walked out into the street and looked for more of the king's fighters to attack. When it saw them all it crouched down and growled viciously. A large group crawled out from behind it and stared at them from down the road with their glowing red eyes.

Everyone drew their weapons. Malcolm's sword and armor turned fiery as Herex formed an orb in his hand. Beck chambered a shell and took aim as Archer pulled an arrow back in the string of his bow.

Helaina walked out in front of everyone and stole the attention of the undead. She gently kissed her palm and a small red orb formed over her hand. She leaned in and blew it out in front of herself.

The undead became mesmerized and they silently watched as it floated toward them. It lit the storefronts as it passed by, then it stopped and hovered just in front of them. Their eyes were glued to it as it slowly faded to black, and smoke rose off the top. A moment later it exploded, and it shredded half the pack, sending their bones ripping through the shop windows.

"Love hurts," said Beck with a giggle.

Malcolm charged at the remaining fighters as everyone else started to fire on them. The battle lit up the road and flashed into the sky.

A group of the king's fighters came out on the rooftops above them. They fired on the undead as another lit the fuse of a bomb and dropped it into a crowd of the undead. It exploded in a bright blue flash and took down a dozen fighters. The men saluted Malcolm then they went back to firing on the enemy. The explosions were so bright it seemed as if the undead fighters had disappeared.

Herex held his mace into the air and a bolt of energy shot into the clouds. The wind started to gust, and the clouds churned. Thunder began to stir and suddenly a large bolt shot down and struck his mace. He directed it toward the rest of the undead fighters and their bones ignited. In a blinding white flash, they were gone. The force blew all the doors and windows out of the shops and nearly knocked everyone else off their feet. The only thing left of the undead was their old robes and armor now spread across the ground.

"Well, I guess that's that," said Beck.

"Well done, Herex and thank you, gentlemen," said Malcolm to the fighters on the rooftops.

"Glad to assist you, Lord Cahpra," said one of them as the others saluted them.

They all went back to the entrance and looked out at the Starlite valley. Dark clouds from powerful spells rained fire and even ice down on the enemy fighters throughout. Colorful explosions lit up the hills from the orbs being fired in every direction.

Malcolm called his bird and everyone else did the same. They all flew off in an arrow formation with Malcolm in the lead. As they reached the center of the valley, a bolt of thunder shot down from the clouds and electrified a large group of the undead fighters.

The king's fighters around it were lost, but the

undead weren't harmed. Hundreds of them mended together to form two large skeletal fighters. They turned into legs and torso, then arms and a skull. Their eyes lit up bright red like the smaller fighters and they wielded large bone axes with shiny steel blades that reflected in the moonlight.

They both let off fearsome growls.

Everyone landed in front of them and unmounted their birds. The king's army began to fire on the huge skeletal fighters with everything they had. Orbs flew from across the valley and struck them all over their bodies. The explosions pushed them back and chipped away at their bones, but they were able to withstand it.

Gamon watched them from the ship.

"What in the world is that? Captain, bring us over there," he said as he ran down to the cannon room and put his goggles back on.

As the Captain reached the fighters, he turned the ship to face the cannons their way. Malcolm went to the closest fighter and prepared to attack. His armor turned fiery from head to toe and right up to the tip of his sword. He pointed it at the fighter and as the blade extended, a firebolt suddenly shot off the tip. It struck the fighter in the chest and sent it falling back to the ground. He gazed down at the sword then he looked up at the ship where Gamon was watching him through the goggles.

"Oops! I forgot to tell him about that," said Gamon.

Arlo waited impatiently beside him since he couldn't see what was happening.

"What's going on down there? Let me shoot that thing! How hard can it be?" he asked.

The fighter got back up and Malcolm charged. It swung its axe, but Malcolm slowed enough for its blade to pass right in front of him, then he counter swung and shattered the fighter's hand. The axe fell to the ground and the fighter quickly picked it back up with the other hand and swung wildly.

Malcolm deflected the swings as bright sparks shot off the blades each time they crossed, but the strength of the large fighter began to tire him. It pulled the axe up over its head and swung straight down on him. He deflected it with all his might, but the impact knocked him to his back. The fighter went to swing again, and Beck quickly pulled the trigger on his rifle and fired all the barrels at once. The recoil threw him right to his back, but he knocked the fighter clear away from Malcolm.

Malcolm stood back up and struck the fighter's leg to send it off balance. He quickly swung again and hit the same place, slowly chipping away at the bone. The fighter swung back, and Malcolm dodged, then he struck its leg again. This time the bone broke, and the fighter fell to its side. Malcolm leapt into the air and came down with a powerful swipe that severed the fighter's head and the red glow faded from its eyes.

Everyone else focused on the last fighter. The whole valley was lit up bright from all the orb fire. The fighter growled and swung its axe angrily at the fighters in front of him. In one swipe, a dozen of the king's fighters was knocked halfway across the valley. Gamon fired the cannons and knocked the axe from its hand. Another shot took off its arm and a third separated its head from its shoulders. The skeletal body collapsed to the ground and all the fighters cheered aloud, then they ran off to finish the rest of the undead army. The battle had now moved to the southern side of the valley as small groups of the undead wandered throughout the hills.

More bolts of thunder suddenly shot down from the sky and struck the airships that sat over the observatory platform.

Everyone watched as they exploded and fell from the sky. Malcolm looked to the clouds as the lightning flashed and he saw the silhouette of an airship.

"We must get up to that platform. There's something happening up there, and I have a feeling we will find our answers at the old observatory," he said.

Everyone made their way to the base of the hill, and they prepared to make their way to the top.

CHAPTER 19
TO THE OBSERVATORY.

They began their push up the hill to the old observatory. The path they traveled was somehow untouched by the battle and the luminous foliage lit their way. When they reached the halfway point, Malcolm stopped to look around.

"Let's close the door," he said.

Beck took a small steel ball out of his satchel and lit its fuse. Everyone watched as it burned away and disappeared inside. A small pop made Helaina jump and smoke began to pour out into Beck's face. He coughed and choked then he quickly rolled it down the hill, leaving a thick cloud between them and the rest of the battle.

"We are now invisible. Complements of Gamon," sobbed Beck as he wiped his watering eyes.

They were about to make their way to the top when suddenly the captain flew the ship overhead. Gamon fired on the hill above and cleared the rest of the fighters between them and a white stone stairway. The Auburn sailed back into the sky and took a position over the center of the valley.

Everyone made their way up the dirty old steps with comets and stars engraved in their faces. When they reached the top, they saw the fallen ships still burning nearby. They walked out onto the platform and all the trees around it began to illuminate.

"It's twilight," said Helaina.

They all looked out across the gleaming valley as the battle raged throughout. The plant life began to glow bright green and blue and purple. The trees with yellow leaves seemed as though they were on fire and large flower pods bloomed in the hills. Thousands of white butterflies that laid dormant, now rose into the sky. The Starlite valley had come to life. Even during destruction it was still a beautiful sight to see.

When they turned back to the observatory there were two men standing at the entrance. One wore a blue robe and only the lower portion of his face could be seen under their hood. A yellow aura lingered off a staff that hung on his back. The other wore a black robe with a gold pattern and his staff let a purple aura into the air.

They were unsure of who they were at first, but then Malcolm made them out. It was the sons of the banished king and the man who betrayed Herex, standing before them.

"Ethan and Morgan Westmore?" asked Malcolm in bewilderment.

"You're the ones responsible for this mindless army of the dead?"

"It was set in motion long ago," replied Ethan. "We only took advantage of the situation. A little organization and now we have you right where we want you. You're all, right in time to die."

He pulled back his hood and glared at Malcolm.

"You both will die with them, tonight," Malcolm said angrily as he moved toward them.

The observatory doors suddenly swung open behind them. Five skeletal fighters in black robes exited and formed a line in front of them. Each one held a long staff with a smoky black crystal. Everyone drew their weapons and stared back at the fighters. The red eyes peered back from under their hoods, and they spread apart from each other. A click of their staffs on the ground and they multiplied across the platform into lines of fighters. Malcolm swung his sword, but it passed right through them. Beck fired his gun and Herex a dozen orbs, but all of it disappeared into the trees.

All their staffs started to glow with a bright purple aura. Helaina formed a dome around everyone just as they fired. Dozens of orbs deflected off it in every direction, then the lines of fighters faded away and she lowered the dome. Beck fired back and hit one of the fighters. Its bones ignited inside the robe, and it crumbled to the floor.

Malcolm charged and swung his sword at another, but the fighter dodged him. Malcolm came back around and took out its legs, then as it fell back, he impaled the fighter and it burst into flame.

Herex and Archer fired on at the last three, but it was all diverted into the walls of the observatory.

One of the fighters fired a black orb into the air and a dark cloud formed over their heads. Helaina quickly reformed the dome just moments before a fiery rain poured down on them. It covered the dome and rolled to the ground like water. She waited for it to stop then she dropped the dome and Beck fired again. The fighter waved its staff and the bullets stopped in front of him. Another wave and they fell to the ground.

"Oh, yea! Try this on for size!" he said as he fired the launcher.

The orb rolled right up to the fighter's feet. It formed a shield in front of itself to avoid it and the orb just sat dimly on the ground. After a few moments, the fighter disregarded it and dropped the shield. Immediately the orb started to glow. He tried to reform it, but the orb exploded and in a bright green flash, the fighter was gone.

One of the last ones formed a bright aura in front of itself and released it toward them. A powerful gust of energy pushed them back. Helaina lost her balance, but Archer was there to catch her. Malcolm and Beck crouched down to keep their footing and Herex stayed planted to the ground as if it didn't faze him.

He stared back at the fighter and made a pushing motion. The fighter was shoved into the wall of the observatory. He stumbled to get back to his feet then he fired back. Helaina stepped forward and swung her wand. The orbs stopped right in front of them and one by one she fired them back and hit the fighter with every single one. Its bones ignited and left only its robe smoldering on the ground.

They all turned their attention to the last fighter. It lifted its staff into the air and as the crystal lit up, Herex swiped his arm and ripped it from his bony hand. It landed off to the side and the purple aura faded. Helaina fired a green orb at its feet and vine sprouted up and wrapped around its legs. As it tried to free itself, Herex fired one last orb and in a bright red flash, the fighter was gone except for its legs that remained entwined in the vine.

They all turned back to the Westmore brothers and began to walk toward them. Morgan called his bird and quickly climbed onto its back. He looked at Herex and glared as the bird leapt into the air. Herex watched him fly away and as he scanned the sky, he saw the silhouette of the hidden airship in the clouds. He quickly summoned a portal and went through.

The portal closed behind him, and it rose back up from the deck of the ship. He exited in the middle of the undead crew. Immediately he saw Morgan at the wheel. As the crew started to realize his presence, they drew their weapons and charged at him, but Herex just stared at Morgan. He threw his arms over his head and the entire crew was lifted in the air.

He slowly walked toward the stern with his eyes still locked on Morgan. The undead crew panicked, and they dropped their weapons to the deck, but Herex didn't flinch. When he reached the center of the ship, he threw his arms out and the crew was flung overboard. Morgan turned the ship abruptly. Herex stumbled but he grabbed the mast and held on tight as they rose up into the dark clouds and sailed away at full speed.

Nothing could be seen on deck as Herex stared into the darkness and tried to reacquire Morgan. He held his mace in the air and when the rubies began to glow a purple aura lit up the stern and Morgan fired an orb. Herex deflected it away and quickly fired back where it came from, but Morgan had moved.

Herex shot a white orb into the air above the ship, but the dark clouds stopped it from lighting the deck. The ship was silent except for the sound of the wind that blew against the sails.

"Herex, my old friend. I wasn't expecting to see you after all this time. You haven't faded yet," said Morgan.

He held a vial into the air that contained a luminous blue fluid inside.

"If you leave this ship, I'll give you the antidote that you need to return to your body. It's the only dose in existence. That is what you want, isn't it?"

Herex stared at the vial and briefly pondered to himself, then he raised his mace and the rubies started to glow. With a slight flick, a bright red orb fired at Morgan and shredded the railing in front of him. Morgan was thrown to his back, and he dropped the vial on the floor. It slid across the deck and became lodged in the boards.

Morgan's staff went dark and again nothing could be seen in the stern of the ship.

"The last time we met, I took your body. This time, I will take your soul," said Morgan from in the darkness.

His staff lit back up and he fired again. Herex deflected it away and it tore a hole in the deck behind him. They began to fire back and forth, destroying the ship all around themselves. Herex threw his arms out to his sides and the clouds were suddenly shoved away from the ship. He fired another white orb overhead and this time the deck lit up brightly.

Herex summoned a portal then he ran inside. It closed behind him, and it rose up beside Morgan. Herex jumped through and struck him with his mace, sending him falling back to the floor.

He stared down at him with his glowing red eyes and Morgan looked back up at him nervously. He held the mace against his chest and formed an orb in his hand. Morgan tried to reach for his staff, but Herex just slapped it away. He began to move his mace in a circular motion and a dark swirling hole formed under Morgan. A funnel of smoke reached up into the sky and as he fell inside, he grabbed the railing and tried to pull himself out.

Herex dropped the orb into his hood and with another wave of his mace, the hole enlarged, and Morgan was pulled down into a whirlwind. As the orb exploded a massive flame shot up into the sky and the ship started to sway. Herex grabbed the wheel and brought it back under control. After the winds died down and the funnel closed, he noticed the glowing vial was stuck in the floor and he went over to pick it up. He brought it back to the wheel and gazed at the luminous blue fluid inside as he turned the ship back toward the observatory.

The moonlight lit the deck as he sailed on with the thought that he'd now be able to return to his body. He could live a normal life and no longer would he have to worry about fading away. He clinched the wheel of the ship and looked up at the moon with newfound hope.

Back at the observatory, the others made their way toward Ethan. Malcolm's sword went fiery as Beck chambered a shell. Archer took an arrow from his quiver and Helaina poised her wand.

Ethan thrusted his staff into the air and a bolt of thunder shot down from the clouds. It electrified the staff and lit up so brightly that it blinded them. He touched it down to the metal frame and the current surged through the entire platform. Archer was struck and he fell to a knee. Helaina cast healing spells toward him and a glistening aura surrounded his body. A swipe of her wand and a bed of moss grew below him to heal the wounds.

Malcolm swung his sword against the ground and a wave of energy ripped through the platform. It cracked up the floor below Ethan and knocked him to the ground. He hurried to his feet and fired carelessly behind himself but hit no one. Beck fired his launcher back and the orbs rolled right to his feet. Ethan quickly formed a shield around himself, and as they exploded, he just watched, knowing that they couldn't hurt him.

Archer regained his strength and stood up as Helaina cast a final spell to complete his healing.

"Glad to have you back," she said.

"Wouldn't miss it. Thanks for the help," he said.

"Anytime," she replied with a smile.

Ethan whistled aloud and four skeletal tigers came out from behind the observatory. They had the same glowing red eyes as the rest of the undead and they stopped beside Ethan and growled.

"These are my little friends. I'm sure you won't get along," he said as the tigers scratched their large claws on the ground.

Ethan went back to the entrance of the observatory and the tigers charged. Beck fired his rifle and the bones of the one that came for him were shattered. Malcolm plunged his fiery sword into the one that leapt toward him. The blade flared up and its bones burned away to ash.

Helaina formed a wall around herself as one of the tigers reached her. She stared deeply into its eyes and was able to tame the wild animal. It lost all its violent tendencies and sat beside her. She lowered the wall, and the tiger rubbed its skull against her. She gently petted its head, then it walked off down the stone stairway and disappeared into the hillside.

The last one jumped at Archer and as it flew, he fired an arrow. When it exploded, the bones became a wave of sand that splashed over him. He froze in surprise then shook himself off and swiped his hand through his dusty hair.

With the tigers all down, they turned back at Ethan and ran toward him. He thrusted his staff into the air and the clouds above them began to swirl. Bolts of thunder struck aggressively and electrified the frame of the platform. Everyone dodged the powerful blasts as they tried to reach him.

Ethan flicked his staff at the steel frame around Helaina and Archer. The bolts began to arch over them to form a cage that held them inside. They were both impacted with large bursts that knocked them to the ground. Malcolm and Beck continued to make their way through. When Ethan saw them getting closer, he gave another wave of his mace and the bolts around them intensified. Both were struck numerous times and they fell to the platform beside each other.

As Beck fell to the ground, the orb he got from Rebecca rolled out of his pocket. The one she had lit up over her kitchen table and she saw the vision of Beck in terrible pain. She watched as the enormous bolts jolted through his body.

"No, Arthur!" she screamed as she fell to her knees.

His eyes became more and more distant after every strike. Helaina tried to heal them, but the current stopped her from casting. They were forced to watch helplessly, both unable to blink. They tried to get up, but constant shocks knocked them back down. When the bolts subsided, Malcolm and Beck rolled around but they were unable to get up.

The current around Helaina and Archer increased and it struck them again and again, leaving them immobile.

"I'm going to finish the great Malcolm Cahpra and his loyal companions. Now it's time to die," said Ethan.

He waved his staff and a dark cloud formed above them. Large shards of ice began to rain down and crash against them violently. As they shattered around them, the broken fragments began to glisten in the moonlight. Malcolm deflected some of them with his shield, but Beck took every hit. One after another the shards slammed down on top of them.

Helaina and Archer looked on in shock, knowing that they couldn't take much more. Rebecca could hardly watch as Beck endured the final blows that he could handle. His eyes stared off as if he were dreaming. Suddenly a shard landed on the orb and shattered it. Rebecca's vision went dark, and she was sure it was the last time she would ever see him. Her head fell against the table as she wept uncontrollably. The dogs sensed her sadness and went over to comfort her.

Malcolm turned to Beck and saw him lying motionless.

"I'm going to take your soul," said Ethan.

He watched as he took a vial of green fluid from his pocket, and he tossed it into the air. Malcolm quickly threw the shield to Beck, and it floated in the air just above him to protect his body from further harm. The shards began to strike Malcolm all over his body. His arms and legs jolted into the air as the vial shattered on the ground and a thick black cloud rose up around him.

Malcolm slowly looked over to see Beck one last time as the smoke engulfed his body. His head dropped to the platform and his spirit drifted into the air. Helaina let out a piercing shriek and Archer watched in horror as Malcolm's spirit stared down at his battered armor in confusion. At that moment, they knew that things would never be the same.

Suddenly, from out of the clouds came Herex with Westmore's airship. He was coming into range, and he saw what was happening on the platform. Ethan looked down at Malcolm's spirit with a grin of satisfaction, then he looked up at his airship and formed a portal that would bring him to it.

Herex noticed Malcolm and Beck were lying on the platform, then he saw Helaina and Archer being held prisoner. He became infuriated and turned the ship on a collision course with the observatory. He sailed it just over the platform then he summoned his portal and walked through just as Ethan's rose from the deck. Ethan walked out and turned to see that the ship was only moments from crashing. With no time to react he could only watch in awe.

"Oh my," he said as the ship disappeared into the side of the observatory.

Herex's portal rose up between the others and the fiery explosion. He walked through with his arms firmly out to his sides. His eyes shined red like never before as he held a protective wall in place to keep everyone safe from the blast. His portal smashed against it and flung out onto the platform in pieces.

Ethan died in the crash causing the cage that Helaina and Archer were trapped in to disappear. She ran to Malcolm and Beck and cast healing spells all around them. The bright and sparkling energy lit up the platform as she hurled everything, she had at them. Beck moved slightly and he strained to look up at her.

He noticed Malcolm's shield lying beside him, then he looked over and saw his body a few feet away.

"Nooo. Nooo! Malcolm. Noooo! Is he alive? Tell me he's alive, Helaina. Please!" cried Beck.

He looked up at her for an answer as the tears filled her eyes, then she dropped her head in sadness, and they rolled down her face.

"No! Nooooo! He gave his life for me!" wailed Beck.

Herex was in disbelief at what had become of his friends in his absence. He watched as they grieved over Malcolm's body. His eyes were lifeless, and they stared blankly into the sky. Helaina slowly leaned over and closed them. A few moments later, Archer stood up in anguish and signaled to the captain that they were ready to depart.

Herex suddenly remembered the vial he got from Morgan. He immediately pulled it out and kneeled beside Malcolm. He uncorked it and poured the blue fluid down his throat till it was empty, then they gently laid his head back on the platform and waited.

A short time passed, and Malcolm's spirit slowly sank back into his body and a slight cough was heard from him. Helaina quickly checked him for a pulse.

"His heart is beating! It worked! He's okay!" she yelled joyously.

Relief came over Beck's face as he laid his head back down and fell unconscious. The Auburn descended to the platform and Voodoo's carpet rolled out to make a plank for them to come aboard. Helaina formed two small green orbs that lifted Malcolm and Beck from the shards and brought them to the ship. Archer picked up the shield and followed behind them as Herex took a stone from his satchel and dropped it onto the platform where his portal last stood. He looked around at all the pieces of the broken frame then he turned away and boarded the ship.

Malcolm and Beck were brought into the ready room and laid on the floor. Helaina waved her wand, and a fresh bed of moss grew below them. Another wave and a clear capsule formed around Malcolm to better help him heal. Just then, Gamon and Arlo came running in and saw them.

"What happened? Are they okay? What can we do?" asked Gamon in a panic.

"They're okay, but they need to rest. They'll be just fine," said Helaina.

"Thank goodness," replied Gamon.

"Please have the captain to take us back up to oversee the rest of the battle," said Helaina.

They both ran out of the room and a few moments later the ship rose back up into the sky. Everyone went out on deck and looked down at the Starlite Valley.

The last few orbs flew back and forth in the hills and domes still filled the ground where the medics treated the injured fighters. As the final spells were cast and the last orbs hit their targets, the valley fell silent. Skeletal birds still flew around the sky and the other undead animals now grazed peacefully on the quiet side of the valley.

"Light the lamps and sound the horn. Send our

ships in to get our people. Let the undead animals be. They don't seem to be causing any harm," said Helaina.

The war-horn sounded and signaled to the fighters that the battle was over. The ships lit their lanterns and began dropping in all over the valley to pick up the fighters. A few of them had the grim task of receiving the dead.

Herex stood off by himself at the bow and stared out at the sky.

"I don't know how Herex got that potion, but I'm sure it would have done the same thing for him," said Archer.

"I was thinking that too," replied Helaina sadly. "I wish there was something we could do."

Voodoo overheard them talking and he took a seat across from him. While he watched him, he saw Herex take the empty vial from his satchel. He looked at it for a moment and then he dropped his head in despair as he tossed it overboard.

Voodoo quietly disappeared into a dark part of the ship and leapt off. He unrolled his carpet under his feet and flew toward the tiny sparkle that the vial made in the moonlight. He reached out and grabbed it just before it was lost in the trees. He crashed through some branches and flew off over the treetops as he looked closely at the vial. He saw a tiny drop of the blue fluid still inside and a curious look came across his face. He placed it safely into his pocket then he flew back up to the ship and landed where he wouldn't be seen.

"Let's get some light down there," said Helaina.

She began to form white orbs and fire them all over the valley. Each of them floated below the trees and shined a light onto the ground below. Soon after, the whole valley was lit, revealing thousands of fallen fighters.

After a few hours, when the last of them were found and brought aboard the ships, the orbs dimmed out and fell to the ground as the searches were completed.

"Bring us up, Captain," Helaina said.

"Destination, my lady?"

"Home," she said with relief.

The captain brought the ship higher in the sky and turned it to the west. The rest of the armada got in formation, and they sailed off into the early morning air. The landscape of the Starlite Valley still glowed bright as the shipwrecks smoldered throughout. The battle with the forsaken army was over and there were no more threats to the people of Cahpra Isle.

CHAPTER 20
ADAPTING TO POST WAR TIMES.

Every star in the sky was shining as they made their way home. The reflection of the moon on the ocean seemed like path that would lead straight to it. The lanterns dimly lit the decks of the ships and a green aura streaked through the sky for as far as the eye could see.

"What in the world is that?" asked Archer.

Gamon climbed up on top of a barrel to see.

"That's an aurora. Solar winds from the sun. They take about two days to get here, and this is what happens when they interact with the magnetic field and the gasses in the atmosphere."

"It's so beautiful," said Helaina.

"Yea. It's all just charged electrons, gases and magnetic waves," replied Gamon.

"Follow the aurora, Captain. It will lead us home," she said.

The captain adjusted course and flew just below it. Everyone sat on the benches around the deck, and they looked out at the scenery on the ground and in the sky. Helaina and Archer talked together in the bow as Gamon and Arlo discussed the things they wanted to build.

A low flying cloud fogged the deck as they passed through it and Herex was suddenly ripped toward the back of the ship as if he were a leaf in the wind. Voodoo got up and tried to grab him, but he was moving too fast. When he reached the stern of the ship the captain gripped his robe and stopped him from floating off.

Herex kneeled and held his hands against the deck boards to steady himself. As everyone else arrived he stood up and went back down the stairs to the bow with haste then he anxiously pulled out the skull flask he got from Marta and took a swig. He placed it back into his satchel and held tightly to the railing as the captain dropped altitude to keep away from anymore clouds.

"What just happened?" asked Arlo.

"He's fading away more than we thought," Helaina said sadly.

"I don't know what we can do to help him now that the Westmore brothers are gone."

Voodoo felt the vial inside his satchel as he looked over at Herex. A short time later everyone settled back in, and they continued on their way home. Soon after, Pirates Cove was coming back into sight. The port now held many ships, and a dreary aura filled the air. Hundreds of people filled the dock as if it weren't abandoned.

"Captain, take us down there, please," said Helaina.

He turned the ship and headed toward the cove. Two smaller ships broke off from the armada to accompany them. As they flew closer, people could be seen in the windows of the inn and out on the balconies. When they arrived, they all realized what was happening.

"Ghosts!" said Helaina.

A ghost that was sitting on a bench saw the ships dropping down and turned to another ghost beside him.

"Hey, Jack. That's a flying ship there, that is," he said.

"Yup, Moe. Wow! That's great." he replied and paid no attention.

Moe watched as it came in and hovered just over the dock. Everyone went to the railing and looked curiously around the cove.

"Hey Captain. I guess you're not the only ghost around here," said Archer.

"Apparently not, but I've never seen this many in one place," he replied.

"Well, that's quite the lady you have there," said an old, bearded ghost that sat on a dock piling. He tugged on his pipe and blew some smoke rings as he looked up at the ship. Then he saw Helaina.

"Quite the lady you are too!" he said as he puffed his pipe some more.

He laughed and Helaina smiled back at him.

"So, what's going on here, friend?" she asked.

"Oh, we're just some merchant sailors trying to

make a living. Well, maybe more of an unliving, but today I made a killing!"

He laughed hysterically and shook his pocket full of coins. Helaina giggled and looked out at the cove. Some of the ghosts sat around a white flamed fire and listened to a man play the banjo as others talked and told stories. Some of them seemed to have spent their night drinking in the old Dockside pub and they fell into the water as the crews on the ships loaded and unloaded their ghostly merchandise.

"Everyone seems harmless here, as strange as it is to see a port full of ghosts. I don't think we need to worry about this right now. We'll investigate it more in the future," said Helaina in disbelief. "Please bring us back up, Captain."

The captain ascended the ship back into the sky and all the ghosts watched as the Auburn sailed away.

"I'd like to get me one of those someday," said Moe, just as Jack finally looked up and saw the ship.

"You're dead, Moe! You're not getting a ship like that," he replied and went back to not paying attention.

They soared back up into the sky and the two other ships followed behind to rejoin the armada and continue their way home.

A few hours later and not far from the ruined castle, the morning sun was almost on the horizon.

"Take us down to that field ahead, please," said

Helaina to the Captain.

The captain brought the ship to a stop just above it.

Helaina formed a white orb and fired it into the center of the field to signal the other ships that it would become the gravesite of the fallen fighters.

The ships that carried the dead descended and docked around the outskirts. The crews began to set up large tents and the fallen fighters were moved inside. A wave of Helaina's wand and a wall of flowers grew around the field to add a little beauty to the dreary task.

"Alright, Captain. Bring us back to the castle."

"Yes, my lady."

Herex took a stone from his satchel and dropped it overboard as they flew off over the trees. When they reached the ruined castle, the captain brought the ship down and docked it on the north lawn. Helaina formed two orbs to carry Malcolm and Beck off the ship. Herex called his bird and quickly flew off into the sunrise. Archer and Helaina slid down the ropes to the ground and they watched him as he flew over the plain.

"It won't be easy for him now," said Helaina. "All he's wanted for so long is to get back into his body to live a normal life."

Voodoo heard them talking and turned to look as he disappeared in the distance.

"I need to put some things in order at home, but I

will return," said Voodoo. "It has been an honor to have accompanied you all on this journey."

Everyone thanked him and they expressed their fond goodbyes then he rolled out his carpet and flew away toward the Teardrop Forest. Malcolm and Beck were brought into the ballroom and placed gently by the fire. Helaina lowered the capsule around Malcolm and they both sank into the bright green moss to rejuvenate them further.

Malcolm's eyes opened just enough to see Helaina standing over him and the broken ballroom ceiling of the ruined castle above.

"What happened? Is Beck, okay?" he asked with concern.

"Yes! Beck is fine," replied Helaina.

"Where are Archer and Herex? Are they okay? he asked as he began to panic and tried to sit up.

"They're all okay," she replied as she held him down.

"Gamon, Arlo, Voodoo?

"They are all fine! You need to rest. Everything is under control," she replied in a comforting voice.

"What did Herex do?" he asked intently.

Helaina paused for a moment, unsure of what to say.

"He saved you. He saved us all. That's what friends do for each other," she replied as she held back her tears.

"That potion would have given him his body back and he gave it up for me!"

"It was, selfless, but you know Herex. His decision doesn't come as a surprise," she replied.

Malcolm's anguish was apparent on his face as he laid his head back down and fell unconscious from exhaustion. Helaina cast another healing spell and a glistening aura formed in the air around them. After that she went over to Archer and they both went back out into the square. Gamon and Arlo were talking with each other just outside the door.

"What do you say, we build Herex a new portal?" asked Gamon.

"That's a great idea!" Arlo replied.

"We just need to build the frame. He does something else to make it a portal. It's a warlock thing," said Gamon.

They walked through the square and down the alleyway to the shop. Gamon went right to his bookcase and scanned the shelves for a certain book. He pulled one down and the cover said, 'Watson's guide to Portals and Teleportation'.

He opened it up and looked through a few of the pages, then he flipped right to the back and stopped on the most intricate portal there was.

"This is the one we're gonna build. He would like this one," said Gamon.

"That'll take a few days, but let's do it," replied Arlo

and they both started reading together.

Outside Helaina and Archer were in the square where all the injured fighters were now being taken care of. A white carriage with the red medical symbol sat in the center by the old fountain. It was filled with different colored potions. Some were green, some were red or yellow and others even bubbled. The medics consulted each other in a circle then they went back to treating their patients. Helaina offered their assistance then her and Archer began to help with the injured fighters.

Just north of the castle, Herex landed on a cliff high above the beach.

He leaned against an old decrepit tree that sat a few feet from the edge. His eyes were dim inside his hood as he stared out at the ocean. He couldn't feel the morning sun on his face or the gentle breeze that blew past him.

An overwhelming feeling of guilt came over him after what had happened to Malcolm and Beck. Along with the realization that he would never be able to return to his body was too much for him to handle. He was tired of living at the mercy of his curse. He wanted to be the one to choose what happened in his life. He stood back up and slowly went to the edge. He looked out at the ocean and down at the jagged rocks below, then he gazed up at the morning sky and stepped off.

His descent seemed as if in slow motion and he

fired a black orb at the ground below himself. A swirling hole formed over the rocky terrain, and he closed his eyes as he fell toward the swirling oblivion. Flashbacks of the life that he once knew flickered through his mind in his last seconds. He opened his arms wide and welcomed his fate.

Just as he fell inside, his bird appeared below him and with the swift flap of its powerful wings they narrowly escaped the funnel and flew off over the beach. Herex revered the bird's loyalty as he gently pets its head in appreciation for being there in his darkest moment. The bird peered back at him proudly and they glided off along the shore.

Back inside the Teardrop Forest, Voodoo was almost home. He could see the smoke rising from his chimney as he coasted through the newly grown forest and landed on the porch in front of his hut.

The Teardrop Forest had fully grown back beyond its former beauty. As his carpet rolled up, he looked out at the thick forest all around his home. A freshwater brook ran through the bright green moss that covered the ground. Lotus flowers sprouted by the dozen along its banks. Tall ferns fanned in the breeze and new wildlife roamed throughout the forest. He took a deep breath of fresh air then he went inside and down to his lab.

He went right to his desk and held Herex's vial up to a lamp to see the one small drop of the blue potion that remained. He carefully dripped it onto a glass slide and placed it under a microscope to examine it.

"Hmmm. I see!" he said as he started to write some ingredients on a piece of parchment. He began flipping through a large black book then he stopped on a certain page and started to read.

"That will take some time to cure," he said.

"I better get started. Lots to do!"

He began pulling bottles from the shelves and placing them on the table. He looked back into the book and pointed at one of the ingredients.

"Okay. That should be exciting," he said in an uneasy tone.

He threw his satchel over his shoulder and went right back out the door. He leapt over the railing as his carpet unrolled below him and he flew off into the forest.

Back inside the castle, Beck opened his eyes and he saw that they were back beside the fire.

"Rebecca!" he said nervously as he struggled to stand up.

He looked over at Malcolm still healing in the moss and he opened his eyes to look back.

"Go get her, Beck," he said in a weak voice as he lifted his hand.

Beck grabbed it tight and the look of acceptance they gave each other spoke measures of the respect they had for one another. Malcolm fell out of consciousness and Beck pulled his blanket back up to his shoulders. He stumbled away to the door and went out onto the steps.

"She would've expected to hear from me by now," he said.

He called to his bird, and it landed beside him. He quickly climbed on, and they flew off toward Rebecca's.

A short time later, her house was coming into sight. They dropped down below the trees and landed by the fence in the front. He ran right to the door and knocked, but she didn't answer.

He became anxious and went to the back of the house to look for her. He checked by the table where they ate and all around the yard, then he looked down by the creek and saw the silhouette of someone sitting on the dock with a dog on either side. He quickly ran toward them, and the dogs heard his footsteps in the grass. When they saw who it was, they both ran to him as fast as they could. Rebecca turned to see what was happening, but the sun glared in her eyes. As Beck walked closer, she saw that it was him. She stood up and ran to him with tears of joy rolling down her face. The dogs tackled him to the ground and started to lick his face.

The dogs moved away as she reached them, and she and Beck gazed at each other for a moment before she reached down and pulled him back to his feet.

"Hello, Rebecca," he said bashfully.

"I thought I lost you," she replied.

"It was close, but we did it."

They looked happily into each other's eyes.

"Can you stay now?" she asked as she took his hand.

"I can stay forever," he replied gently.

"That's all I ever wanted and you're right in time for lunch, Arthur. I have something special cooking."

"That sounds great! I'm starved," he replied.

They held hands and walked back to the house. A bashful but very content look filled Beck's face as they all went inside together.

Back at the castle Herex landed on the north lawn where all the ships were docked, and the medics were about finished unloading the last of the injured fighters into the town. He went past them and right into the great room to see how Malcolm was recovering. Herex looked him over and saw that he was okay, then he settled into the moss himself and kept Malcolm company for a while.

Over the next few days, the fallen fighters were laid to rest in a beautiful ceremony. People from all around the isle came to pay their respects to them. A group of masons began the construction of a memorial tower in the center of the field to honor the fallen. After the ceremonies, the king's fighters boarded the airships to start their journey back to the new kingdom.

Everyone talked together inside the great room one last time before departing from the ruined castle.

"I just heard from Beck," Malcolm said. "He and Rebecca are headed off to stay at her place. It's time for us to leave here too, so we'll need to say our goodbyes to this old place. Its walls have provided us a home for the last time."

"I'll miss this castle," Helaina replied.

Just then, Gamon and Arlo kicked the door open and walked through with the new portal and they placed it in front of Herex. It was made from mahogany wood with two dragons carved into it that climbed up each side and met at the top. Their eyes stared down at whoever was to walk through.

"Herex, we know you gave up so much recently and we just wanted to give you something to make things a little better," said Gamon.

Herex glared at the portal in amazement. He slowly walked up to it and touched the hand carved trim.

"This is the most powerful portal in existence. It can also be duplicated so you can have a few open at one time if you want!" said Arlo.

Herex lifted his arms into the air and smoke rose from the ground and twisted all around it. It engulfed the frame and then it dissipated, leaving a smoky aura drifting off the top of the frame. The dragon's eyes turned red, and a blue swirling cloud formed inside. Herex went to Gamon and Arlo and knelt to shake their hands and graciously thank them.

"You're welcome, Herex. Just take it easy on me from now on. No more ripping me through them without warning!" said Gamon.

He gestured that he agreed and giggled then he stood up and turned back to everyone. Malcolm went up to him and grabbed his shoulder.

"You saved my life and sacrificed your own. I am truly blessed to have you as a friend, Herex. I will travel to the ends of the world to help you find that potion. You have my word."

Herex summoned another portal that led to the new kingdom.

"No, but thank you, friend," said Malcolm. "I think I'll fly back on the Auburn. It'll be a nice trip for the time it takes."

Herex put his hand on Malcolm's shoulder and gave a squeeze, then he went over to Archer and shook his hand with respect. Helaina grabbed him and hugged him tightly as he got near her. He gently patted her back and embraced her for a moment. She was clearly sad, but still managed to smile. He went back over to the portal and stopped in front of it.

"We will see you soon, Herex. There will be a gathering at the new kingdom that you cannot miss," said Malcolm.

Herex turned back and shook his head to agree, then he walked through. In a flash, he disappeared inside and the portals both sunk back into the ground and bolts of energy coursed through the floor in every direction. Malcolm and the others walked out of the castle and across the lawn to the Auburn. They climbed aboard and greeted the captain warmly.

"Bring us up, Captain, and to the south," said Malcolm.

"Destination, my lord?"

"The new kingdom."

"As you wish," he replied.

He brought the Auburn up into the sky and they all looked across the plain as the other ships rose up around them. It was a beautiful sunny day as they began their journey back to the new kingdom and they all flew off, leaving the ruined castle vacant once more.

Somewhere deep in a forest, Herex's portal emerged from the ground inside a small hidden room that was made of stone. A dirty glass roof allows just enough light into the room to let some plant life grow. Vine that was covered with small blue flowers overgrew the walls. In the center of the room was a dirty glass coffin.

He went over and wiped some of the dust away to reveal his body that was being preserved inside. He feared there was no hope of getting back into it since the last of the potion was gone. He laid his head down on top of it for a few moments, then suddenly he stood up and wiped all the dust off the coffin with one long swipe. He went over to the portal and looked over at the coffin one last time before he walked back through.

The portal sank into the ground and rose from the observatory platform in the Starlite Valley. He went to the edge and looked down at the valley below. All the skeletal animals stayed there, and they made it their home. The birds nested at the top of the trees, and some flew around the sky.

He pulled out his orb and let it out in front of himself. His bird appeared and he climbed to the top. They leapt off the platform and swooped down past all the wreckage of the ships then they landed by the entrance of the old town. The skeletal animals watched him intently.

He slowly walked toward them, and a large skeletal mammoth went right up and looked down at him. Herex slowly lifted his hand and touched its tusk. The mammoth backed up for a moment but then it stepped closer when it realized that he meant no harm.

A skeletal bird flew in and landed a few feet away from them. As it did the force caused an egg to break free from its decaying body and land on the ground. It began to move and roll around and suddenly a baby skeletal bird cracked its way out of the shell. It wobbled to its feet and looked up at Herex, then it chirped and flapped its little bony wings at him.

Herex picked it up and when he wiped away some

of the decaying skin, he saw that beneath it was a bright white skeleton. He went over to the old distillery and found a long handle broom, then he went to the shore of Orion Lake and as some of the animals started to come closer, he began to scrub them down. All the ones that trusted him enough to approach were rid of the rotting skin and only fresh clean bone was left behind.

Soon after, many of the animals lined up and quickly accepted Herex as a friend. He spent the rest of the day cleaning them and the sun was setting. A large portion of the remaining skeletal animals were now clean, but a few were still too timid to go near him. He set up a camp just inside the entrance of the town and a group of skeletal animals settled down around the fire with him. The baby bird rested on a branch that protruded from the wall beside him. Their eyes no longer had the evil red glow. The sun fell behind the hill and the foliage of the Starlite valley lit up brightly as they spent the night by the fire.

The following day the king's army arrived back at the new kingdom. The ships settled down and tied up to the docks all around the castle. The large troop ships landed nearby in the plain and the fighters walked back through the front gate to find their families waiting to welcome them home.

The captain docked the Auburn on the same balcony that they left from days before and the king and queen waited there to greet them.

"You did it, Malcolm. The isle is at peace once again," said the king.

"We have much to do now, father," Malcolm said.

"Yes, we do, son. Yes, we do," he replied.

The queen went over and hugged him tightly.

"I'm so happy you're home," she said.

"It's good to be back," he replied, and he smiled at her as they all walked into the castle.

"I have something to do, but I will see you both for supper," said Malcolm while they all continued inside.

He went right up the stairs to the crystal ballroom and went inside. The fireplace flared up as he walked in then he went over to the crystal ball that was floating over the pillar. He picked it up and looked at it closely, then he placed it onto the next open shelf on the wall. Just below it, the current date engraved itself into a small copper plate below the title,

'THE RISE OF THE FORSAKEN.'

He stepped back and thought for a moment about the amazing tale that it would tell, then he turned away and walked out. The fire went out and the room turned dark again. Suddenly, in a flash of light another crystal ball appeared over the pillar and started glowing brightly as it recorded everything that happened on the isle from that point, on.

CHAPTER 21
THE TWILIGHT MEMORIAL.

Gamon and Arlo knocked on Voodoo's door and waited for him to answer so they could leave for the three-month anniversary of the Twilight Forest battle. Voodoo was sitting at a table in his lab that was covered with glass beacons and vials that were filled with different colored potions.

He went over to his bookcase and waved his hand over an empty spot on the shelf. A bottle of blue potion suddenly appeared inside a protective bubble. Another wave and the bubble dissipated. He brought it to the table and with a small dropper he took some of the liquid and dripped it onto a glass slide, then he placed it under a microscope and looked through the eyepiece.

"Nope. It's not ready yet," he muttered to himself as he leaned back in disappointment and wiped his eyes.

He corked the potion and as he got up to put it away, he heard the knock at the door. He placed it back on the shelf and waved his hand in front of the bottle to reform the bubble, then in a flash it disappeared.

He went to the door and opened it to see Gamon and Arlo staring up at him. Gamon was dressed in his normal attire, but Arlo had on a shiny black suit with a top hat and a matching cane that he twirled in his hand.

"Where ya been? We've been standing out here forever! We gotta go!" said Arlo. The ceremony starts in an hour!"

"Actually, we haven't been out here that long, but it is time to go," Gamon added.

"I'm ready," said Voodoo.

He closed the door and followed them down the steps. Parked in front of the hut was a small two seat helichopper that Gamon and Arlo built together. They climbed in and put their seat belts on. Arlo cranked the engine, and the propeller began to spin as a crystal from Teardrop Lake glowed brightly between the seats.

Voodoo jumped onto his carpet. Gamon and Arlo put on their goggles as the engine powered up and they slowly lifted into the air. Voodoo rose up next to them and they all flew off over the forest as a small puff of smoke trailed behind the helichopper exhaust.

"Hey! You wanna try the little red button?" Arlo asked.

"Hmm. Yea, sure! Let's give it a shot!" replied Gamon as he reached out and pressed it.

Rockets in the backfired up and blasted them off through the forest. They both yelled at the top of their lungs as the helichopper disappeared out ahead of Voodoo. They were out of control as Arlo dodged the huge trunks of the trees. He pulled back on the control with all his might, and they shot out from the canopy of the trees, far ahead of Voodoo. Gamon struggled to reach the button as the force of the wind pushed against him. He gave one strong lunge forward and he managed to press it, slowing the helichopper back down to a safe speed.

"Maybe we should have put the button a little closer. On the center console might have been a better idea," said Gamon as he looked over at Arlo.

Arlo was still looking straight ahead as he grinned his teeth and held tightly to the controls.

Voodoo caught up and they both looked over at the same time. Their hair was pushed back, and broken branches stuck out from all over the helichopper. Voodoo just laughed hysterically as they flew off, only a little slower now.

Back at the new kingdom, Malcolm sat in his study and looked over the plans for a new town that was to be constructed on the isle. Helaina came into the room with a jug of water.

"We need to leave, Malcolm. The ceremony is about to start," she said as she watered the flowers on the sill. "We have a surprise for you after it too," she added.

He rolled up the blueprints and got up.

"A surprise? Should I be worried?" he asked.

"Not a bit. You're going to love it!"

"Where is everyone else?" he asked.

"They're already there, with your parents," she replied.

"Good! Well, let's not keep them waiting."

He walked to the door and turned back to her, still watering the plants.

"We must leave, Helaina! The ceremony's about to start!" he said jokingly.

She placed the jug down and gave him a smirk, then they walked out and down the hall together. At the end of it they came up to a large wooden door with a bright light that shined through the gap at the bottom.

Malcolm opened it up and followed Helaina inside. The room was dark and empty except for a row of pillars that led to one of Herex's portals in the center of the room. They walked through, and in a flash, they exited the burial site. A huge crowd covered the field as an orchestra played in the background. Fresh flowers filled the grounds, and each grave had its own colorful bouquet.

The memorial was a white stone tower that reached high above the trees. A large glass shard stuck out of the top and acted as a prism that shined a spectrum of colors onto every headstone across the site. The names of the fallen were engraved on the walls around the base. It was surrounded by an octagon platform with a single step on each side that let down to the thick green grass.

They observed the memorial for a few moments then they went up onto a mezzanine to join everyone else. The king and queen sat together comfortably with a small two seated airship docked just behind them. As they reached the top, they were greeted by everyone, except for Herex.

"Where is he?" Malcolm asked intently.

"I saw him the other day," replied Archer. "He had a small issue with one of the people that moved back into Andromeda. The man mistreated one of the animals and Herex saw it! Let's just say the man ended up wetting his trousers, but Herex did hold back. It was getting a little busy there anyway so I helped him move all the animals north into the hills so they could live in peace."

"We found an old cottage in a hidden valley with a huge stable that houses all the skeletal animals now. It could use some cleaning up, but he and the animals seem happy there. He's gotten quite attached to them and he always has that baby bird with him."

"Well, I'd like to see that when we're finished here," replied Malcolm.

"Me too! Anything we can do to help him," Helaina added.

Herex's portal suddenly rose from the ground, and he walked through with the baby skeletal bird on his arm.

"Here he is now," said Arlo.

The portal disappeared into the ground behind him, and he made his way up the steps. He bowed to the king and queen and greeted everyone kindly.

"It is good to see you, Herex! Have you given that bird a name yet?" Asked Malcolm.

Herex pointed to one of its bones.

"Bone?" Malcolm asked.

Herex pointed to a few other bones on the bird and looked back up at Malcolm.

"Bones?" Malcolm asked.

Herex gave him a thumbs up then he sat down with everyone else.

"Bones! Quite suiting!" He added.

Helaina took a seat next to Gamon and Arlo and they all awaited the speech. Malcolm went to the podium and took another moment to admire the memorial as the orchestra faded and the people gave him their attention.

"We all gather here to pay our respects to the brave men and women who were lost just three months ago. On this tower before you are the names of fifty-three hundred men, women and companions who fought courageously and made the ultimate sacrifice to help bring peace to this land.

They are the very reason we are now able to travel the isle from corner to corner in safety. We're able to reopen the mines and give our people work. We've opened our ports to welcome others to come and share in the freedom we are now blessed with every day. Construction of a new railway system will begin soon, and it will allow everyone to explore the isle as they wish. All of this is only possible because of them.

So, let us all never forget what they gave so we can prosper and the reason why we all now have the chance at a great new day. We present to you, the Twilight memorial."

Everyone clapped aggressively.

"We dedicate this site to all the brave mothers and fathers, sisters and brothers, friends and companions who were lost that fateful night. May they be at peace. To all of you who have lost, may you find comfort here. Thank you."

The crowd clapped again for him as Malcolm sat down beside his mother and the king went up to the podium.

"Good afternoon, great people of Cahpra Isle. I'll be brief so you all can begin to visit the memorial. I'd like to ask everyone to join me in a moment of silence for all the brave souls who were lost."

He bowed his head, and all the people below did the same. The field went silent and all that could be heard was the wind blowing through the trees. After a few seconds, the king looked back up at the crowd.

"This memorial marks a dark day in our history, but it also marks a new beginning for everyone in the land. Here we will honor those brave men and women who went fearlessly into the night. Who fought bravely with courage and honor in the face of evil. They fought till their ends to assure our future and therefore, they will never, ever be forgotten. May this place bring peace to everyone who lost someone that can never be replaced. This memorial will always remain open. If anyone needs help coping with their grief, please alert your town jester and arrangements will be made to help you. You are not alone. Thank you and please enjoy the memorial."

Again, the people clapped aggressively as he went back to his seat beside the queen.

"We should go down to the tower and pay our respects," she said.

"I agree. Would you all join us?" asked the king.

Everyone got up and followed them down to the memorial. The people watched as they took a knee at the foot of the tower. They bowed their heads and touched the wall where the names of the fallen fighters were engraved.

One by one they slowly stood back up. The king helped the queen to her feet and all the people began to clap and cheer for the heartfelt gesture that their royal family had shown them. Everyone looked back and waved to acknowledge them, then they made their way back up to their seats to watch the rest of the ceremony.

The people started to go up and view the tower.

Some traced their loved one's names and others took photographs in front of it. Bright flashes and puffs of smoke burst from the bulbs on the cameras.

"Herex, what do you say we go and see your new place?" Malcolm asked.

Herex shrugged his shoulders and summoned his portal. He held out his arm to welcome all that wanted to go, and everyone got up and went through, including the king and the slightly hesitant queen. They exited into a valley that was surrounded by tall hills on every side. An old broken-down cottage sat in the center with a large wooden stable just behind it.

As Herex walked to the back of the cottage a skeletal mammoth came running out to greet him. Everyone was shocked by the enormous skeletal creature as they realized how gentle it was. They all went to the back of the cottage and saw that the entire valley was filled with skeletal animals. They grazed the land and birds flew in the sky and nested in the trees.

Herex went to the fire pit in front of the stable and shot an orb inside to get it burning. He went into the broken porch in the back of the cottage and got some chairs for the queen, Helaina and Jenny, to sit by the fire.

Everyone gathered around it and observed the old farm and how rundown it was.

"Herex, I won't have you live like this," said

Malcolm. "We have to fix this place up for you."

Herex waved his hands to decline since he really didn't mind it.

"I'm sorry, Herex. It's already done. It'll be quick. Leave for a day and I'll have a hundred carpenters here and by the time you get back it will be a nice place to live. I insist!" said Malcolm firmly.

Herex shrugged his shoulders and unwillingly accepted. He threw his arm into the air and the side wall of the barn lifted to form an overhang. The animals sat around another fire that had burned in the center of the barn. There were stacks of hay all around them along with a thick layer that was spread across the floor to make a comfortable bed for them to lie in.

All the animals mixed. No matter if they were a horse, tiger, bear, bird or mammoth, they were all part of the pack and completely accepted each other. Some of the skeletal animals came closer to everyone and they sat in a group not far away. One of the tigers went up to the queen and began to sniff her.

It sat beside her and lifted its paw up to her thigh as it let out a gentle chuff. The queen looked around to see if anyone was worried and the tiger chuffed again to get her attention back. She slowly lifted her hand and pet its spine as it chuffed again in approval.

"This is amazing!" said the queen.

"They seem completely tame," said the king and

Herex quickly shook his head to confirm what he said.

Everyone talked around the fire and enjoyed the company of the undead animals for a little while. A few of the horses stuck their heads out of the stable and Voodoo went over to them. A tiger came running from out of the valley and went right up to Helaina. It took her by surprise for a moment, but then she realized that it was the same tiger that she tamed at the observatory, months before. She pets its head and it happily nestled up and sat beside her.

"I'm sorry that the town became too busy for you and the animals," said the king. "We will surely remedy this by making it a nice home for you all. I hereby name this valley to be yours, Herex. May you and the skeletal animals live happily here."

Herex bowed his head to show his appreciation.

"I'm sad to say, but we should be getting back before the people start to think we left without saying goodbye," the king said as he put his hand out to the queen.

They all said their goodbyes to the animals that had warmed up to them and as they walked back to the portal, the queen couldn't take her eyes off the tiger.

"We simply must visit this place as often as possible," she said, and the king agreed as he pulled her through the portal.

"I guess we should get back to the ceremony too,"

said Malcolm.

Herex went into the stable and put some wood on the fire then he closed the overhang with another wave of his arm. The door of the stable was wide open for all the animals to come and go as they pleased. Malcolm and Helaina went back through the portal and everyone else followed.

"There's something I want to show everyone that will surely change the mood. You're all going to love it!" Helaina said.

They looked at her in curiosity as she called to her bird and everyone else did the same. They all climbed on and flew off over the trees with Gamon and Arlo sputtering alongside in the helichopper.

A few minutes later the ruined castle came into sight. Each of them began to see that it had been entirely restored along with the town. The Auburn was docked high up on a balcony in the new towers and Helaina's beautiful dome of vine and orchids still covered the square. The Cahpra family crest was stitched on a flag that blew in the wind atop the highest tower and another by the docks.

The port was full of ships that unloaded supplies into the castle. The medical ship that was used in the battle sat beside a dozen smaller ships, each with the red medical symbol on their hulls. They all stopped for a moment and hovered in place.

"The smaller ones are designed to respond to any

medical issues throughout the north side of the isle," said Helaina. "The building next to the dock is where the medics will stay while they're on call. In the case there is an emergency they will take one of the ships right to the patient."

"Whose idea was this?" Malcolm asked.

"Gamon and I came up with it. The hardest part was keeping you away for so long," replied Helaina. "There were hundreds of carpenters and masons who volunteered to workday and night to finish it."

"It's amazing!" Malcolm replied in awe.

They circled around the castle once more before swooping down by the steps of the ballroom. The birds flew off and everyone went inside. The entire room had been refinished but to their surprise, the moss they slept on and the fire pit that kept them warm was still there. Only now with a proper chimney and the ceiling was fixed like new. Even Gamon's table sat in the center of the room just like before.

"We wanted to keep the things that became sentimental to us," said Helaina.

"It's perfect," replied Malcolm.

They made their way through the room and out into the square. Helaina's white orchids hung down from the dome and the strands of vine still stretched down the roads. Old man Wilson waved at them from in front of his shop and everyone happily waved back as he went inside, surely to his beloved wife.

The town was brand new and filled with goods for the people who would soon live there. The fountain was repaired and the peaceful sound of running water filled the square.

"The shops were all rented inside an hour after we opened the gate, and you wouldn't believe who rented some of them," said Helaina.

As they made their way down the road, they saw a new flower shop that Helaina was noticeably excited to show them.

"Carol's Wild Forest moved back in!" she said joyfully.

They all looked in the window and saw the exotic plants from floor to ceiling. A balcony in the front was covered with flowers and an outdoor garden in the back rose high up over the fence behind the shop.

"The next one is going to be your favorite, Malcolm. Merlin insisted on making it his new headquarters!"

"Really? Merlin's bookstore! Here?" he said.

They made their way over and the sign above the shop was a large wizard hat with twinkling stars on it. The wooden plaque that hung over the door said, 'Merlin's Bookstore. est. 1579.'

They went to the window and saw the shop filled with his books. Each section emitted a different color aura depending on the genre of story. There was a green section, blue, yellow and even a small area of red that shined all the way in the back. In the center of the shop there was a large fireplace that was surrounded by stadium seating for the people to sit and enjoy a tale. A lantern dimly lit a small wooden counter in the front of the shop.

"This is great! The people will enjoy this place. I know I did when I was young," said Malcolm.

"The lab's been upgraded too! So, Arlo and I are ready to get back to work," Gamon said.

"I can't wait to see what you both come up with next," he replied.

"There are so many more shops I want to show you guys," said Helaina cheerfully.

They all made their way further down the road to a shop that resembled a birdcage. As they got closer, they could hear the chirping of birds getting louder and louder. Everyone looked inside and saw hundreds of birds in separate enclosures around the room. They filled the walls and covered the floor. Only a thin path led from the front door to a clerk's desk in the center of the shop.

Bones saw the others inside and he tapped his beak gently on the glass. A bird just inside stuck out its long yellow beak and tapped back on the window at him. Bones flapped his bony wings and looked up at Herex with excitement.

"Aww. They like each other!" said Helaina.

"So, this is home," said Malcolm.

"This is home," Helaina replied contently, and they all went off down the road to explore the new town together. It was the beginning of a bright future on Cahpra Isle.

ABOUT THE AUTHOR
C. Iannuzzi

Chris is a New York native and has enjoyed the fantasy genre for most of his life so now he's spent the last few years creating a magical world of his own.

Some of the things he holds dear are spending time with his family, friends, and of course his beloved dog, Mya.

He was deterred from writing at a young age, but he's found his way back and the story that he's always had inside, has been brought to life. He's truly found his passion as a writer and plans to breathe life into the Malcolm Cahpra series for years to come.

IF YOU LIKED THIS

Please visit the Malcolm Cahpra Facebook page. I look forward to interacting with my readers there.
It's been an amazing journey for me, and I hope you've enjoyed it too!

Made in United States
North Haven, CT
03 July 2025

70313898R00201